THE SPREAD

Walter is the New York publisher of a sex magazine called *The Spread*. He sells about 100,000 copies an issue. This glossy, pornographic weekly provides him a platform to work out his fantasies while fulfilling the dubious needs of his readers. The way he sees it, Walter provides a service—he is in demand. He has sex with his secretary Virginia in the office, and services his wife at home. But Walter has become both a spokesman for the sexual revolution, and a victim of it. He has become trapped by his own creation. He begins to harass the readers who send in classified ads. He ignores an advertiser who may be selling dangerous goods. The times are getting ahead of Walter. And he is the last one to know it.

HORIZONTAL WOMAN

She has good thighs, good breasts, a striking if somewhat affected face — she knows all of this because she has been told so by clients many times — but she knows what they can never tell her: that her best feature is her compassion and she wears it like armor through all the streets... Elizabeth Moore is a social worker. Her supervisor, Oved, is trying to train her to be a dedicated investigator. After all, her job is to protect the city and reduce public assistance. But Elizabeth has another mission, to help her clients with their self-esteem. She is a caseworker who takes her caseloads very seriously indeed. The trouble is that so many people need her. But how can she explain to her boss that the kind of therapy she provides her clients can only be offered in bed?

The Spread

Horizontal Woman

BARRY N. MALZBERG

Stark House Press • Eureka California

THE SPREAD / HORIZONTAL WOMAN

Published by Stark House Press
1315 H Street
Eureka, CA 95501, USA
griffinskye3@sbcglobal.net
www.starkhousepress.com

ISBN: 978-1-944520-82-3

Book design by Mark Shepard, SHEPGRAPHICS.COM

First Stark House Press Edition: July 2019

FIRST EDITION

Contents

Spreading the Social Worker

■　■　■　■　■

BARRY N. MALZBERG

I used to think of these retrospective essays (Stark House and its ever tolerant publisher have already granted this twice) as soaring over the various scattered monuments of what in antic moments I would call "my career" but of course that was the wrong simile; these essays are more like stumbling through the graveyard of my published work, the not so luminous detritus of ambition if not accomplishment. These two novels, not science fiction (for which I am better known) or of matters criminal (there were 17 of those, three in collaboration with Bill Pronzini) but rather situated temerariously in what we call "the mainstream," are refugees from a period, almost half a century ago, when I was producing novels with frantic haste and usually from a position of social observation. Both *The Spread* and *The Social Worker* were written within the last two months of 1970 and could—like two previous works published a year ago by Stark House—alternate means of dealing with the crumbling circumstance of New York City as it lurched toward its most venomous and deteriorative decade. Two versions of hell glimpsed through a glass lightly.

As was to be expected (I was counting on it) they met a horrid fate with the same publisher about six months apart, dumped on the market as paperback originals, not quite pornographic, but not quite un-pornographic either, both of them centered on characters who were going to take that rotten zeitgeist by its figurative neck and shake it into a kind of attention. The social situation was one in which the cauldron of America's hidden desire and secret life was bubbling sullenly into the central sphere: Vietnam was coming home and occupying the streets, the Living Theater productions were inviting audiences to join them onstage and commit rape (someone took them up on this and was arrested), the Presidency then as now but a little more subtlety was up for sale and somewhere in Williamsburgh, Elizabeth Moore, the idealistic social worker, was eagerly, hopefully, wantonly, religiously screwing her male clients as her private program of lending hope if not wealth to the disadvantaged. Elizabeth (like her creator) was a young Dept. of Welfare Investigator, just out of college, something like Skidmore, and eager to repair the social fabric but she found quickly that it was not the fabric but those it entrapped which most needed her services.

Infused with what had to wait decades to be known as "political correctness," Elizabeth wanted to suture the rent fabric in the most expeditious fashion, one which would best suit her talents (she had not the money of a dowager nor the musical skills of Michael Rabin) and she earnestly, without merriment but with great dedication, humped her way through selected cadre from her client load, always with warmth and dedication and an insistence upon repair of the social structure. Eventually she became entangled with an Orthodox Rabbi (Orthodox Rabbi's collecting welfare were no rarity on my own caseload) and that is when her dedicated, marginally satisfying quest became dangerous. The Orthodox Community and the Rabbi himself looked with less tolerance and far more agita upon her quest. It all ends or ended (the novel is fifty years old and Elizabeth would now be 73 and settled in some terrain inaccessible to me) rather embarrassingly, certainly badly, with a riot in Williamsburgh, as infuriated Rabbi's, Rebbitzens and their children came streaming from the streets to accost the hapless Elizabeth during one of her field trips. Like Sol Yurick's great 1968 novel, *The Bag*, a marginal influence, it terminates in a great riot of Rebbitzens, Rabbis, children and police into which Elizabeth disappears insisting upon her continued belief in social justice. But I do not want to spoil the ending beyond that. Somewhere the lady may still be drawing breath and repenting but repenting for what? And why? With such anomalies and like Elizabeth I struggled fifty years ago and struggle to this moment. Another Elizabeth in another novel warns the narrator of *Screen* as he walks out on her in search of more thrills at the Bijou, "I', your last chance." No she wasn't. But it seemed so at the time. Not that this was any brake on the Bijou for *Screen's* intrepid narrator, Martin Miller.

The Spread is similarly entangled with a zeitgeist seen by its central figure as being hopelessly *fubar*. But lucrative. A roman a clef about a wholly imagined Al Goldstein, the publisher of *Screw* Magazine (who I never had the fortune of meeting), this guy is the founder and successful entrepreneur of a pornographic newspaper sold on the same stands as *The New York Times* or *Cosmopolitan* and dedicated to similar purpose: information, entertainment and all the news that is now fit to be print. Goldstein, who died on welfare, confined to a wheelchair, entrapped by history, was a remarkable figure, one who interested me from his emergence in 1968, a figure who had all of Maurice Girodias' revolution in his bosom and not a shred of rationalization. "I am a pornographer," Uncle Al would say to any interviewer who could find him (he was not hard to find), "I am a smut peddler, that is all I am, the Supreme Court has given me the right, they have certified that I have a social purpose and I'll give them all the tits and ass they can handle. More than they can handle." A centerfold in the first or second issue of the newspaper was a double-page black and white photograph of the female organ, telescopically enlarged for convenience and disclosing all of its wonders in pulp. Uncle Al was as serious as Girodias, he saw sex as the wedge to force the society open; it was the wedge which would open a new life. "Look at all these people" Uncle Al said to an interviewer who was covering the elegant annual *Playboy* Christmas party at which he was a semi-invited guest, "Hefner, Guccione, all of them talking about *literature* and *First Amendment* and a *freeing culture* with their foundations for justice and their hors d'oeuvres and champagne. Let me tell you what they are, they're just a bunch of smut peddlers in tuxedos and so am I and that's not a bad thing to be."

Uncle Al had no pretensions, he had a vision as focused, however, as that of Elizabeth Moore and if there was a tree to be shaken or a grenade to be tossed he would do the deed. Eventually and exactly as Maurice Girodias had predicted to me in 1970, visual pornography, tapes, home devices put static or textual porn on the downslide and by 1980 *Screw*, a foundation shaker, had become an irrelevant if not scandal-free publication. Uncle Al hung in though. He continued to publish, he downsized his offices, he moved ever further downtown, he traded in the stewardess wife for the model wife for the writer wife but he kept on until not the market but his health completely collapsed. It did not end well. Did I write that already? Write that twice for a man who was a cultural force, who was the mirror held up to Hefner and even his true model, Larry Flynt. "I am in it for the money," Goldstein told the world. Eventually there was none.

A fascinating and (in the early years) unpredictable figure, however, and screamed into my (eventually more hearing) right ear for a novel. So I wrote a novel. In fact I wrote *The Spread* which the great writer read on a California to New York flight for a publicity tour and told me "This is a novel which obviously was not fighting the writer on every page." It came as quickly as almost anything and when it was done, it was done.

(That this was not true for Elizabeth or Uncle Al was their one great mistake.)

Uncle Al's odyssey was a kind of morality play and of course so is *The Spread*. It ended as badly ultimately for Goldstein as it did for my own protagonist but when I wrote the novel in late 1970 I had no idea how it would end in the culture biography, only that it would have to end badly here because this guy, this horseplayer, this wrecker of lives genuinely hated himself and Calvinism required his descent. It only became obvious to me much later that Al Goldstein hated himself even more and that he had his destination fixed from the beginning. (Maybe Elizabeth did too. I am not sure of this.)

Both books sought the invisibility their protagonists had sought. (The author too.) Perhaps it made them happy. (The author too.) Social nihilism had bigger plans. Everyone got what they wanted. Or so they thought. It is even more gratifying now, we are living in the consequences of that nihilism which Elizabeth so eagerly battled, which Uncle Al so desperately sought and in that bubbling cauldron we will not necessarily perish but we shall all be changed. At last: in a moment. In the twinkling of an eye.

December 2018: New Jersey

The Spread

BARRY N. MALZBERG

I

To come to the point (such as it is), I publish a dirty newspaper: a pornography sheet which sells approximately 100,000 copies an issue. This does not mean, however, that my intent is purely sexual. On the contrary, I devolve upon simpler, darker matters: returns, distributor weakness in the Bronx, judicial reform, the interpreted limits of the First Amendment and so on. Sex is peripheral to all of these issues although without it, of course, none of them could exist. Sex put us to 200,000 copies a week in the first four months and would have taken us further yet had it not been for certain illegal maneuvers in the office of the District Attorney, certain pressures, that is to point out, on wholesale outlets and so forth. Even at our present standing, we make money although things could be considerably better. They could also be considerably worse, matters in this business being relative.

I concede the value of sex while unwilling to be entrapped by it. This is not to say that I lack normal tendencies, normal outlets, I am a devoted husband, a careful adulterer, an admirer of many of the photographs we print and so on. What must be cultivated is a sense of perspective, an awareness of a larger scheme in which we are but one minor facet. The system is breaking apart: somewhere between scatology and revulsion lies the truth around which we will reassemble. I am devoted only to illuminating one pole to the limits of my ability.

In this sense, I have a certain assurance of mission although the realization that I have more in common with those on the opposite pole than with anyone in the middle occasionally induces a complicating headache, a dismal woe. It is not easy. Nothing is easy. But in fifty years, all of these will be artifacts, frozen in perfect and contained time, available to all of those who will care to investigate a past that made them whole. All passion spent, all *amicus curiae* denoted, the pages alone will speak, and they will speak in the calmest and most level of tones: tones of reassurance and hope. Souvenirs of the tour available in the gift shop below; facsimile prints carved upon stone, the stone cool and timeless in the suspended palm.

II

I have no sense of guilt. All of that was overcome a long time ago. It is a business like any other business. I am performing a service. Masturbation is a harmless outlet for unrelieved sexual tensions;

masturbatory materials lend harmless pleasures to lonely millions while saving any number of attractive girls from violent and bestial rape. I see my audience as gentle men in small rooms, surrounded by haze, sinking into wonder as they stare at my pages and with sure, ample strokes, bring themselves past desire to the perfect abscess of memory.

III

I am having an affair with the secretary in my office. It is a small office consisting of only four full-time employees plus a number of freelancers who provide photography, text, layouts and so forth. The other two members of the staff are homosexuals, I believe, although I am not absolutely sure of this; in any event they pay no attention to the secretary, leaving me a clear, unembarrassed field.

The secretary is named Virginia Nelson. She is twenty-three years old and very pretty, attended graduate school for a while but grew tired of the academic life and came to New York in order to make entrance to the world. Being of a new generation, she suffers from neither guilt nor stifling cultural taboos and took this job when offered because it paid well and was interesting. In addition to taking my dictation, filing correspondence and running the subscriber service, Virginia writes text for the newspaper under a pseudonym, talking about the female attitude toward orgasm, penetration, breast-play, etc. I have no idea whether she has the experience she claims but find her columns consistently rewarding and they are one of the most popular features in the newspapers, judging from the small quantity of reader mail we receive. For these services I now pay her $200 a week plus occasional bonuses. I also copulate with her often, sometimes in the offices after working hours and sometimes, for atmosphere, in a large nineteenth-century hotel several blocks from this building into whose canopied beds we can literally sink, moaning and descending against one another. We are not able to go to her apartment since she lives with two roommates whose hours are unpredictable, and we cannot go to my own apartment since my wife lives there and would be likely to interrupt us just when things were getting started. Also, she would ask questions which I do not care to answer at this stage of our relationship.

Hovering over Virginia — who is really a terrific fuck, the tone of my description of her notwithstanding — feeling her breasts, tonguing her neck, preparing to make that first and last of entrances, I sometimes think that I am on the verge of making some enormous equation; something which will connect the real and the illimitable so tightly that never the gap to be broken again … but then, as the first sureties of orgasm overtake me in the familiar way, I realize that it was all a cheat and that as ever I am suspended, caught in the trap between heaven and earth, trying to piece out that small beneficence which is all we can know of the final connection.

IV

The office contains a huge bulletin board on which are thumbtacked selections of our best pictures. Often, while fucking Virginia, the angle of our conjoinment has me facing this board; prowling into her I see the gape of newsprint cunt, newsprint tits, the open, stunned mouth of a model as she holds her breath, the desperate cleavage of a male ass as it constricts against thighs pinned below. The pictures, at these times, lend urgency to my coupling, and gasping, flowing, unwinding within her, I think of the stricken eyes of the masturbator as, fistward, he plunges himself home over and again toward the very pictures I glimpse and yet, prowling her, can never touch.

V

My wife does not approve of what I am doing. Our original plan, when we married some years ago, was for her to finance me through graduate school while I took a master's degree in business, but a false pregnancy and a siege of academic panic spelled the end of that; also I did not want to attend school. Instead I obtained a job as an editor of a men's magazine and that led in turn to an executive capacity at a whole chain of men's magazines until I decided, two years ago, to take the plunge into publishing myself. Now my wife does not know what is going on. "Don't bring it home," she says, "that's all I ask of you, don't ever bring it home. I don't want to know what you're doing."

"But you'll take the money, right?" I say, not tactfully. "The proceeds are all right as long as you don't have to grapple with the source."

"I never asked you to do this. It was going to be entirely different. You did this on your own."

"You'll take the money," I say. "The money doesn't worry you in the least." In the last few years, my wife has picked up rather expensive habits. To a certain degree this is a compensation for loneliness and the loss of central urgency in our marriage which is why I do not begrudge her any of this. Nevertheless, I sometimes like to tease her. "You're like anyone else," I say, "as long as you don't have to face the consequences of your acts or the source from which they come, you'll do anything.

But you're on a higher emotional plane, of course."

"You are a disgusting cold man. You have no feelings. All the feelings have been squeezed out of you a long time ago. All you do is analyze; analyze and torment. How can you take yourself seriously? Don't you know what I think of you?"

"I'm tired," I say. "I don't want to discuss it. Am I not entitled to some relaxation on a night home? Do I have to start all over again with pain and accusation? Get me a drink. Give me the newspaper. Sit by and comfort me with caresses. What's wrong with you?"

"Oh, Walter," she says and something breaks slowly within her; I can see her surfaces waver, reassemble at a different point, "Walter, I can't stand this anymore. What's happened to us? Where are we going? What is to become of us? Oh, Walter, I want children. We must have children, Walter, before what has happened becomes solidified in the cells and then our children would be monsters. We must — "

"Now you are being naive and sentimental," I say and stand, go to the sideboard, mix myself a drink. Straight scotch and drink it slowly, feeling the even fires of alcohol burn me cleanly, sever me in two. "We must work out our fate in the present time; it is too late to pass on solutions to the next generation. We live here in this world and in this world we must make our accommodation. I will not allow you to ease the problems along, shelve them once again on abstractions. Do you understand? Live in this world."

This is cruel of me and I am not so beyond feeling for her that I do not know it, that I fail to see what saying this does to her. Nevertheless, I cannot become sufficiently interested in the situation to retract what I have said; the concern that gave me patience is long gone and now, more and more, I feel that we must hasten in our marriage toward endings. Past the balance wheel of a relationship, this always happens. When you get to the center, the urgency is to get outside again.

VI

Pausing at a newsstand to admire the prominent display given our current issue and its competitors, I see my newspaper in the process of being bought. A small, scholarly man carrying a briefcase leans over toward the newsstand, plucks my newspaper from the top of its pile and reaches to hand fifty cents to the dealer. The dealer, however, is engrossed in a magazine and does not, for the moment, see him, inducing a kind of restlessness that verges on panic. The purchaser grunts, shrugs his shoulders, leans forward to tap the dealer on the shoulder. Before he can,

I intervene.

"Pervert," I say in a monotone, pulling the brim of my hat all the way down to the eyeline. "Fool. Idiot. What are you buying that stuff for?"

"Please," the purchaser says, trying to stuff the paper under his arm, "I'll thank you to — "

"Don't kid me," I say, implacably. "I saw. We see everything, you know. We've got our eye on you people, every single one of you, and we have for a long time. There's a special branch which does nothing but keep up files on you people. You're heading for trouble sooner than you think."

The purchaser puts the paper atop the pile, trembling, and turns to flight. "Hold on," I say, seizing the sleeve of his overcoat between thumb and forefinger, nailing him into place with a single determined yank of the head. "It's too late now. You can't run away, not ever. You might as well buy it. Take it home and perform upon it your unspeakably brutal acts while dreaming of the limbs of the untouched child. Do you think that it would make any difference at this point?"

"You're blocking my newsstand," the dealer says, looking up from the magazine. "That's not allowed."

"Please, my friend," I say, taking the newspaper back from the pile, handing the dealer fifty cents and putting it in the purchaser's arm all in a swift, blurred series of motions, "please take it with my compliments. We want to do everything to ease your burden in this world."

He takes it, mouth compressing, and turns to run, his shoulders hunched against the cold. I watch him go while standing in place, then take a copy of our largest competitor and give the dealer his money before withdrawing to a more neutral position under a streetlight. There I open the newspaper to an innocuous inside spread featuring lines of text, turn it around and shield my face while I watch the newsstand further.

Three more purchases of my newspaper are made over the next hour. One is by a cleric in full dress, one by an ambiguous middle-aged man with a pained and convulsed face and one by an elegant Negro lady who thrusts it into her armpit and goes tap tap tapping down the avenue, heels hitting the pavement like glass, ass high, wide and handsome to the avenue, the compressed features of her face like stone as they recede. I think of common destinies and then think of nothing at all, leaving the demographics of the issue to our circulation manager who is trying to open up certain outlets in the midwest.

VII

A short story is submitted to us for our consideration. From time to time we run an appeal for material from readers; our own capacities for invention are almost nil after two years of publication, and most of the scripts and photographs submitted to us through the agencies lack vitality, lack any kind of conviction other than the writer or photographer's need for money at the given moment. Our regular contributors, sad to say, are a group of weary hacks and now, after over a hundred issues, the same models are beginning to reappear in the photographic submissions; blond for black, smirk for sneer, the familiar attitudes remasked. For all of its seeming pervasiveness, this is a small repertory theater which we run, and most of the actors have reached that stage where they are completely dependent upon gesture.

The short story is by a young man whose covering letter states that he is an unpublished writer but has been following our newspaper for a long time and is now eager to break into print via the wealth of experiences he has had. The story describes his first sexual experience at the age of fourteen with several animals and a parish priest and then goes on to detail an orgy which the writer visited two years later and at which he had the act of sexual intercourse fifteen times within twelve hours with ten female partners. As we are entitled to hope, the script does have a certain conviction and vitality, and we decide to publish it although not quite in its submitted form, we change the names of all the characters since the author has used his own, and we relocate the events from the east coast to the rural south. One section, in which the writer describes masturbating a rooster to climax, we decide is not credible and we eliminate this although we do leave in his description of his fifteenth orgasm at the orgy which he describes as "ferocious and stupendous and almost the very best of them all although I thought that my prick was going to fall off inside her with the force of my desire." Virginia, signing herself "associate editor" and using a pseudonym, types a letter of acceptance to the author and advises him that our payment of $10, due thirty days after publication, will reach him with a complimentary copy of the newspaper in due course.

Afterward, perversely excited, for reasons I do not understand, I level her panting on the office couch and have her not once but twice within a span of fifteen minutes. At the peak, I hear a dim clucking and seek to shelter her with my feathers, feeling the stir and rustle of her body trapped below.

VIII

In the army, many years ago, a vision assaulted me during the nights and the vision was this: somewhere up on the hill, within the very sight of the barracks, the captain's wife was lying with the captain, and he could be, at any instant, entering her groaning; the knowledge that the captain's reality and my own could coexist within such a small area was astonishing, and toward the dawn it seemed that all things were possible, even that I, a private in basic training, could fuck the captain's wife if only I had the strength to demand it. Knowing the captain's limitations from close association with him, sensing the psychic impotence that oozed like slime from every crevice of his being, I could not believe that she found him desirable or her life with him happy; if it were only possible for me to carry my gifts up the hill and attend to her alone for an hour I could have everything that I wanted. Lying in the barracks toward the dawn, hearing the groaning of sleeping men around me, I felt that I could see her flesh, know the angle of her breast, know the slick tension of her thighs as they encircled to grasp but then reveille would come, and after reveille the pain and standing in the company street at noon, wincing against the sun, the day not a third over, listening to the captain scream, I knew that all of this was misdirection and lies and that no matter how close I came to her in the night, I would never have her in the real. Sometimes we would see her in the company area, coming to pay the captain a fast visit, exchange a quick confidence or two, and a gaze of perfect blankness would pass between us; her wide and empty eyes staring past the assembled troops and then to the greenery and then to the gardening orderlies picking up weeds outside the orderly room, and for all the discrimination she made between the three, she could have been in my bed that night, and I reaching out to overcome her.

IX

At the track: noise, color assault me. I am here to play a tip given me by Tony, one of the wholesalers for the Bronx district whose brother runs a handicapping sheet out of his home in Bay Meadows and who claims that he could make a small, effective living out of the racetrack if it did not fundamentally bore him. The tip is on Gemini, a bay filly out of Revoked who has been running in straight claimers but is today being dropped into a filly maiden for the first time; the word is that today, and with blinkers, she will atone for past deceits. I am here to play $50 for Tony and anything I wish for myself.

Unfamiliar with the races, I am nonetheless eager to learn. What marvelous passions, what heights of misdirection, what strange peace seems to afflict these people as they wander in the grandstand between bar and restaurant, tote board and window, rail and garden! Everything seems simple here; none of the complexities of the social organism and all of it reduced to figures, besides, in a paper which I can comprehend and worked out in races which I can see. Not for a long time have I permitted myself to believe in immediate outcome, but I am interested, hopeful; the office can wait for two hours and the payoff from the tip will more than cover me for my time. As I wander down toward the rail, a blond woman in a tight dress gives me an absent look compounded of desire and fear; vague but constant adulterous impulses churn, I wonder if I should ask her the time. I decide not to. I intimate from other sources that sex is nonexistent at the track.

By the rail, jammed cheek to shoulder with hundreds of others, I watch the running of the second race. My tip is on the third and for interest I have bet $2 on the longest shot in the race to show. The horses break from the gate opposite us and run down the backstretch, into the turn, and all the way through the unfolding stretch, hitting the finish wire some yards from where I stand. This is a simple enough act; as basic and straightforward in its convolutions as fucking or sleep but it seems to overwhelm the crowd; they scream and curse, shake their fists into the air and pray, do everything within their power to urge their horses on. A small man beside me seems to faint but before his head has even hit the rail he is awake again, bright-eyed and desperate, saying something about the seven horse. I try to clear a little space around me with knees and elbows, looking for my own number, but it seems hopeless. The race is over before I am even acclimated and I have no idea how my horse has done. Numbers come on the board and it turns out that my horse has placed. The numbers turn the screams of the crowd into dull rumbles, analyses, excuses. The race is declared official and my horse has paid thirteen dollars and eighty cents to show. I get in line to collect.

In the line I find further mysteries: no one seems particularly happy. Some feel that they should have bet their horses to win, others are convinced that they did not bet enough. They know that some person or forces have done terrible things to them, but I can see their advantage over me; they feel that this person or force is at the track this very afternoon and that there is still the possibility of intercession or, at least, of divining motive. It is something like being at God's elbow while the

Book of Life is made out for the coming year and you are able to discuss
the issue with him as slowly the names of friends, acquaintances and
relatives are written in, along with those of several enemies. Perhaps your
name will not appear. Then again, very possibly it will. The book is open
and God is writing; he is willing to hear your position on the matter.

I take my thirteen dollars and change and go forward to the seller's
area, seeing the blond woman for the second time that day. Her glance
is more meaningful; there is no question now that she is trying to get my
attention. She is not particularly attractive but there is a demented tilt
to her breasts under the tautness of her dress which excites me, and I
go to her side, ask her if she has any ideas on the next race, explain that
I have come out to bet it. She touches my wrist and leans against my
elbow, whispers something that I do not hear. We then make
arrangements to meet by the rear grandstand cigarette counter, ground
level, after the race. She shows some interest in staying with me, but I
explain that I have to meet associates on important business before the
running of the race and she is content. I hand her a cigarette and she
leaves.

I go to the $50 window and bet Tony's money on the horse to win.
Then, abstracted, I move over to the $100 window some feet down and,
under the glum face of a Pinkerton, bet $200 on the horse to place. As
I do this, feeling a faint warmth to the tickets, I feel a distant excitement
within me, but the excitement is hardly enough, and on the instant I
decide that I will play the horses no more. It does not seem worth it.

The betting completed, I return to the rail and watch the horses circle
the paddock and then move to the track for the post parade. The
jockeys sit uneasily on the horses, shake their heads, look at the sky while
around me people make comments on their riding in the last race and
beg them to do better or worse. Gemini turns out, through some error
in Tony's information, to be not a bay horse but a roan, a series of
uneven red blotches marring what would otherwise be a dirty gray. She
moves unsteadily, her feet trembling on the dirt, her head tossing now
and then to the opposite of her stride. I decide on the basis of the little
I know about horses that she is probably hurting, but for this too there
must be a reason; possibly only the question of pain will inform the horse
with terror and the need to run. I think of a veterinarian creeping into
the horse's stall at midnight to inflict brutalities upon her hips and hocks,
a cigarette dangling unhealthily between his lips as he cunningly inserts
nails into the bottom of each shoe. There is a certain air of disreputability
to the track which I like, although most of the people who surround me

seem to think that it is killing their chances.

In due course the horses get into the starting gate and across the track break for their seven furlongs. The filly is on top all the way but begins to stagger in the stretch and barely hangs on to finish third, beaten by several lengths by the second place horse and only a nose in front of the fourth horse. For the first time it occurs to me to look at the toteboard, and it turns out that the horse was 25–1, certainly enough to make a show bet very profitable. Sullenly I hope for a disqualification but this is not to be and once again the race becomes official. Gemini pays $14.60 to show, meaning that I would have won $1260 for my $200 if I had only been cautious as I had been the first time. It is, however, too late for considerations of this sort.

I begin to wonder why I am at the track. I decide to leave. I have forgotten the woman already but passing the Stevens cigarette stand I see her by herself, casting darting glances through the crowd, her hands fluttering as she reaches into her handbag for a cigarette, a certain fine beam of despair in her glance. I find that I have no stomach to leave her there and instead go over and tell her that I am now ready to leave but have lost several hundred dollars on a bad tip and am therefore unable to entertain her.

She gives me a complex look of bitterness, pain, and communion and says that I have obviously had the situation all wrong. That she is not that kind of person at all. That she would not permit herself to go around with a person who saw her in that way. That I have done nothing less than cheapen her in such a way that she literally is ashamed of herself for ever having spoken to me.

She moves to slap my face but I dodge agilely enough and move quickly down the stairwell and to the ground level, then out to the parking lot. My stride is loose, easy, a certain space seems to lay between my feet and the asphalt; unforeseen, a strange, manic tune begins to burble out of my throat. If I did not know better — but surely by this time I know better — I could almost swear that I have had a good time at the races and that like everyone there, I have found exactly what I was looking for.

X

Not since our fifth issue have we run pictures showing couples actually engaged in the act of sexual intercourse. The law of the land, as interpreted through the Supreme Court, seems clear enough: nothing that has socially redeeming value may be denied the rights of publication and mass distribution and all published materials have this socially redeeming value since they are an expression of certain phases of the culture, social obsessions, so to speak, and an index of the taste of thousands. Despite this, the District Attorney of Kings County, through his minions, seized several thousand copies of our fifth issue, the centerfold of which showed a man and woman lying side by side, his erect penis in the act of penetrating her vagina. The contention of the District Attorney was that this picture was pornography *per se* and unentitled to the protection of the First Amendment, and the efforts of our attorneys to block the action at the level of the first hearing were unsuccessful. The case went on appeal to the next highest court, but in the meantime the District Attorney carried an injunction enjoining all newsdealers in his borough from carrying further issues of our newspaper since the offending publication indicated that we were likely to print pornography in the future. Because of this, several of our outlets in the other boroughs became panicky and substantially cut down their orders for issues, while all hopes of out-of-town distribution were lost. Our attorneys stated that the action of the District Attorney was illegal and the case, when it got into the higher courts, would certainly be decided in our favor, but in the meantime we were faced with the possibility that the actions of the District Attorney could put us out of business. Sales of our sixth issue were off 75 percent from those of the fifth and of the seventh were even worse, and the clearest projections showed that we would hardly last another month unless the pressure on us was removed.

Our attorneys, then, worked out an agreement with the District Attorney whereby he would withdraw his injunction if we in return would promise not to run offending material in the future. We were not to show couples in the actual act of intercourse, we were not to show manipulation of the genitals and we were not to depict any acts which in the opinion of the District Attorney could be labeled an incitement to riot. Naked bodies, male and female, were permitted, as were pictures of males and females, females and females, or males and males together as long as intercourse, sodomy, or pre-coital play were clearly contraindicated. By agreeing to this compromise, we were able to recover our circulation and eventually paid only a very small fine. Our sales have never returned to the level that they reached at the point of offense, but on the other hand the newspaper has been extraordinarily profitable, and we would clearly be misguided if we were to risk our position for a principle whose finding would come too late to save us.

These are part of the compromises of publishing and I have little guilt or self-recrimination about the action which we took. Nevertheless, now and then, looking at proofs of the pages or the newspaper in actual distribution, I feel a sense of loss overtake me; it is not so much the act of connection that I find missing as a certain expression which seems to come to the faces of all couples engaging in sexual intercourse or even miming it. It is an expression of knowledge and cunning, complex apperception under the fact of connection, and for that which is missing, the pain and knowledge which overtakes even the ugliest and most professionalized model, I feel loss and wish that it could have been different while knowing that this can never happen.

XI

With a priest, a television producer and the moderator, I am sharing a panel on a late-night radio program, broadcast live over a network hookup from a small, shadowy, gutted studio in midtown Manhattan. The subject of the panel is the new libertarianism in the arts, and I have been invited as a demonstration case. The moderator, an ugly man in his fifties who intersperses insults of the most personal and vicious type with off-the-air reminders to us that there is nothing personal here at all and that he is only trying to get a discussion going, the moderator, as I am saying, has momentarily stopped the discussion to read an ad for a hamburger chain in New Jersey which serves a complete meal for nineteen cents and tosses in a hospitalization guarantee. The moderator's facial gestures are totally out of accord with his material as he speaks; he gives us to know, through a horrid series of winks, twitches and contortions, that he is a serious man given to serious purposes and that all of this nonsense is only the price that he must pay for the boldness of the discussions he hosts, the positions he takes. When he has finished the advertisement, he returns to the issue at hand, which happens to be my sense of responsibility for what I am publishing, and asks me if I would like to have my daughter read an issue of the newspaper I publish.

"I don't have a daughter," I say, "but if I did, I am sure that I would not object to her reading anything that happened to be in my home and, yes, my newspaper is often found in my home. I must take a lot of the work with me; what you have to understand is that this is a difficult business." The priest breaks in to say that he thinks that the moderator is arguing *ad hominem* and is misdirecting the issue which deserves to be taken on its own merits. He is a very libertarian priest, who is in favor of clerical marriages and the breaking down of the old Italian control of the Church although he, personally, observes the vows of celibacy. I hate to say this but I find the priest something of a bore; a bore and a fool as well, he reminds me of nothing so much as certain boys I knew in college who were afraid to go out with girls but had a kind of relentless jocularity about sex in general and believed that their social failures were personal rather than something to do with the scheme of things. That is what the priest is; a dormitory boy who has discovered the reality of sex at the age of forty and now, hopelessly too far behind to ever catch up, can only submit to it by laughing the question out of court. "The thing you should be asked," he says, "is not about your daughter because you're obviously too young to have a daughter who could be influenced by this newspaper in any way, but about your wife. Do you let your wife read your publication? What does she think of it?"

"My wife reads anything she wants to," I say, "I could hardly control her reading. She reads the newspaper, yes. I think she rather likes it although we've never discussed it in those terms. Mature adults don't feel they have to take *positions* on sexual material, you know." This is, perhaps, an unfortunate thrust, but it has been a long session, the studio is foul with our breath, and since there is no payment for the broadcast, one must take his compensation where he may.

"Exactly," says the television producer. He is a stunned little man who, many years ago I understand, directed a loathsome situation comedy into the top ten ratings; when the package changed hands and he was fired, he took a position with a university journalism department and appointed himself an academic critic of television; in due course he became associated with an educational channel from which he was never heard again except for occasional freelance articles in Sunday newspapers deploring the progress of the medium. "That is exactly the point." Then he folds his hands, takes a look down at an intricate doodle he has been composing and sighs further into the microphone. "I would think that one would ask his wife," he says. I find it difficult to understand exactly why he was added to this panel although the moderator, before the show went on the air, hastily whispered to the priest and myself that the "original" guest who was far more interesting had taken ill at the last moment and that in the interests of "balance" this is really all the network can produce at short notice. "If his wife is askable of course," the producer says.

There is a dead spot of silence into which the moderator moves quickly to question my sexual adequacy and wonder whether my newspaper has as its basis a psychic need in me to make sex ugly and degrading and punish all of its participants. It is somewhat subtler than this, of course, but I get the idea. I point out to him that my sexual life or lack of it has nothing to do with the significance or value of my work and that a similar statement could be made about, say, Karl Marx or Ernest Hemingway without in any way managing to come to the point. The priest says that he agrees with this wholeheartedly and the moderator makes a nasty, veiled comment about the code of celibacy. The producer says, "I think that we're all being dragged down to a gutter level now by our publisher-guest." The priest says that this is disgusting and offensive, the moderator says that the whole problem with sex nowadays is that the basic sacredness of the act has been utterly lost along with a sense of self-respect, and I feel the program literally beginning to dissolve under me; it is hard to maintain a proper sense of attention anymore and the room is wavering, voices are wandering; sounds are pulsing in the air as in the instants before deep sleep, and when I come to myself, my cigarette is being lit for me by someone who has come out of the control booth and I am talking passionately, floridly, about the reasons for my establishing the newspaper. It seems that I was sick of hypocrisy, sick of cant, sick of the whole insane bent of the culture which made death visible and glamorous yet shielded the act of love and the naked body as something despicable. It was a sickness in the culture which was symptomatic of the whole mad misdirection since the time of the industrial revolution and I had had enough of this, quite enough. I founded the newspaper because I wanted to do my part to tear open the windows and let the cold breath of sanity into the room of America. I realized that often the publication was perverse and offensive, but this was the way that it had to be if it were to have any vitality at all because the price of freedom was pain, the price of liberty was the blasting of cultural cant, and I was willing to do this because through the centuries it had been men like me who had restored human culture, periodically, to sanity through upheaval. I listen to myself with astonished interest; I appear to have a social conscience. Also it seems that I am making very little money from the newspaper, virtually every cent being plowed back to the distributors, the employees, the paper itself and most importantly the legal fund which is reaching massive dimensions as we face the necessity for a large number of court cases to prove that people have the right to their own thoughts and desires. The few dollars which I am making from the newspaper I could have made just as easily and at less strain on a payroll elsewhere and, in fact, did for many years, but decided when I passed the crucial age of thirty that I had to do something useful for my life, take a position at the barricades and try to save America from her own madness. The moderator listens to this with nods and winks reminiscent of the gestures with which he delivers the commercials and says that on that note he will wrap things up for the night and thank you very much all of you for attending; we cannot always agree with one another but we can learn to respect each other's motives, and this is the purpose of his program, to shed light on issues through people. The priest says that he is moved by my statement and on his own level is trying to do exactly that kind of thing within his impoverished Brownsville parish; the television producer coughs, struggling with a cigarette and says that he has learned through the years to take men seriously only through their acts and not so much through their rationalizations. I show him with a nod that I see his point and may even agree with it and the moderator signs us all off the air with a jingle for Howard Shoes which are not for cowards but for men who want to beat the blues. We stand up stiffly, twitching in the heat of the studio and shake hands. The moderator says that he thinks that this has been a very good show, interesting show, useful show, he must have all of us back soon for another go at it. Bearded men pour from the control booth, giggling, and ask me if I have any spare issues of the newspaper in my attaché case, or failing that, the numbers of any of the models. Once again things dissolve, although in full color this time, and when I come back to myself I am having a martini in an empty bar with the priest who seems to be drunk and who tells me in desperate tones that he was thirty-five years old before he understood that the flesh could no longer be denied, thirty-five wasted years, and another five to struggle through as far as he had come, but I have to understand the terrible guilt of a strict Catholic upbringing and it indeed would have happened to me if I had grown up in his circumstances. I am smoking a cigarette, appear to be agreeing with him, although with a quiet smile now and then for the bartender who appears, however, to be engaged with other business. Later I am in a taxicab alone going home and later than that I am lying in the bed, next to my naked and sleeping wife, listening to the playback of the radio program on which I have just appeared. I listen to my voice with quizzical interest; I have no idea what I am getting at. My wife is a light sleeper and I could, at any moment, reach over and with a touch on her buttocks turn her toward me and reach for her breasts, take the obligatory act of love that at three in the morning comes from whatever source as full of mystery and need … but I do not want to touch her, I am lying bolt upright in the bed at three in the morning, listening to the radio, listening to my voice, trying to understand what I am saying, and it seems that if I could only get to the sense of it, I would come to a sense of myself which would answer all of the questions, but I know that it is not that easy and listening to the bland, shrieking confidence of my intonation, so self-righteous that I could cut it, I begin to come to a different perception, and the perception is one of confusion and loss, and finally I fall asleep although not for a long time and not to an easy awakening.

XII

During one of our afternoons, I ask Virginia to blow me to climax. I confess to her, with some embarrassment, that although my wife is willing to try this she does it so inexpertly that I am unable even to maintain an erection and that never, in my whole life, have I come in a woman's mouth. "Please," I say, touched with an awkwardness which I rarely feel with her, "please, I'd really appreciate it if you would."

"Oh," she says, leaning over me, her breasts hobbling, her mouth a thin opening line above mine, "oh you poor dear, you don't have to beg. No man should ever have to *beg*. See, there's nothing to it at all." For the first time she puts her mouth on my genitals, my cock uncoils to readiness, a truly murderous need overtakes me, and before I have even attained control of the situation I find that I am pouring semen into Virginia's mouth, grunting, feeling my body press into the bed, a high whine somewhere between embarrassment and passion overtaking me. Silent, she wags her head back and forth, motions me to quiet with a gesture and then drains me of every thread of semen, leaving me slack and gasping against the sheets. When she is finished, she smiles carefully at me and goes to the bathroom to do something, comes back and joins me under the sheets, a hand falling across my chest, her mouth curling against my ear. "See," she says, "it wasn't so much after all. It's very simple."

I say nothing. I am in a half-sleep. I want to dream the moments away, establish some connection within myself between what has happened and what I thought it may have been like. If I can do this, I will have come one step further toward knowing what kind of person I am. But Virginia is insistent, talkative. This is usually one of her more endearing traits — I cannot bear silences most of the time — and I am in no position to tell her to keep quiet.

"You have to make a decision, you know," she says. "This can't go on. It can't go on this way at all, we have to reach an understanding."

"What understanding?"

"Your wife. You have to do something about your wife."

"I love my wife," I say and realize that this is true. "My wife has seen me through all ages and stages. There is nothing simple about what we have constructed, where I have come from."

"Did your wife ever do this for you?"

"No," I say, "but that isn't the most important thing. The important thing is what you build up through the years; you owe a relationship something, it has dimension you know. Anyway, I don't know if I liked it."

"You wanted it, didn't you?" she says. "And she wouldn't do it for you. It's always going to be this way. You've got to make a decision, Walter. Things can't go on this way; they have to reach some kind of a resolution sooner or later. Try to think of me."

"You didn't have to come to work for me," I say, "You knew what the situation was. You knew what you were getting involved in. If you don't like the job, you'll have to get yourself involved with something less degrading." This is cruel of me, I know, but I take a certain pleasure in punishing Virginia and never so much pleasure as when she has just seen me in moments of great vulnerability. It is perhaps the only weapon I have, this ability to make her vulnerable emotionally as she renders me helpless sexually. "You didn't seem to have any objection," I say.

"Oh, Walter," she says, putting her cheek against my neck, raising herself with a slow motion that puts her breasts against my chest, running her hands up and down my stomach until I feel something intricate within break and begin to spill out in small, shocking waves, "Walter, you don't have to be this way if you don't want to. There's so much pain in you; we should try to cleanse the pain rather than make you hurt. You don't have to hurt, Walter," she says and comes against me. I can feel the wetness of her box as she flexes and unflexes her legs. Momentarily limp, there is nothing that I can do but hold her, look at the walls, look at the window, look at the outlines of the city as I listen to the creak of the hotel elevator and wonder how many scenes have been enacted in this very bed, scenes that to be sure, all of the participants felt to be consequential, and now many of those participants dead, locked in ashes, facing the sky, all passions resolved in the simple cloak of renunciation and mystery.

XIII

The most popular feature of our newspaper and its competitors is the "personals" section, five or six pages of classified material at the end of the issue in which a diverse group of individuals and corporations advertise services or make pleas for companions. Most of the acts or goods solicited are obscene, of course, but a network of euphemism has grown up around the suggestions over the past decade and since the newspaper itself emphasizes that it takes no position on its advertisers and no responsibility for outcome, we stand well within the law of obscenity on this point.

The ads, for all their seeming diversity, break into two groups: there are corporations which (under several different names) advertise sexual goods and satisfactions, masturbation machines, dildoes, creams to retard orgasm, life-size inflatable female dolls to take into the shower and so on ... and then there are individuals (almost always male) who conceive of sexual connection as a more random, less systematized kind of affair; they call for companions of various inclinations and advertise their own qualifications which usually have to do with the size of genitalia although the question of emotional sensitivity is not to be overlooked. The ads come in steadily, a mournful stream of mail, checks for advance payment enclosed, across my desk, and replies to the mail come in as well to the box numbers which our newspaper maintains at an additional charge to facilitate communication between interests. The mail to the box numbers seldom equals in volume the number of original ads, and there are whole strings of advertisements (usually taken by single men in search of afternoon female companionship) which never receive any replies whatsoever, filling me with a kind of vagrant sadness. It seems to me that for an individual, the act of placing an ad is in itself such a difficult admission that our advertisers are entitled to all the help they can get. Of course this may be projecting a trifle; I cannot conceive of placing such an ad myself at any stage of my life although it is true that I found Virginia herself through an open call for employees published in the classified section of the newspaper. In this way, I was sure that I would find someone preselected, so to speak, for the job.

As I occasionally do, I opened a letter at random the other morning and found that it was an advertisement requested by a young man in search of a homosexual partner. (Homosexuals in the columns of this newspaper seem to severely outnumber heterosexuals although the paper itself is purely heterosexual; I do not know exactly what to make of this. Are our homosexual readers settling for second best in their choice of reading material or in their selection of a sexual partner? This might be worth working out at length at some time in the future although I hardly have the time to come to grips with abstractions.) The text of the advertisement read: *Young man, 29, slim build, well-hung, is a member of the rear-guard. Seeks similar partner for fun and games, possible longer-lasting relationship. Interested in French and Greek cultures as a sideline and also has some curiosity about water-sports. Call NNFGOST anytime.*

I was alone in my office at the time, Virginia at one of her long lunches and the two homosexuals involved in a legal conference having to do with true sales figures and the exact percentage of purchases to returns. (This is difficult ground to walk; on the one hand we want to show the District Attorney that there is very little profit in the newspaper and that his illegal actions have severely hurt our business; on the other hand we do not want to circulate the impression that we are not doing well or are in any kind of financial trouble. The true sales figures, of course, are a mystery and we can only seek a figure which would be an appropriate metaphor.) Nevertheless, I locked the outer door and then closed the door of my office before I picked up the phone and dialed NNFGOST.

A wavering, uncertain voice answered. This is to be expected; the more insolent or outlandish the ad, the less can be expected from the proprietor. "Hello," I said, "I saw your ad in the new issue. I'm calling up in reply."

"Oh," he said with a giggle, "I didn't even know that it was out yet. The new issue. I just placed the ad a couple of days ago."

"Well it is," I say. "What do you mean about water sports? Exactly what did you have in mind?"

"Oh, that was just an extra. Something that I put in. A lot of the fellows are interested in that kind of stuff. It really isn't my thing, but I'd be happy to cooperate. Are you, uh, interested in water sports?"

"What are water sports?"

There was a thick, clamoring pause on the other end, then the voice said, "I thought that everyone knew."

"I don't know. I'm very interested."

"You haven't told me anything about yourself. You've got my number and know what I want and everything and I don't know anything about you at all."

"That's perfectly all right," I said. "You think that people take pleasure from being pissed on. Is that what you mean?"

"I don't," he said rather hysterically. "It isn't my kind of thing at all.

French and Greek — "

"French and Greek," I said, "I bet that it's French and Greek. Listen you lousy, stinking pervert, we've had our eye on you for a good long time. You don't think that you can live unobserved in this country, do you? You don't think that there can be any secrets from us, do you? Think of the most private, unspeakable act you have committed, the act which is locked deepest in your memory and which you are sure no one but yourself can ever know and *that act*, that very act, is written down somewhere in a file folder in black and white in an alphabetized drawer and can be reached by us anytime we want to look you up. You think that we can take this kind of thing seriously?"

"You're a prankster," he said weakly, his voice modulating now to the perfect and predictable faggart's shriek, just as I had expected. "You're just out to torment me, to take advantage because I have the courage to come out in the open. I'm going to hang up on you and call the police."

"Don't give me that gay liberation crap," I said. "You're a lousy stinking homosexual, that's all you are and that's all you're ever going to be and you can dress it up with French and Greek and water sports all you like but you know exactly what you are. You disgust me. You are committing a crime against nature and God, do you know that? You are placing your soul in jeopardy, you are risking your eternal future because you don't have the strength to control your bestial and stinking impulses. Well, you take a tip from me, friend, we are watching you with the closest and greatest interest and the biggest favor you could do yourself is to get the hell out of the newspapers. Your private nightmare is your own affair but when you start pandering — "

"You're crazy," he said in a shaky, quavering voice. I could see him, the bastard, trembling over the telephone, his thighs and mouth caving open, his whole body curved to a position of entrance, the sheer weakness of him oozing from every pore. "You're crazy. This can't be real. This is America."

"Yes," I say, carefully meshing an older concept with a newer, "yes, my friend you are right. This is America."

Then I hang up on him, chuckling from a sudden weakness of my own which causes me to stagger to the window in search of fresh air. Through the vents the city pours over me, the clear, stinking gray of it clearing my head and giving me a better orientation. I put the phone back in the center of my desk, toss the ad into the out bin, take the check to give in to accounting and then for a while I merely sit, hands behind head, chair tilted toward the window, looking at New York spreading out underneath me like a fish abandoned on shore, gasping for air.

This is no easy position into which I have gotten myself, but it has certain narrow compensations which, after a fashion, can keep one going.

XIV

On the streets in the summer I am overcome by seizures of lust, follow strange, pretty girls for blocks on end muttering to myself and watching their bodies move ahead of me as if they contained all light, all purpose, all sense and structure. In their dresses the girls look untouchable, the vulnerability of their flesh and soft breasts masked by a slow hardness which begins at the eyes and descends through all areas and levels of their faces, ending at last around the waist from which fulcrum they move in urgent, contained motions that simulate but have absolutely nothing to do with intercourse. I have noted this hardness more and more in recent summers; it seems to me that girls, when I was younger, did not look this way but faced the streets with demureness and fear. Now there is something else, something almost shattering, an air of malevolence which marks them as both dangerous and desirable. The hardness only makes them more sensual; I yearn to touch, to cleave myself against them, to tell them secrets.

Following them in stunned gaze, my whole body poised to attention, the mind only a numb chatter in the midst of the sensibility, I feel that if I could only somehow go up to them and lay before them my fear and desire, my uniqueness and pain, they would submit to me, for I know that what goes on inside of me when I look at these girls is the churnings of an emotion more profound than ever they have known before. I am sure, at the moments of pursuit, that I love them more than their parents or boy friends, fiancés or husbands, children or employers; if only given the chance I could sculpt out for them that love in a way which they could not refuse … but I find it impossible to speak to them. Sometimes, heads swinging from side to side, they nail me with a gaze, and in that gaze is such complacence, protectiveness and contempt mingled that it is all I can do to keep from gasping on the street and holding onto my sides for comfort. I cannot speak to them. There is no way, I understand this, no way in which I could ever establish myself with these girls, for the messages they send out in midsummer casualness are not those which can take any reply.

"Listen here," I want to say to them, pinning them against a wall, holding out my hands, showing the streaked, innocent palms, the fine, intelligent crinkle of my forehead. "Listen here, I am a college graduate, thirty-four years old, highly intelligent with a good income, and I feel for you more deeply than you could ever know. I have wit, a good deal of background, have had my small successes with women and am considered good in bed. Perhaps you would not approve of my occupation or source of income *in toto*, but the fact is that I am doing very nicely and am less corrupt than any of the account executives or copywriters who catch your attention; I am at least meeting existing desires rather than trying to create them, and I am meeting those desires on their only level of comprehension. I had a terrible time in the Army, almost losing my life when in Europe, I had high marks in college, I was a successful editor, I performed a unique and courageous act in giving up all of that to found my own business two years ago. You can be led to appreciate this. It is not only your breasts and eyes which engage me, not your hips and walk, the fine density of your upper arms bare to the sun, no, no, it goes far beyond those perversities and has to do with necessities of the spirit. But even if it did not, what is the difference? Do you think the account executives or copywriters who are laying you steadily on Friday and Saturday night within the context of a relationship, do you think that the aspiring writers and artists with whom you are shacked up in a meaningful situation, do you think that any of them are thinking of your *mind* when their hands encircle your breasts and, groaning, begin to take possession? Have none of that my dear; they are informed only by the basic lusts and urges which sent me into flight after you… but there is so much more to me than lusts and urges, there is a whole range and depth to my personality which you will never understand unless you give me a chance, a chance, that is to say, to explain myself to you, to connect to you on my own terms. Oh, God, give me that chance." And I would throw myself in front of their hard little shoes for love and necessity's sake, would have them stamp the very life out of me with their magnificent knee-length leather boots but none of that, of course, not a bit of it; after a time, I tire of the hopelessness of it and duck into a sidestreet or a store, return to the office to perform my sullen tasks.

And if I were to speak to them, at the moment of completion I know this: that I would look up toward their faces yearning and would see spreading from eyes to cheek, brow to mouth, the most perfect expression of querulousness, and they would say to me, "I don't know what you're talking about. Get out of my life before I call the police."

As if they were not an incitement to riot. As if they were not glittering stone against which a man could break himself for desire, savaging the polished surfaces, looking for the smallest crevice into which he could sink his fingers, grab hold before the Fall.

XV

In the Army, in Germany, three whores came to us on field maneuvers and took customers on in a tent a few hundred yards from the main bivouac area. We were in training for a fortnight in the field, cold and snow driving the days to flatness underneath us, and it was inconceivable that the whores could survive that German winter without protection, but somehow they did. No one knew where they came from or where they went after they had hustled a weekend's work; it was certainly not to the tent which they broke and abandoned, but there was no town within many miles of the bivouac area and no way, seemingly, in which they could be out again in the early morning, preparing for a quick, covert fuck before reveille. Nevertheless they survived; they were part of the training maneuvers, as consequential as the rifles, the snow or the helmets, and as we were apt to do in the Army at that time, we took things for granted. If Germany provided us whores, we (or some of us) would use them; if Germany wanted its slab of reparations in this manner, we would pay them. There was very little to do with the money and the whores were reasonable; $5 American, fuck until you come, quick or slow one price, all means and methods utilized, if it were necessary. The whores were libertarians who did not understand American cunning. I was not the only man who masturbated an hour before going to their tent and who spent half the afternoon inside, staring at the tent wall in the act of fucking, trying to embarrass the mind out of all thought, canceling any question of sexual imagery as one shoved it into the German cunt as one might have pressed it against the rough impassive surfaces of the tent. The whores were not pretty, but under the circumstances this hardly mattered; they had hard, useful bodies and the absence of prettiness meant that the question of emotion would not enter into and complicate the matter. I was never able to get their identities straight; they all had thick, Teutonic names, closed their eyes while in the act of copulation and squeezed with small, grunting yanks of the pelvis to urge the semen forward.

The whores had one interesting effect upon the company; they converted all of us — married, unmarried, young, middle-aged, talented, untalented — into whores ourselves because like prostitutes we began to think and live solely in terms of the sexual act, and there was very little else that interested us at that time. Gambling fell off, so did insults and jockeying for favored positions among the men, goldbricking fell off, the only thing that was important and which involved people were the whores and the question of arranging for their time, making sure, days in advance, that a guaranteed fuck was there. Fucking has never been as important to me as it was during this time, which may have something to do with the metaphysics of proximity or then again only with the dull, numbing effect of the German landscape upon us in that cold, diminishing winter.

Of the two hundred in the company, only seventy or so were actually cohabiting with the whores; the others talked wisely of disease or loyal wives or the cheapening effects of paid, predictable sex or the danger of consorting with ugly women who, for all we knew, might have been spies… but this majority was as affected by the whores as those who were actually using them; they were forced to reexamine, no less than the customers, the question of their lives as controlled by the whores, and it was not a cheap period in anyone's life. If one of the benefits of the Army is its ability to provide a heightening of experience, a continuing reappraisal of action under the influences of pain and boredom, then surely the whores were as effective as any platoon sergeant or insane colonel in making metaphysicians of the least of us. They were also wholly unconcerned with question of rank; officers and enlisted men alike paid the $5 fee, and officers received no preference in making appointments. It was like the open latrine privileges during combat.

Hunched over my whore, working toward the slow throes of orgasm, certain vicious German insects buzzing wintrily around us in the night, I opened my eyes to the burlap and had an apprehension, a vision so dark and full that it explained all consequence, fixated me in time and space, made clear the question of my destiny, and I reached toward it groaning, but as I was on the verge of touching it, something broke within me and spasmed out along with helpless seeds of climax, and the lights behind the vision faded; I found it yanked from me before I could touch it and was left with only the small clutching whimpers of the whore against me as she touched my face and wished me good; staggered then from the bed in the lamplight to find my clothes but, stumbling on the dirt, fell to Earth and lay there for a time too weary to get up, post-coital *tristesse* locking my limbs, and when the whore said to me in the darkness, "hurry, hurry," I did not know for a moment from where her voice came or whom she was talking to, and the vision of the Captain's wife came upon me; the Captain's wife as she must have looked under him as she spread and took his agony within, but before I could get a glimpse of her face it all winked out again and I was struggling with my boots and thinking helplessly of the Captain's wife who in no way could be equated with the whore … but the captain's wife is a different story altogether and does not fall within the context of this memoir.

XVI

A small, disheveled girl from one of the consumer magazines comes to interview me in my offices. She cannot guarantee that the magazine will be doing an article on us, but our kind of publishing is becoming an increasingly important phenomenon, affecting increasing numbers of people, and the magazine, which is devoted to covering the whole panorama of American madness, is beginning to gather material for a feature. Perhaps they will run it; if so I can look for it in about three months. On the other hand, if I do not wish to cooperate with the interviewer, that is perfectly all right with them; they have already obtained interviews from several of my competitors and the article will cover the whole spectrum of sex publishing, meaning that one element more or less will not affect the overall veracity of the piece. This is a summary of this magazine's attitude toward publishing. I tell the girl, whose name is Rona Milliken, that I am perfectly happy to cooperate with the magazine in any regard they ask, and that there was no need for her disclaimer or explanation. At this she relaxes a trifle although a continuing jangle afflicts her wrist-bracelets, a jangle that increases slightly in tempo as I lock the door of my office for privacy and sit behind my desk in a position of modified alertness. "When did you start the newspaper?" Rona Milliken asks. "And precisely what did you have in mind when you started it? Were you merely trying to exploit the new libertarianism or did you have larger purposes in mind?"

"I was the first, you know," I say. "I opened up the doors to the whole genre. If I hadn't had the courage to yank the shoestring, none of these other thieves would have come in behind me. They've just used my convictions without giving anything back to them. They merely wish to exploit. I have a definite philosophical purpose. I was the first of them all you know."

"Yes," she says, "I know that. I mean, we've done a lot of basic research already. We don't go out on a story until we know enough about it already to feel that we want to give it full coverage."

"Well then what do you have to say about it?"

The jangling stops and she gives me a trapped, birdlike twitch of her head. "About what? What do you mean?"

"About our newspaper being the first? Doesn't this count for credit? Just as your magazine was first in its field, we were first in ours. This should induce some sympathy, no? I wouldn't want you to do one of your sarcastic, satiric articles on us, you know. We're entitled to a little respect."

"I don't set editorial policy. I'm simply a researcher and interviewer. Then I turn the findings over to someone else who writes it."

"You mean you don't even write?"

"I *write*," Rona Milliken says with an uneasy twitch of her feet, "it's just that I don't write for the *magazine*, if you follow what I'm saying. I do a lot of writing on my own. Short stories and articles. I'm trying to get a novel started but it's very hard."

"Maybe you'd like to do some writing for us."

"Oh, no," she says, "they wouldn't permit that. Under your employment contract you can't sell anything until you leave employment. The short stories that I'm writing are just for the *future*."

"We can give you a pseudonym. No one ever has to know that you did some writing for us. You can do it under a pen name. We could use some feminine first-person stuff. The trouble is that almost everything we publish lacks vitality. Sex writing is an unexplored field. Almost everybody doing it is there because they can't make it anywhere else or just to turn a few dollars until they can do something useful. No one takes it seriously."

"I don't think I could be a *sex* writer," Rona Milliken says and puts her pad in the other hand, brings down the pencil, tries to look businesslike. A slow, uneasy flush spreads out over her cheekbones bringing for the first time the taint of sexuality to her face. Her breasts heave slightly. I begin to understand how a man could, after a fashion, have sex with Rona Milliken and not feel that his time was entirely wasted. Might, as a matter of fact, see it as a Significant Experience.

"I'm sure you could," I say. "I'm sure you have the talent and I have no doubt but that you could bring some very interesting background to your writing. Certainly you'd have a lot of interesting first-person material to share. Where did you go to college?"

"Wellesley," she says and then shakes her head, focuses on the pad. "Listen," she says, "I'm supposed to be interviewing *you*. Now if you don't want to cooperate, if you don't want to talk about yourself — "

"It's all nonsense," I say, leaning forward, slipping the pencil from her fingers with the most delicate of gestures, fixing my eyes upon her face and then moving them slowly downward toward the thrusting slope of her breasts, nicely supported by an expensive brassiere which gives them a tilt I was sure they could not have in the real … and am nonetheless excited for all of that. "You're making a $105 a week after taxes and you're restless. Unhappy. You feel somehow that your talents are not being utilized, that you are wasting the most capable years of your young life in foolish tasks presided over by uncaring, bloodless men. Every now and then you wonder if you have any purpose whatsoever; if what they taught you in Wellesley applies at all. Then you try not to think about it and tell yourself that you're beginning to come to grips with the world. But the thoughts still will not go away. Sometimes at night you can't sleep; you get up and stare out the window for hours, looking at New York and wondering if you can survive it or whether it is only using your hopes to destroy you. Sometimes, quite often as a matter of fact, you spend the evening with men, in their places or yours, but it is not satisfying. There seems to be no future to it. Also, they never slip out of gear. What you are looking for, although there is no way that you can understand this, is for something irrevocable to come into your life and to change it past the possibility of redemption."

"Get away from me."

"No, I will not get away from you," I say, moving my hands gracefully up her soft thin arms, twirling my fingers in her careless, fine hair, blowing my breath upon the bland sheen of her forehead. "I will not get away from you because you don't want me to, you see. Not at all. Actually, I entice and excite you; my tasks are mysterious, my person disturbing to you. You don't know if it's me or the very ambiance of this office; the half-bared pictures you can see peeking out from spaces on the desk blotter, the displays on the wall of some of our most notable centerfolds, the obscene sampler on the wall behind me. You find this unbearably exciting because it comes utterly outside of the confines of your life and functions as some externalization of your need. The truth of the matter, Rona, is that you want me; you want me desperately. They all want me, all of them. Now put that pad down and stop acting like a child. Begin to seize your life. It is the only life you have."

And I go toward her then, strip the pad from her palms, drop it with a crash and crinkle on the floor and falling across the chair where she is poised, pin her toward the rear, then, slowly, slowly, begin to ease her toward the couch itself. And all the time, with small whimpers and gurgles she works with me, her fingernails scraping my chest in small convulsions of assent, her mouth unevenly taking in air and exhaling it in sighs of cooperation. "I won't, I won't," she says, "this can't be, you're crazy, this is impossible, what do you think you're doing; who do you think you are?" And at last, onto the couch itself in which her moans transmogrified into caws of submission and finally triumph and in the end it is her flesh that overcomes mine, I lying perfectly stunned and open on the couch, looking once again at the ceiling as huffing and humping she forces me to climax, the small freckled breasts of her bobbing me into small shrieks of woe as I stare at the pictured newsprint on the wall and imagine myself seized by a giant fist, a fist gone mad, yanking the last drops of fluid out of me and the fluid dry, wrenching sputum of the soul as I heave and moan into the very center of Rona Milliken.

There is a whole new brand coming out of the women's colleges nowadays. Afterwards, we finish the interview. It is a good one and she says that she is sure that we will be given due credit in the final treatment.

XVII

Out to the track again on Tony the distributor's second tip. Poor information, a crooked jockey, an inept stable source contributed to the disaster on the first, but this time the word is that things are straight and that amends are made. Out in the subway special this time, I look at the people with interest; they stare, quivering, at tipsheets and the *Morning Telegraph*, occasionally mumbling "bastards" to themselves. Once I took this kind of hatred for granted, but now I see it as unique and motivated; I am beginning to see their point. Life examined from their point of view is eliciting some very sane responses. At the track I go directly to the windows, make the bet on the first race and walk to the rail, a sense of purposefulness overcoming me. No waste this time around. People make way for me, smoking cigars, picking their noses, examining the lights on the tote under the shade of hands. The horses break from the gate and the tip wins by seven lengths, galloping, in near track-record time, paying $21.40. I collect Tony's $2,140 and then go to the $5 show window to collect my own winnings of $14. I feel that I have learned something although I am not sure exactly what. Tony's two thousand will apply to his long-standing debt to us so that part of it is all right. No, it is something else I have learned, something that is either subverbal or beyond the poor artifices of words. It has to do with the question of timing, and if timing is merely another word for mortality, then I have learned almost all of it, although it will almost certainly take me several years to get it straightened out in mind and codified to a set of principles which will do me any good at all.

XVIII

About the two faggarts of whom I have said little there is even less to say. One is circulation director and the other accountant although their jobs are often interchangeable and they actually work as a team in performing those mechanical, mathematical tasks, which permit us to remain on the newsstand week after week, adding our own dosage of liberation to the general mix which is contemporary America. I hired one on the recommendation of the other, and when I saw them take to twittering in the corridors and exchanging meaningful, yearning looks over papers in the midday, understood that I had been utilized, but since both of them are competent at their jobs and since neither engages in any questionable activities in the office, I have no reason to complain. One advantage of their condition is that I have a clear field with Virginia (who despises them) and another is that they lend a certain rococo elegance to the offices; a tired tilt of the finger bringing back to me centuries of medieval or baroque charm, a hint of classical music wafting through the air when they whisper to one another. Homosexuality is a convenience these days, perhaps even a minor social asset, and although I have never been able to comprehend men who want one another's flesh, I do not sit in judgment of them and find the activities themselves unremarkable. There is so little to visualize that I do not even speculate. The faggarts keep the office going, they provide our lawyers with unending lists of figures to show the District Attorney, and they lend my life a certain smugness, a certain low security which I accept without probing deeper. I do not think that either one of them has the slightest comprehension of what is actually going on in the newspaper or has ever done more than scan an issue or two. They seem to think that we are in one branch or another of trade publishing. One of them is named Donald and the other is Jim. We all call one another by our first names in these offices.

XIX

My wife has joined some kind of feminine activist movement whose meetings and rallies she attends once or twice a week, and in the evenings she is home, she moves about with a new sullenness, a kind of grim determination around the mouth and eyes that is new although not entirely discomfiting. "Now I understand," she says, "exactly why I've lived with you all these years; why I've put up with this kind of thing from the first. I'm afraid that this is the best that I can do and my training is to unquestioningly accept the supremacy of the male ego. What a fool I was! but it is of course never too late," And a wise expression causes her mouth to purse. "Never too late," she says, "although all of us have a long, long way to go."

I find the whole thing vaguely uncomfortable, but we have had too much trouble ourselves with the feminine activists recently to make me anything but very cautious in all of my dealings with them. The feminine activists assaulted our office in a body, some weeks ago, three or four miserable girls who said that we were degrading the female form and figure and pandering to the chauvinist impulses of diseased men to use women as mere outlets for their poisonous desires. I pointed out calmly enough that both males and females were shown nude in our pages and that women were as free to masturbate in or upon the newspaper as men; it was sheerly a matter of choice or taste. This seemed to satisfy the girls or at least to confuse them. They withdrew, mumbling to one another and stealing several copies of the current issue which happened to be available at that time. I thought that our difficulties were resolved, but it seemed that they were only biding their time; very shortly after that they got my wife, and now things around the house are more difficult than ever, although I try to spend a minimum of time there in the first place.

"You went into the business to degrade women," she says, turning after an hour of silence in the bedroom, to face me across the covers. "It was as simple as that. All your life you were looking for an image of degradation and you found it. It was so simple, really. I should have figured it out a long time ago."

"You take the money," I say, but with a feeling of tiredness; the standard response no longer seems appropriate to the circumstances.

"It was male power mania," she says. "The whole thing is so easy to understand when you look at it the proper way. I was a fool. It was in front of me all the time."

"We print naked men, too."

"That's rationalization. And men are always pictured as the aggressors."

"What do you do during the days, Dorothy? I don't even know any more. You never tell me."

"I do a lot of things. Recently I've been going to meetings. What do you care? You never ask me."

"That's because you never tell."

There is something of a silence and then she says, "We are going to have to re-evaluate our entire life together. Things can't go on this way. We're going to have to have a long look at this and then put it together in another way. It can't be taken for granted anymore."

"You have no idea of the pressures."

"All our lives we're trained to be inferior. To be submissive and docile. We learn that the tactics of inferiority will be rewarded, that those of assertion will be punished. We're nothing but the new slave class."

"It works two ways."

"They pay off on submission. The other things don't interest them at all." She twists in the bed, moves her face from side to side, an old symptom of distress although, strangely, it also occurs during moments of passion. "I don't even know why I'm talking about this to you. It doesn't serve any purpose. I wish I didn't feel that I had to talk to you."

"Go to sleep then."

"It didn't work, did it Walter?" she says quietly. "It just didn't work out the way we hoped it would, did it?"

"No," I say, "but then it never really works out for anyone."

"I believe in female liberation, but it's not the whole answer."

"No," I agree, "it isn't the whole answer." I run my hands up the panels of her body, feel her small breasts curve into my palms; she whimpers against me with a helpless jerk. "No," she says, "not now. Please don't do that to me now. I don't want to."

"Yes you do. I do." I feel her nipples rising with a slow sting against my fingers. "I know you do."

"Oh, nothing works out," she says with a cry and comes against me. I feel her body opening up all along the line, I lean over her and begin to remove garments; in due course, naked, we press against and into one another, her thin cries at climax falling like birds into the spaces of the room. I withdraw slowly, inching my way out, feeling her close behind me and then for a while lie against her, looking at the pattern of the night lights against the wall, hearing the rumble of trucks on the highway. In the distance my wife is weeping softly, the sounds so faint that, near as she is, I can hardly hear them; far as she is, I cannot misunderstand why she is crying.

Consorting with the enemy. Moving across the lines. The cowardly spy, the faulty saboteur. Ruined espionage and a campaign destroyed.

XX

An unusual advertisement comes into the classifieds and I decide to check it out. An attractive blond divorcée 42-24-38, is seeking male companionship in her home by appointment with people who can show their appreciation for her in the establishing of a meaningful relationship.

Prostitutes rarely advertise in the newspaper. The majority of our readers either are looking for something more bizarre or are oriented entirely toward masturbation, the idea of contract-and-expense somehow repellent to them. The day the issue comes out I phone the number she has given and make an appointment. She lives on the fourth floor of a building in Greenwich Village and tells me that the fee will be $20 for a quick engagement, $50 for all night. We settle for an afternoon rendezvous and at the proper hour I tell Virginia that I am going out to appear on a panel and leave the office. I must explain my days to Virginia as I must explain my evenings to my wife — there is no end to the little cubicles I must construct for myself, you see — but fortunately Virginia has no true conception of the internal workings of the business and will accept any explanation as plausible. Besides that, she enjoys being in the office by herself; the faggarts are usually with the attorneys or out in the field scouring up business, and with the doors closed and shades drawn, Virginia can imagine herself to be, somehow, an empire maker. She has total control anyway of the assignments made to the freelancers and over the piles of manuscripts which we receive daily on submission, but this is not enough for her. The fact is that she wants a feeling of total control over a business situation, some sense that she is connecting with and influencing a whole series of lives. This trait of hers makes me sentimental and indulgent because in my own life I have no feeling of control whatsoever and am happy to turn it over to almost anyone who thinks that he does.

The apartment turns to be a walk-up in a dismal building jammed between a psychedelic shop and an Italian restaurant, flooded with sounds and grease and small deadly implements which the tenants of the building seem to have left on the stairs. The prostitute turns out to be strikingly attractive, twenty-five or so, with breasts truly as large as she has advertised, a waist only slightly thickened through dissipation and an astonishing pair of hips which manage to be simultaneously hard and soft as they jut out of the thin pants she wears. She is also wearing a sleeveless sweater without a brassiere. Her name, she says, is Rochelle, and she is an actress who finds New York almost impossible although she will not allow the city to defeat her. She does not consider herself a prostitute but merely someone who is performing a service as legitimate as any other. "I could go to television work," she says, removing her sweater, "commercials, you know. There's always a call for people to do commercials, but to me that's the worst thing. To turn your art into something to sell products that people don't need and don't want. It's not honest, you know what I mean? This way at least I can do something honest which makes people happy. I'm not helping them to make further lies of their life." Her breasts are enormous, descend only a little in movement, the nipples as large around as tea saucers, glinting at me. She is chatty, distracted, as she moves around the studio apartment, taking off the remainder of her clothes, flicking spots of dust off the wall. "I hate to ask you this but I have to, like, make you pay me first, if you know what I mean. You don't mind, do you? It's just better that way."

"How much?"

"I told you over the phone. It's twenty for a straight and fifty for an all night. That's very reasonable. You can't get a good-looking white head for that kind of price in New York. Even semi-pro action costs more than that to promote. Twenty and fifty, that's it. Those are my only two prices. And none of the S-and-M bag. I don't like dig that stuff at all. Otherwise anything goes if you make sure that you take care of me."

"But it isn't night yet. So how can we have an all night at three in the afternoon?"

"Well," she says, putting the cigarette out, looking from side to side, then taking another cigarette and lighting it, "it's like this. All night is just a euphemism, if you understand, for a longer session. Now, the way we'd do it if you wanted an all night is that you'd stay here until seven or eight in the evening. Or for an extra ten, sixty altogether, you can stay until midnight. You have to leave at midnight, though. I make it a rule that no one can really stay overnight with me; it's just better that way. So what do you want, it's your choice?"

"You have large nipples."

"Yes, I do. I always did, but when I was eighteen they started to grow so fast that I thought they'd never stop growing, if you know what I mean. I thought I'd have two breasts that would just be all nipple, and I was embarrassed because I didn't think that men liked that. Of course they stopped after a while, and I learned that lots of men do. It must have something to do with the milk supply. What's your bag by the way?"

"Oh," I say, "I'm a businessman, I guess."

"I didn't want to get personal. I mean, you don't have to take offense.

I just find that it's a little better if you, like, get to know each other first, then it's like you're fucking someone instead of just doing it against the wall. That's why I told you I'm an actress."

"No, I really didn't take offense," I say. "I am a businessman of sorts, that's the truth. I work for the government and the government is the biggest business we've got."

There is a short, thick pause during which she shrugs. The nipples pucker expressively although her face is impassive. "I work for the police department," I say and remove a twenty from my wallet. "Here it is."

"Wait a minute," she says, withdrawing, "what do you mean, you work for the police department?"

"I'm in an investigatorial branch. A special division. Do you want to take this twenty or not? I want to see you take it and place it in your possession now. How about that?"

"Now wait a minute," she says, getting up and backing toward the wall, taking another cigarette from the table, "I don't think I understand the bag here. What do you mean investigatorial work? I don't like this kind of gig, if it's your idea of a joke."

"Take the twenty," I say, following her and putting it lightly on her left breast; the fortunate bill seems to crinkle sympathetically from the slight bobble of the breast. "Just take it."

"Look," she says, "I don't want any trouble at all. Trouble isn't my kind of thing. I'm not taking any money from you. I only do it with people I like, and I don't like you very much at all. The money is like a gift, see, that people I like give me after it's all over to show their appreciation. That's what it is. I don't want to make it with you so get out. I'm not taking your money so that's the end of it. I want you to go."

I back her full into the wall and say. "Prostitution is illegal, you know. It is a misdemeanor and carries a maximum penalty of six months. Also, it takes an enormous toll of human lives in damage, deceit and disease. It must be eradicated."

"I want to get dressed."

"You'll get dressed in due course. You listen to me. You may think that all of this is perfectly innocent but you're wrong. You're leading men into decay. You are wrecking human lives. We don't like this kind of thing in my division. We're starting to get very serious about this in an effort to stamp it out once and for all."

She begins to cry now, more or less at the time I had predicted. Perhaps she is a little bit slow on the draw, a bit more hardened than I had thought. Still, amateurism leaks from her. "I'm not a prostitute," she says, "I'm an actress."

"An actress without work, right? Like a writer without books. No, I don't think it washes. You'd have been better off doing the commercials. Commercials aren't illegal in our society, you know. This is. And you've got to live in society although more and more of you people nowadays have the disgusting idea that you can take the blessings of America and pay none of the dues. We're going to stop that kind of thinking. We're beginning to get very serious about this now; it's gone on too long."

"Please," she says, "please go away. I'm frightened. I don't want to hear this anymore. If I did anything wrong, I apologize. It was stupid of me. I'll stop. Just please leave me alone."

"Taking the ad was really stupid," I say. "Don't you think we monitor that sheet? Don't you think that every agency in the world has an eye on that rag knowing that it will bring every creep, fanatic, rapist and pervert out of the woodwork to spread his disgusting filth in their columns? Didn't that ever occur to you? Don't you understand what that sheet really is?"

"I never read it. I just heard about it and thought I might as well take an ad. Please, can I get dressed? I don't want to stand this way."

"You really don't understand it, do you, baby?" I say, stepping back from the wall and allowing her to scurry in the direction of the couch. She seizes her sweater and puts it against her chest, cradling it like a child, trying to get inside of it but not willing to bare her breasts to me again. "You don't understand a bit of it, do you? You miss the whole point. You people think that you're so clever and so advanced and so liberal with your life-styles and intellectual and so on but you don't realize that we were around long before you came on the scene and that we've forgotten tricks you never knew. We have our hands on *everything*. Everything, do you understand me?"

"Go," she says. "Please go."

"That's *our* magazine," I say, "*our* publication. We created it, we own it and we run it. How else do you think we're able to keep an eye on every creep and pervert in New York? We get their advertisements, we get their mail, we get everything from them. They trust us, you see. They think that they've found an outlet. They think that we're their *vox populi*. And all the time we're keeping an eye on them, keeping the files up to date, getting ready to make a move anytime we want. We have the whole thing right in our hand, you know, and how do you like that?"

She has succeeded in getting the sweater on, pats it into place, smoothing it over her breasts, hanging tightly inside. She seems to have recovered some particle of her manner. "I don't know what to think. I asked you to go. Please go, I promise you I won't do it any more."

"You bet you won't do it anymore." I say to her with a flourish, taking one of her cigarettes and sticking it into my mouth for effect, although I have not smoked for several years, considering the habit extremely dangerous. "And you know why you won't do it? You won't do it because we've got our hand on everything. Nothing escapes our sight now; nothing vanquishes our control. Look at every newspaper on the stand. We've got them all. Everyone."

I go over to her, rest a hand on her shoulder, squeeze lightly and feel the soft resilience gathering under me; for an instant I regret that I have not been able to lay her. From the feel of her flesh, she would have been an extremely good fuck. Nevertheless, there are larger purposes assigned here. "Just remember," I say, "Remember this. Remember everything. Consider this a warning. We won't let you off like this the next time. The next time we go for the big wheel. This time you can consider yourself lucky."

"I don't like New York," she says. "I never wanted to live this way. There's something about this place that makes people crazy. Maybe I've been crazy."

"Maybe," I say, "maybe, maybe." And I take my hand off her, back to the door, give her a farewell tilt of the hand, reach behind me with the other hand, deftly pull on the knob and in a single motion am standing on the threshold, tilted in profile toward her, cigarette dangling, an air of pure menace sifting from me and hopefully throughout the room. "Remember," I say, "there is no escape." I give her a wink, salute her and pull the door closed, dart down the steps quickly and into the jangle of the psychedelic store music. Behind me I hear the sound of a bolt being thrown, kicks against wood, the grinding sound of a chain; behind me she has quite clearly locked up for a long time.

It is all really too much, and I find myself laughing almost hysterically on the street, but the laughter turns to somberness when I begin to think that she indeed would have been a wonderful fuck and I could have done everything that I did after instead of before and saved the $20 to boot. But then I remind myself that to do it first and then pull the stunt would have compromised my integrity to say nothing of the clarity of the role I have established for her, and these purposes above all must be honored. This makes me feel a little better although not entirely resigned, and I return to the office to find Virginia still alone, lock all the doors, pull the shades, put the tapes on high and at four o'clock on an October afternoon bang the living shit out of her on the floor, my eyes closed in convulsion as the pure surging arc of the orgasm overtakes me and moves me far from there. Making all the changes, the colors of the day.

XXI

One of our advertisers threatens to get us into difficulty. It is a large mail-order house in California which advertises under several corporate names and box numbers; maybe two thousand dollars an issue of advertisements all told. They also use the personals column, employing names and box numbers to induce dirty correspondence for a fee. Our relationship with them is admirably cool, admirably distant; every week their typesetter mails in their new copy, ready for the printer and every other week, without comment, their check arrives, always including an extra six cents reimbursement for the formal bill they have us mail before they pay. In many ways, what we have established is the most satisfying and humane connection I have ever known.

One of their regular ads is for an orgasm-retarder, a kind of prophylactic cream which, when massaged over the erect penis, will dull the nerves and prevent premature ejaculation. It seems that this preparation is dangerous; in any event, we have received several letters from readers independently saying that the cream has caused scales to appear on their genitals and in one case produced pus and bleeding so serious as to necessitate an embarrassing and painful operation. Also three of the letters say that the female partner had discharge and pain for several days following the intercourse during which the substance was used. One letter even states that the cream resulted in an immediate loss of erective power which continues to the time of writing, two months later; the correspondent is still unable to have satisfactory sexual relations of any kind with any partner, male or female. Because the letters have come in at different times from widely disparate areas of the country, it is reasonable to assume that they are legitimate. It is also reasonable to assume that many more such letters would have come in if most of the purchasers did not simply buy the cream in the *hope* of sexual outlet.

After consultation with the attorneys who say that we might indeed be criminally liable if formal complaints were brought, I write a cautious letter to the company, addressing it to the president. It is the first letter I have ever written them and I point out the history of complaint, the way that the letters, coming in at different times, seem to corroborate one another, the possible penalties which both the company and I might incur if some of the complainants were to seek recovery. I keep the letter courteous and to the point; it is no more than four paragraphs altogether. I end by asking him to withdraw the offending ads from the newspaper while assuring him that we maintain the warmest interest in working with him closely and hope that the ad withdrawn will be replaced by one for something else. I close by advising that if I do not receive a reply within five days of the date of my letter, I will assume that he concurs and will remove the ad.

Two days later a special delivery letter arrives in the offices. It is signed in an illegible scrawl over the words FOR THE B&E CORPORATION and states that if we do not run the advertisement as we have done previously they will be compelled to remove all other advertisements from our newspaper.

Without much hope, I attempt to contact the B&E Corporation in California over long-distance phone, but find that there is no listing for them or for any of their subsidiary names. The information operator and I go through the various names carefully for half an hour to establish this, the operator in a mood of rising rage, my own a descending embarrassment. I write a second letter to the corporation, special delivery, pointing out that their product appears to be dangerous and that they, no less than we, would not want to be responsible for injuring people or incurring legal action. I advise that if I do not hear within two days of the date of this letter, I will assume that they agree with me that it would be in the best interests of all parties to remove the offending advertisement and that certainly their relationship has been valued over these past years and we hope that it will continue as previously. The following day, while I am going over a photographic agent's latest submissions (pictures of nude women posed with zoo animals, the animals exhausted and seedy, giving the women shy looks devoid of ferocity or determination), Virginia informs me that I have a long-distance person-to-person phone call, and while these are generally only people who wish to pose for the newspaper or who want to know exactly what we are up to, I make it a matter of policy to accept as many as possible, wanting to know now more than ever what is going on in America's deepest heart. A hoarse man tells me that he is Mr. B&E or perhaps that he represents B&E Enterprises. I do not quite catch which but assume that it makes little difference.

"The ad," he says, "the ad stays. That's the word. It stays in."

"I've already written you a second letter," I say, trying to sound as reasonable as possible. "There are some other facts — "

"We got the second letter. The second letter came in already and they had a discussion. They told for me to tell you that the ad is staying. That is their final decision, it stays in and that's the decision."

"Look," I say, "I take no position on the ads. You know that. And we've done a lot of good business together. But still I think it's best — "

"You don't do business with me," the voice says harshly, "you do business with *them*. Me, I am only the messenger. I don't know anything. That is their message. It stays."

"It could get very dangerous. If this stuff is poisoning people a lot of us could get sued and then — "

"Listen, mister, you can't argue with me. I don't even know what's going on. It's not my business to know what's going on, I just deliver the messages and it's healthiest for everybody that way. The message is that the ad stays and that if it does not stay, then all the ads go. Every single one of them. We will pull all of the ads out of the issues starting right now. I mean, they will pull them out; I just work for them and that's why I say we."

"The issue's already made up. I couldn't take the ads out."

"Then you take them out the next time around. Listen, I have no further instructions. I can't go on discussing this. This is what they want me to say and I've said it."

"Is there anyone else I could talk to? Maybe if I were able to speak to someone in the offices — "

"They're all out to lunch."

"When they get back from lunch."

"They go out for long lunches. Sometimes they don't come back until the next day. By the next day it will be too late."

"If I could only talk it over — "

"That's all they wanted to say, friend," the voice points out and hangs up on me.

I replace the receiver on the stand and walk to a side cabinet in which a sample of the prophylactic cream has been placed. As a matter of policy, recommended by our lawyers from the start, we obtain a sample of every product advertised in the newspaper. Most of them have never been opened but certain of the photographic materials have given me endless amusement and have been placed in my private stock at home, one which not even my wife knows about.

I remove the tube from the box and shake dust off it. Opening it I am assaulted by a peculiar smell midway between glue and wax, oddly penetrating and somehow refreshing to the nostrils. I squeeze the tube and a small, deadly squirt of grayish jelly lands in my fingers, cold and only faintly sticky to the touch. I rub the jelly between thumb and forefinger and then examine. Everything looks pretty much the same in the translucency of the jelly although it is possible that I see miniscule cuts and bruises on the fingers. It is hard to tell. So much of the efficacy of these preparations has to do with a matter of attitude.

I wait five minutes and my fingers neither wrinkle nor fall off. They do not seem to feel any pain under pressure and remain firm when pressed. I use the treated hand to put the tube back in the box and the box back in the cabinet, and then I close the cabinet and take Virginia to lunch. We discuss our relationship. I tell her that I am beginning to reach a point in the situation with my wife where I think things will break the other way very quickly now and it is only a matter of timing. In a good mood, sipping her second Gibson, she looks at me with wonder and says that that will be fine, she is willing to be patient. She has, after all, not even truly begun her life.

The ad stays.

XXII

We run an advisory column, something in the lonelyhearts tradition but strictly for laughs as most of the queries are invented in the office and the few that aren't are too dull to print. (*What is the difference between a sadist and a masochist? What is shrimping? Is there any street action on the East Side? Are streetwalkers dangerous; would it be smart to go with one to a hotel?*) I write the questions and answers myself and to the degree that I have any writing talent at all or interest in personal expression, believe that I have found the outlet here. Today, however, a letter arrives in the offices, addressed to our advisory service, which puts me at something of a loss for one of the few times since I got into this branch of publishing.

The writer is a twenty-eight-year-old white male of Jewish extraction. He lives in New York City, has a college degree in accounting from one of the city university, drives a fairly new automobile and is well employed by a large firm which specializes in accounting for the jewelry trade. The writer works with several female secretaries in his office, he attends mixers and parties advertised in the columns of the evening paper, he goes to dances and has essayed singles weekends at the resorts. He makes, before taxes, $11,500 a year. He has never had intercourse with a girl in his life. He has never had "heavy petting" (his phrase) with a girl in his life. Because of a deadly fear of sudden impotence, he has never used prostitutes although now "more and more I find myself looking at scarred black women of the streets with desire." He finds it difficult to procure dates; girls seem uninterested in him, but on those occasions when he does pick up a girl at a mixer or by prearrangement, he finds that he has nothing to say to her and absolutely no idea of how to make a date progress. Sometimes he will make a sexual advance, but despite everything he has read and heard about the "New Morality," he finds that these advances are repulsed as violently as they were ten years ago when he was in college and trying to get girls in dormitories to neck with him before curfew. At other times he has tried to take a more direct approach, telling the girl he is with about his problem, his sexual suffering, his loneliness, his deprivation, in the hope that the girl will have sympathy for him and, as he has read in certain publications, then try to "protect" and "mother" him and "prove his adequacy" out of her own ego. He has found, however, that this approach is even less successful than direct advances since it fills the girls with unspeaking, uncomprehending horror and they obviously no longer want to be in the company of someone as abnormal as he.

He masturbates frequently — two or three times a day, in fact, on weekends, and almost once a day during the week — but has found a slow decline in his sexual powers over the past few years; whereas he could once have thirty orgasms a week he is now lucky to have ten or fifteen and furthermore the masturbation is no longer satisfying since he finds himself possessed after climax with a "strong psychic urge to have intercourse" which the masturbation has in no way reduced. Also, masturbation is now beginning to make him feel increasingly inadequate; he is convinced that something in his life has been irretrievably taken from him, and sometimes he is so full of bitterness and loss that he finds himself crying in his sleep, something that he never used to do. He cannot believe, in this age of easy sex and relationships, that something like this can be happening to him, and he is driven mad by the sight of men far uglier than he in the company of attractive women who are obviously having sex with them.

Our newspaper is "probably the only breath of fresh air in my life at the present time because I see in your pages something that I have never seen in any other publication or admitted in public, namely that there seem to be a large number of men in my condition, men seemingly normal in appearance and manner, who simply cannot get a woman and for whom masturbation is their only sexual outlet. That you can take for granted the fact that this is so and that masturbation is a perfectly sane activity under the circumstances gives me hope; for the first time you have begun to show me that I am not the only one in my condition, and if this much is so, then there must be another conclusion: that there is hope. No one could have the philosophy expressed in your newspaper unless someone working there had been through the same thing and had passed through it. When I was eighteen people told me not to worry because some people matured socially later than others and eighteen was very young. When I was twenty-three I reminded myself that many men had their first real involvements in their late twenties. Now at twenty-eight, the only thing I find I can remind myself is that George Bernard Shaw did not have sex with a woman until he was over thirty, but this somehow is no comfort to me. What I want to ask you is this: how can I get out of this? How can I find a girl who will have sex with me and who is not repulsively ugly? I am perfectly willing to get married if that is the price of sex; in fact I am dying to get married, but since I cannot establish a relationship with a girl for even a second date I obviously find it very difficult. Can you help me? I promise that if something changes in my life and if I am able to stop masturbating for release, I will not stop buying your newspaper. I will in fact buy it faithfully, all the time, as a reminder of my origins and a constant reminder to me that no matter what happens, where I go, how things work out, how much I am suffering, I yet have much to be grateful for and will never suffer in this way again."

I looked over the letter for a long time and then I dug up an envelope from the drawer, addressed it back to him (as expected he included his full name and address and I settled quickly with the phone directory that it was real) and stuffed it back into the envelope. Then I took a sheet of letterhead stationary and typed this note to him:

Dear Sir:

I have read your letter with much interest. Your condition is ineradicable, your suffering is eternal and there is nothing that can be done to change your circumstances. Certain men are doomed to suffer in this way, just as others are born with clubfeet or low intelligence. It is your cross to bear. Nothing will ever change for you as long as you live. You will never have a woman as long as you live. At thirty-five you will still be standing on pavements outside the Hotel New Yorker on Saturday nights, watching the girls go in by twos and threes and wondering how such attractive girls could obviously be lonely and desperate, but these wonderings will not enable you to get any nearer to them than you are at that moment. Whole generations of girls with whom you tried and failed will get married, bear children and be divorced while you remain outside the Hotel New Yorker. At fifty-one you will be trying to look forty-six with a flower in your lapel as you go to a college graduates mixer in a Fifth Avenue hotel, and when you go to a girl to speak to her, something within you will unwind and you will be without words. At sixty-five you will still be jerking off although by then far, far less and more as a matter of habit than anything else. Like certain old married couples, you will obligatorily engage in sex with yourself once or twice a month just to prove that you have the capacity which you will deceive yourself into thinking is interest. At seventy-five you will look like any other old man and when you sit with the old men on benches in the park will be able to nod and talk of your sexual experiences as you look at the young girls with them and none of them, by that time, will be able to tell the difference. They will believe that you have had a lifetime of sex and love and will ask you no questions. This will give you, finally and at great costs, a perverse sense of relief and belonging, and I urge you to look forward to this because it is about the only thing you have to look forward to. At eighty-four you will die and neither your ashes nor the worms will have any interest in the fact that at the age of twenty-four you screwed up a date in the front seat of your car by begging a girl to have sex with you. Neither your ashes nor the worms will know the difference, either biologically or metaphysically speaking, so you see in the long run you really have no problem at all and must instead cultivate the resignation that, like peace, passeth all understanding. Your friend,

I took the envelope to Virginia and asked her to mail it for me. "I don't understand," she said, "what's the difference? The stuff all goes into the out box and at the end of the day the messenger picks it up and dumps it down the chute. What is this?"

"It's personal," I said, "don't worry about it. It's just something that I want you to mail yourself. It will take you just ten seconds, go to the chute and drop it down there, will you? I'd appreciate it."

She gave me a look and took the envelope and stood and walked out the door of the office holding the envelope delicately in her hand. A fine graceful hand, tapering fingers, fingers meant to grasp the cock with the most fragile of caresses and move it toward its yearning explosion. A fine ass, fine bearing, fine nervous tilt to the curve of her ass as she swings it ever so gently behind her. Long, drooping breasts, nearly down to her navel in certain naked postures, but surprising in their fullness, the arc in the mouth during suckling. Dark, gentle taste, her odors swimming up to me as I immerse myself in her.

XXIII

On an otherwise boring Tuesday morning, I write myself a letter of complaint. DEAR SIR, I address the publisher,

Your publication is one of almost indescribable filth, pandering to the darkest and most evil human impulses. Do you not understand that the body is the Temple of the Holy Spirit, that mild vessel in which God makes himself known to man? To hold the body up in your display of decadent, prurient filth is to distort the word and name of God. Have you no shame? Do the tortured and demented creatures which allow themselves to pose "naked" in your publication have no understanding of the hideous roles to which they will be assigned in hell? Have you no sense of responsibility? There are not only millions of innocent children who can be twisted and injured by your disgusting pages, there are hundreds and thousands of blameless adults, children of God every single one of them, who can be done unspeakable damage by your irresponsible and disgusting greedy attempts to play upon their needs.

A terrible judgement awaits you, I finish, *unless you repent now and turn toward the paths of righteousness. Repent now! lest you spend an eternity in purgatory where it is too late for repentance.*

I sign the letter *very hopefully yours* and then consider it for a while; consider the round curvature of the arguments, the lean tautness of phraseology, the dry immediacy and crackle of its rhetoric. It makes the case well and something within me vaults to meet it, to embrace this truth as if the truth were a lover, thrash with the lover truth on some bed of understanding and finally reach a climax of comity and grace. I *accept, I accept,* I murmur, and hasten to post the letter on the bulletin board where I can consider it for the rest of my days.

Later, Virginia sees it, becomes furious, and rips it off. "I don't see why you pay any attention to these ravings," she says as she curls it neatly in a delicate hand and grinds it into the wastebasket. "You may think it's funny, but I don't think it's very funny at all, Walter." I think about explaining it to her but decide that it will be entirely too complex, let it go then and write myself another such letter in the morning. But in the morning I am tired and have other things to do and I do not pass that way again.

XXIV

I am out with my wife on a Saturday and for once we are having a pleasant time. Part of the reason for my good mood is the wine in the Italian restaurant where we have come for a late supper after the play, and the other part has to do with the fact that I was recognized in the theater lobby by a crowd of people who pointed at me and whispered among themselves to identify me as the publisher of *The Spread.* My face is becoming increasingly well-known, not only because honesty compels me to publish it in the newspaper weekly over the masthead as an attestation of conviction, but because I have appeared at a number of lectures, seminars, panels, radio shows and so on around town although not yet on television. The recognition in the lobby was utterly without laughter; there was a time when strangers who knew my face from the newspaper would giggle but now, more and more, they are becoming respectful. I am a figure of some solidity and weight; the test in America is to be substantial, the origin of your substantiality hardly mattering anymore. Also, my wife was not in the least embarrassed by my identification; she did not turn away but, instead, took my hand with a thin edge of defiance and returned their glances levelly. This is something new and augurs well; it means that she is coming to terms either with herself or with me or even perhaps both but in any event the time of conflict seems to have been put behind us and drinking good wine in the restaurant, listening idly to the piped-in music, I can even feel small surges of my old feeling toward her, a feeling which at the time was the most profound I had ever known and even now, when I am older, stands up well. She is an attractive girl, intelligent, faithful, worthwhile in many ways, and I have no interest in leaving her, something which I admitted to myself early in the relationship with Virginia when things seemed for a tiny instant about to get serious. It is unthinkable for me to leave my wife; I would leave all of my accumulated adult history with her and she would make a very poor custodian. She is not merely a wife; she is a projection of myself and for that, if for no other reason, I could love her a little.

It is a pleasant evening, no indication of trouble at all: even some undercurrent of anticipation for the sex which will follow until, for no apparent reason, she shakes her head, breaking off from a very funny discussion of certain types she has met in women's liberation and says, "You're an anachronism, you know. The whole thing is. It's not going to last long at all."

"What isn't going to last long? I don't know what you're talking about." I am slightly drunk or at least verging toward that line and am trying to preserve the mood, but I know her well and it is clear that the evening has already taken a different course.

"The newspaper, I mean. The whole gig. I figured it out; I don't know why I didn't see that a long time ago. You're just playing out on a transitional state of the culture. The culture is starting to go free, but it's caught between the old Puritan horrors and the new ethics the kids are setting up, the whole question of life-style in the suburbs, and it just isn't making the adjustment yet. So the paper comes into the vacuum. You're just playing on the old Puritan fear and hatred of sex, making it ugly and disgusting, but packaging it in a way that makes it seem new and bold. You're just playing on the sickness of the culture."

"I don't want to talk about it," I say. "I really don't want to talk about it. I thought we agreed that we wouldn't discuss this anymore."

"Oh, but I'm not discussing it," she says. "I'm telling you why I'm not going to discuss it anymore. It doesn't bother me now, you see. It used to when I thought that you had started something entirely new, but now I see that it isn't; it's the same ugly old bag and it's going nowhere. Just as soon as some more people begin to get their heads straight, the whole thing's going to go. It's just a symptom of change."

I am still willing to be agreeable, trying to be mellow, although a certain nasty knife of indigestion has begun in my stomach and the smells of the place have turned rancid. "That's true," I say. "I've pointed that out myself many times. The paper is just a transitional thing; we're trying to shake people up and get them to accept sex as part of life, and when it becomes matter-of-fact, of course the paper is going to go away. It's just a signpost on the way to cultural health, I hope. Maybe within our lifetime — "

She takes a cautious sip of wine and shakes her head vehemently, "That's what I mean," she says, "it's not a question of a lifetime. It's not something in the far-off future. I mean, it's something very soon. No more than five years at the tops, maybe less. Two I would think. And it could be as little as six months."

"I don't think we can straighten out everybody's head in six months."

"No, but enough heads are getting straight without having anything at all to do with the paper. In the first place, the people who read the paper aren't the ones that matter anyway; they just act and react to what's really going on. You have no idea how fast things are happening these days; I think you're too wrapped up in all that nonsense even to take a look around. You know, Walter, you used to be a very curious, interested kind of person; you aren't anymore. Things are changing so fast that you wouldn't even know it. *I'm* changing in ways you couldn't understand. Everybody's changing and you're changing too but not fast enough; it's going much faster than you think, Walter, and it's really just *beginning* to change, if you know what I'm saying. I don't think you have any idea of where we'll be ten years from now. *I* don't but at least I can say that and try to swing with it, but you can only look at the future in terms of the way that things used to be or are now and that isn't enough. You know, Walter," she says, taking a roll and peeling it, looking at me with bright interest as her spectacles take a gleam from the candlelight and cast a wicked dart straight into my eye, "I don't think you understand a single thing that's going on today. You got hold of something which was a little bit of a truth and then you had the guts to act it out and I'll give you that much credit, but you haven't had an idea since and you haven't known for two years what was really going on. And now the whole thing's going to come down around you, faster than you could think, and you're going to be left in the cold without a crutch. Poor Walter," she says and puts her palm over the back of my hand, rubs it absently, looks into my eyes, licks her lips, "poor Walter and it's so cold out there. And they won't even throw you a crutch in the snow."

"You're wrong," I say. "You're all wrong. You don't understand me at all."

"I won't discuss it anymore. I mean, I just wanted to say that one thing, and that was the end of it. There really isn't anything else to say about it. Maybe I shouldn't have, but I wanted to."

"You're all wrong."

"I said I won't discuss it, Walter. Now, let's try to have a nice evening."

So I try to have a nice evening, but the evening is not nice anymore, and much later, fucking her, I try to make her scream. It is almost impossible. I have never had so much trouble that way with her before, and I work her over, tongue to cunt, lips to nipple, fingers to ass, mouth to ear, prick to thigh, holding myself back in a cold agony of suspension which I know I will sustain as long as necessary, move over her finally, skillfully and split her with a grunt and she begins, in the fucking, at last to reciprocate; I hear her making sounds as I fuck her but as she starts the last orgasmic scream I do not know if it is a wail or if instead I have only worked so hard, come so late, moved so stiffly to yank out of her a perfect, sustained bellow of release and triumph.

XXV

We receive a threatening phone call. A bomb has been hidden in our offices and will detonate within fifteen minutes of the time of the call. Oddly, it is the first such incident in our history; perhaps we have been regarded for too long as threateners ourselves rather than victims, but circumstances alter as our status improves. The caller says that he is an agent of the Lamb of God and hangs up. The police are called and in the interim, Virginia, the two faggarts and I stand on the street in the September mist, huddling against the building and trying to avoid the plumes of smoke which come from a manhole opened in front of our building. Within the manhole, workmen swear colorfully, talking about what they think they see in the guts of the city.

The police arrive, unenthusiastically, in two patrol cars and go to check the premises. The threat as reported was not serious enough, it seems, to warrant the bomb squad. In three or four minutes they are down, chewing gum, saying that the premises are perfectly safe and we are free to return. I am invited to file a formal complaint but feel this is pointless since the caller is unidentifiable. I ask what the liability will be if there is a bomb after all and it explodes when we are back in the building, incinerating all of us.

"No bomb, friend," one of the patrolmen says. "Anyway, you'd be surprised what's going on in this city. Maybe ten thousand bomb scares a day now; if you checked every one out thorough, you'd have no one in the precincts and you'd have no one at work. Maybe one out of a hundred thousand is really serious but it's a percentage game. Anyway, you're safe. There's nothing up there except a lotta pictures. What kind of outfit you got there anyway? My brother-in-law buys that paper but I never touch it."

We thank the policemen for their services and go upstairs in the creaking elevator that moves as if it were being dragged up by crippled gnomes, hand over hand. The office is in some disarray; the police have ransacked our inventory and taken several of the choice items, not only off the desks but the walls. While none of it is irreplaceable, it is all quite irritating and one of the faggarts, Donald I think (they are simply undifferentiable; this is not my problem but theirs), says that we should certainly file formal charges against these police; there is no excuse for it and if we are not entitled to equal protection under law, who is? "They still remember that business up in the Bronx," Donald says with an inflected precision and goes back to his desk, shaking his head. He will have nothing more to do with it. Jim goes over to him, leans near, whispers something and Donald seems more cheerful.

"This is such a hateful city, the people in it are so full of hate, how can you live in a city where everyone wants to blow up everyone else?" Virginia wants to know. I find that there is no easy answer I can give her; I tell her that perhaps she is exaggerating the situation and that most people do not want anyone blown up except those forces or institutions nearest their condition, and it is only the accumulation of rage that makes things difficult. She is not pleased with this but, shaking her head, decides to let it pass. We begin to make some order out of the offices; it is quite a mess and we see that certain file cabinets have been ransacked and a portfolio of unprintable photos depicting the act of homosexual love have been spat upon.

An hour later the phone rings and we are threatened again. The caller says that the first time was a dry run but this one is incontestably serious and we have five minutes before the whole building goes at a quarter to noon. This time he has adopted a rich, Slavic accent, somewhat reminiscent of voices I heard in my own humble youth, and something within me instinctively yearns toward him as he completes his instruction and crisply hangs up.

We debate the issue for a few moments and decide not to call the police. We remain at our desks and conduct the business of the morning, such as it is. At a quarter of twelve the building is not blown up so I conclude that we have all been saved.

At three o'clock the caller tries again but finds only me in the office, Virginia having gone home ill and the faggarts to their quarters on some mysterious assignation. I tell him that I have lost interest in the whole thing; I'm sorry but I simply can't be involved anymore and cut the connection on him. He does not call back and we never hear from him again. When a routine police follow-up comes in the mail, I throw it in the wastebasket and put the precinct on the list of complimentary subscriptions, three copies in all.

XXVI

A letter arrives from the midwest stating that the writer has used B&E magic lovemaker salve on his penis and his organ contracted a severe fungus illness which resulted in infection and its near-amputation. He has been told on good medical authority that he is likely never to be capable of intercourse again. His wife has contracted some exotic illness as well and her vagina smells, even after repeated washings, like a "potted palm." The correspondent says that he is canceling his subscription effective immediately and intends to see his attorneys about the possibility of direct legal action against us.

I forward the letter, without comment, to the B&E Company with their bill. In a rash moment, I take the ointment from its place in the cabinet and dispose of it in the incinerator chute. Now and then I begin to think that my thumb and forefinger have a peculiar complexion to them but assure myself that it is only a trickery of light and that all is as it was and will ever be.

XXVII

I attend a special lecture course given at one of the evening colleges in the city as a participant in a seminar on the "new publishing." The publisher of a pornographic book house is on the panel with me as well as an intense bearded man who says that he is interested in the "cinema of juxtaposition," most of the juxtaposition having to do with naked bodies. The moderator, who writes a column of sociology and comment for one of the weekly newspapers, has banded us together to bring some meaningful insight into the changing mores and standards of publishing but quickly finds himself defeated by the energy of the panel and the responses of the audience and retires to one side of the stage taking notes.

A desultory discussion leads us nowhere in particular — the publisher monopolizes most of the time talking about the truly outstanding list of brilliant new literary discoveries he has put together to fight the fight for freedom — and then the floor is thrown open for questioning. The questioning is unbelievably hostile and tends to focus upon our presumed sexual inadequacies. The publisher is asked about his marital history and people want to know why I seem to hate women so much. The cinema director creates a minor break in the pattern by confessing calmly that he is an exclusive homosexual (he calls it, however "monosexual" and, when the floor fails to understand this, must clarify it by shouting "homo, homo, homo!") and that this has increased the truth and clarity of his art, but past the initial sensation of confession he falls completely out of interest; he has given his blood to the audience and there is nothing more. He sits sullenly to the side, his hands folded in his enormous, discontented lap, as the publisher and I, without help from the moderator, push off further questions. The publisher says that a distinction must be made between the erotic and pornographic which compare to one another as scotch to beer or representational painting to television ads but he is unable to make the distinction to the audience's satisfaction, and when he sits I see that he is sweating. I am asked exactly how great are my weekly profits from the newspaper and what percentage of these profits I am donating to the women's liberation movement, the gay liberation front, the black resistance movement and "damaged peoples everywhere." I try to point out that our profit margin is minimal but the audience is not satisfied. "You're sucking the lifesblood from the bowels of dead people!" someone shouts, and a fine Gallic quiver comes over the publisher's resonant face. He turns to me and whispers that it would seem to be a very good idea to leave now. The audience catches his gestures and begins to make cries about cowardice. The publisher rises again, goes to the microphone and says that he has been fighting baboons and philistines all his life and he will continue as long as he has strength, but he did not expect, did never expect, to find them in such a quarter as this. "You're dead, baby, you're behind the times; you'd better liberate yourselves and forget about the rest of us cats," someone shrieks and there is a perfect bellow of applause and cheers at this. When it quiets the voice shouts, "If this is an example of what liberation can make of you, I'd rather stay pure, wouldn't you, friends?" And there is more applause yet and the publisher, swearing, returns to his seat. The cinema director makes delicate gestures toward the audience and pleads for decency and self-respect but no one listens.

I come to the stage and take the microphone, point out that we are living in very difficult times but that the whole complex range of them must be understood. That perhaps the three of us do not represent the ideal types but then again freedom was what you made of it and if it came down to people such as us to stand for freedom, then we would. It made a pretty poor case for decency, perhaps, if it was left to such as us to defend it, but that is the condition of the times today and so be it. This takes some of the momentary pressure off us; the audience is forced to some applause by this and when it comes back it is without the previous energy; for the first time I see a passageway through the evening and out the other side and with desperate glances and motions manage to induce the moderator to bring the session to a close. It closes with a sense of accommodation, even approval, oozing up from the audience in slow waves, but just as I am congratulating myself and the others for getting out of *that* one in a single piece, just before we leave the stage and the stage lights come up, someone shouts from the audience, "Well, you may have done pretty good, Walter, but the shit still stinks; I remember you from way back when and it's the same old jive." I turn toward the voice but the lights come up suddenly, dazzling me, and it is lost in the exiting rumble and shuffle of feet. There is absolutely nothing to do but to leave the stage with the others, shaking slightly. I have recognized the voice; that is to say that the voice connected to me in some profound way, a voice out of history this, a voice from the Army, and if I were only able to reach it and find who carries it, I might have the explanation which would make everything all right, justify everything for once and for all, but the voice is gone, whoever carried it is gone, the audience is gone and the past is gone and I am left with the pornographic publisher and the cinema director at midnight, staring into convivial glasses at the bar next door and wondering how, in the face of all this liberation, we have wound up there at that time, sitting in the best place we can be in at that time, nothing solved and everything questionable, no matter how many question periods we have survived.

XXVIII

Finally, in the subway, coming home one night during rush hour, I do it. It is sweltering in the car, hundreds of us packed against one another; a dull rumble of fear and assault moving through the tunnels and I am jammed against a tall blond girl, around twenty-four or twenty-five with a briefcase under her shoulder, a fine moistness coming from her forehead, a fine heat seeming to come from the damp of her underarms. The car lurches, we press against one another, smile, turn away, slam into one another again at a halt, uncouple, smile, move, smile, jerk, slam, grunt at one another, move away unsmiling, slam to a halt, drive into one another, smile, and I cannot take it anymore, literally cannot take it, her left breast is resting against my forearm, her right less than an inch from my nose and I say, "I could love you, you know, I could really love you, it wouldn't be difficult at all, you have no idea of what goes on inside me, but if I could only make you see, I know that the two of us could somehow come together; you're really extraordinarily beautiful, sensual arms, beautiful breasts, but more than beautiful you're sensitive as well, I can see from your face how sensitive you are and furthermore from the briefcase you are carrying that you are a consequential person, an artist perhaps, or a fashion designer, possibly a model carrying around shots of herself or a writer turning in brilliant crisp samples of her prose style to the top magazines. I am thirty-five years old, a college graduate, industrious, intelligent, I am making approximately fifty thousand dollars a year from my own business, I have lived an interesting life and am really at the verge of my best possibilities. What do you think? Do you think that we could manage somehow with one another? It would be no problem to disentangle myself from my home life and as far as you, a girl so beautiful could have formed no entanglements that she could not break without the others thinking that they were blessed to have known her on whatever terms for however short a time. What do you think? Will you make love to me?" and then, shyly look up at her for the first time as the train pulls into the Fifty-ninth Street station, yawns to a halt, flings open its doors and begins to evacuate passengers.

She adjusts her briefcase, gives me a smile, prepares to join the passengers on the way out. "I think," she says, looking at her watch, "I think that it's about five twenty. But I've been slow for weeks, maybe you'd better ask someone else." Her ass waggles a slow, sad good-bye to me as she steps to the platform.

Before I can get really involved, however, in thoughts about modern alienation, the train gets jammed in the tunnel outside Seventy-second Street, and for half an hour I have nothing to contemplate but the smell of smoke and my own terror, both rising like the winking lights of an incoming New Lots Express bearing out of the tubes, and by the time we finally get going again, a good share of the passengers in the train have panicked or fainted or begun to curse about being late for dinner on the fuckin subway, and comforting the wounded, healing the sick, and talking with the afflicted keeps me quite busy almost all the way home.

XXIX

My wife has now taken an affair. She is not loathe to tell me anything about this although, of course, she will not reveal his identity as a "matter of common decency" and she refuses to give sexual descriptions or comparisons. A long time ago, however, we decided that we would have total honesty within and without our marriage about all of our involvements, and she has kept her part of the bargain. He is a "wonderful English teacher" whom she met at one of the women's liberation meetings; the estranged husband of "one of the girls" who remained on friendly enough terms with her to come discuss himself during "consciousness-raising." After he and my wife were introduced, they began to see one another a bit although the affair itself was not actually consummated until two weeks ago in his furnished apartment near Columbia where he teaches three courses on the modern novel and also gives a seminar on Byronic poetry. Now she sees him three or four times a week, for sex "and other things," usually in his apartment although occasionally in ours; she had no "particular plans" about how their relationship might go but thinks that things are "pleasant enough the way they are right now." This is the second time my wife has committed adultery but only the first time she has had an affair; the other time was at college during the first year of our marriage, when she, an old roommate of mine and I sat around until late hours getting drunk, and when the lights went out and in her drunkenness, she swore, she thought that he was me. I had no reason to disbelieve her, having certain vague scatological memories of that evening in which it seemed to me that I might have thought that he was her. This is something entirely different, however, and I do not know precisely in what way to take it.

In the first place I hardly have any right to complain, and in the second place our marriage has obviously not been right for many years now, at least five or six, and it is a testimony to something or other that she did not go into adultery years ago, and in the third place I am extraordinarily upset, more so than I ever thought I would be. "But why?" I ask her. "Why, of all people with a goddamned *English* teacher. I mean, I can see how you might want to try something different and I can see where you've been unhappy for a long time, but an English teacher? Why that's death! Haven't you had enough literacy over here with me?"

"You don't understand, Walter," she said, "you don't understand how certain things can be with two people. And the women's lib was a very good thing for me even though I see how I can't take it seriously anymore. It made me look at things in an entirely different way. To begin to see myself in terms of my own preferences, my own needs, and not as they were regulated with others."

"You're so damned *reasonable*," I say. "How can you sit there and be so *calm* about it?"

"We promised each other when we got married, Walter, that we'd never use faithfulness as an empty ritual and that if either of us at any time wanted someone else, he or she was free to do so and the other one would understand. *You* were the one who wanted it that way, remember? I would have settled for a perfectly normal conventional-type marriage vow but you felt that marriage canceled freedom and that you had to have control of your options. Control of your options, remember that, Walter? Anyway, I don't think it's very serious. We're just having good times together, it's not going anywhere. The trouble with you, Walter, is that you're utterly unprepared for the future, you know that?"

"Tell me who he is. Just tell me who he is, that's all I ask."

"Of course I won't. You just aren't ready for the future, Walter, and yet it's all around you. You've got to learn, you understand?"

"Goddamn it, you bitch, stop giving me aphorisms," I shout, and overtaken by a high old rage, leap upon her right there in our conservative, neatly furnished living room, find myself filled with the raging need to show her that if I cannot reason with her in one way, I can connect with her in the other; I want to pound her senseless under me but something very strange and peculiar happens; she opens her arms to me and takes me in and before our clothes are even off I find myself utterly out of control; I ejaculate not within her but upon her thighs with a high wail that surely cannot be me, a wail compounded of foolishness and submission, and she gathers me in the aftermath against her breasts and strokes me carefully, comfortingly; I want to rise up and strike her, but I am too drained, too stunned, and so I only lie in the circle of her arms and take small greedy peeks at her face from time to time; her face is implacable, compassionate, the face of a madonna, and I take her breast into my mouth, suckling myself into sleep that way, the stroking all around me, and for several hours I know nothing but the motion and the blankness. When I wake up it is morning and she is gone.

XXX

The priest whom I met on the radio panel show has gotten in touch with me and has invited me to appear at his Church for a weeknight discussion of the new trends in morality and publishing. It is all part of his program to make the Church more relevant and timely, and haunted by the possibility of some young relevant ass seeking topicality, I decide to go. When I appear at the Church, however, it turns out that I have somehow misjudged the situation; the congregation appears to be not young but very old and somewhat demented as well: forty or fifty men and women over the age of sixty are sitting in rows in the vestry mumbling to one another. Now and then amidst the pensioners I see a younger face, maybe thirty or forty, but these faces have the demented, fanatical cast of the kind of people who go to churches because they have nothing else to do, and I take little comfort from them or from the priest himself who greets me with nervous, public cordiality and motions for me to sit beside him at the table at the front of the room. The church is located on a rather elegant sidestreet in Greenwich Village, filled with restored brownstones and quiet mansions, and as I sit beside the priest, I can hear the sounds of a street violin staggering in through the windows to say nothing of the noises of people fucking. That is, I can imagine that up and down this block, attractive young New Yorkers are performing highly relevant sexual acts upon one another while I, publisher of the hippest pornographic weekly in the history of the western world, sit in a church basement surrounded by applicants for the Golden Age Club. It is a very discomfiting phenomenon and leads me to a precarious understanding which is something new for me: relevance is where you make it, and it is, perhaps, wiser to exercise more discrimination than I have been recently. I notice that the priest has turned the meeting over to me, talking about the need for a fresh perspective and new trends in publishing, and it seems that I have to say something. I stand, uneasily, and two issues of the newspaper, open to the centerfold, fall from my lap and to the floor. I scramble for them, hoping that they have not been noticed, and stuff them into my briefcase with the horrid feeling that I have split my pants in bending over. "I thought the best thing would be to simply take questions," I say to the senior citizens. "I mean, I don't have anything really formal to say, I just thought that we could kind of discuss the issues together." What issues? I think but put the thought away; issues are everywhere, everywhere you turn nowadays there is at least one new issue to incite concern and possibly three, and the senior citizens no less than any other segment of the population are surely interested in becoming Involved. "If you want to," I add, realizing that this sounds foolish, and then I snake my fingers around to the crotch, find that I have indeed split my pants. A thin line asserts itself to my forefinger, opens slightly under fumbling. I decide to ignore it as best as possible and keep a full face to the audience at all times.

"Father said that you would have some issues of the paper with you," an old woman says, "so that we could see what you're doing. Could we look at them?"

"I'll pass them around later," I say and with a foot push the attaché case further out of sight under the table. I make a decision to leave as soon as possible, with a violent illness if necessary. "Do only perverts read your paper?" someone says after a pause, having apparently given up hope on examples for the time being.

"Certainly not," I say. "The interesting thing about the paper to me is that it is read by a total cross-section of the population. College professors, taxi drivers, barbers, truckdrivers, artists, writers, models, businessmen, advertising executives, all of them and more read our newspaper. We are talking the language of the streets; we are talking the language that people understand; we are finding people on a common denominator of need. We are, in short, fulfilling a function that was lost to American journalism half a century ago; we are telling a wide range of people the absolute truth in ways which they can understand."

"You don't mean the *lowest* common denominator," the priest says jovially. We exchange a rapid look of sheer loathing, his face convulses, and he whispers, "Only trying to get a discussion started." and I say, "Let me handle this my way." He retreats to a seat shaking his head. I observe for the first time that he wears a large jeweled cross around his neck even though he has taken to a relevant business suit for the occasion. "Just trying to get a discussion going," he says again rather hopelessly and looks down at the table.

"Yes, but exactly what *does* your newspaper publish?" the old woman asks. "No one here seems to be quite sure; nobody has seen it, you see. You're some kind of a radical paper, right?"

"We're a sex newspaper, ma'am. We publish articles and photographs dealing with sex."

"Oh," she says with a giggle and sits. "Oh."

"There's nothing wrong with sex," I say rather defensively. "You know that."

"Of course not," an old man says, "but how much is there to say about it?"

The gentleman is apparently popular and this remark incites a large patter of applause, cheers, scraping of chairs against the floor. A tall girl with mad eyes, somewhere in her forties, wearing tinted glasses, stands in the midst of the applause and says, "Exactly what do you think you're going to accomplish in this way?"

"Accomplish?"

"What do you hope to do?"

"The liberation of the culture," the priest says. "The blasting of old myths and shibboleths, the removing of magic from the unknown by making it comprehensible. Isn't that right?" He smiles, sweats, takes off his glasses and wipes them, gives me a nervous grin. "I think you've made that pretty clear."

"Well, not exactly," I say, filled with a sudden mad apprehension that I know exactly how the evening must end, "not exactly. It isn't quite that way at all. Excuse me, all of you, but I just remembered a previous appointment that I had forgotten about when I arranged to come here and I must get to it. It's absolutely crucial, this appointment. I'm sorry I forgot about it and that I've got to do this to you but I can't afford to miss it. It isn't quite that way at all," I say, seizing my briefcase, patting the clips into place, reaching for my coat which I have flung across a chair. "It's something else entirely."

The meeting seems to have broken down into confusion. Some people are standing, shouting at me that I have no courtesy, others are urging me to go quickly. The room is full of shrieks and breath, small hobbling motions. It is a wonderful thing to see that senior citizens still have left so much energy and involvement. "All that I wanted to do," I say when I get to the door, poised on the parapet to flee, "all that I really wanted to do was to make a buck. The rest was secondary, wouldn't you say? Wouldn't you say so, Father? You have to, after all, focus on relevance."

Then I am gone. Out the door, into the night, briefcase slamming against walls with a clatter. But before I go, for an instant, the senior citizens and I exchange a single look at the door, and it is a look of such total understanding and communion, a look of such utter connection that I feel shudders passing through me as I hurtle down the streets. Never have I felt greater understanding than at that moment. The senior citizens, the priest and I, holding out in the basement, discussing matters while outside conditions persist. What are we holding out against? What is truly going on outside? What did we hope to gain?

I decide to limit my public appearances.

XXXI

Virginia admits to me that she has become friendly with the faggarts. She had dinner at their apartment one night last week and for the past couple of weeks Donald or Jim has been calling her in the evenings for advice on personal matters. Also, they often have lunch together, the three of them. "They have a lovely apartment, quite a large apartment up on Riverside Drive, Walter. And they're really sensitive men. The fact that they are what they are doesn't mean that they can't be nice human beings, you know."

"I'll fire them both," I say. "That's what I'll do."

"You're not being rational, Walter. Why would you do something like that?"

"To keep you from getting involved with them. I don't want you getting involved with people like that."

"Oh, don't be an ass. I'm twenty-five years old and I know exactly how I want to run my life and I've been around quite a bit. I wish you'd stop feeling that you can run people's lives for them. You're not going to fire them and nothing is going on so just cut it out."

"I thought that we had an understanding."

"What understanding? Of course we have an understanding. That doesn't prevent you from living your own life, I've noticed. You go home to your wife all the time. I bet you're making it with her, too."

"That's only temporary. It's only a matter of a little time until the whole thing is over. I'm just paving the way."

"Well, you pave the way. I'm not going to go to bed with either of them, believe me, Walter. I'd just make one of them jealous if I did."

"Come here," I say.

"Come here? What are you talking about?"

"I said, come here. I'm going to bang you right here in this office with the doors closed, just twenty feet away from them, that's what I'm going to do."

"Listen, Walter, if you want to do that you can. I won't stop you, but it's awfully immature, isn't it? What is it going to prove?"

"Nothing," I say, unbuttoning, unzipping, clinging, unfolding, suckling, "but it's something I want to do."

"It's childish of you. It doesn't change a single thing. And you shouldn't have the idea that you can have me anytime you want. I have feelings you know."

"Oh, God I know. I know you have feelings," I say, and plunge thickly into her without preparation, solder her tight, begin the familiar in-and-out motions, but moving sidewise since she is sprawled across my lap on the editorial chair, holding my neck and stroking as I wedge in quickly. "Everybody has feelings."

"The phone could ring, Walter. Someone could knock on the door. Someone could even try to come in. Oh, this is stupid, stupid. It's stupid. Oh, stop that. Oh, God. Oh, don't do that. Oh, it can't go on this way. You're just a bastard, do you know that? You're an absolute bastard. I'm coming. I'm coming open inside me. I'm coming for you, all the way down. Oh, Oh. Oh, God."

Afterward, routinely, we dress and separate, part with smiles. She is quite right, however: when she leaves the office the faggarts are still there, chatting seriously in the corner about inventory, and they give her waves as she passes. It is one more nest of complication is what it is, although I could hardly fire them; they know things about the business that I could never understand, they have close contacts with the attorneys, and they are responsible for the cash flow. Besides that, they are homosexuals and homosexuals have no interest in women. I am positive of this although a strange flush seems to brighten Virginia's cheeks as she sits typing near them when I pass on my way to the elevator an hour later. The flush is not for me; it is not for them; it is, perhaps, only for herself. I say something to her as I pass by but she does not hear me. Small dimples appear in the corners of her mouth; she smiles to herself winsomely as with perfect concentration she places her tongue between her teeth and uses an eraser to make corrections.

XXXII

An advertisement appears in our classified placed by a young man deeply interested in the foot culture and anxious to give lessons in toe talk. Seeks same or females although males preferred. From a phone booth well removed from the office, I call him and make an appointment for the afternoon. He sounds cool, possessed, advises me that there will be a fee. I tell him that there was no such specification in his ad and he says that of course there wouldn't be: do I think he is stupid? In any event, he does not practice his expertise for nothing; the fee will be $25 per half hour, payable in advance, and I am free to do as I please. I like his straightforwardness and tell him that I will be at his apartment at the appointed hour. He says that there will be no such thing and gives me the address of a hotel on the west side of Manhattan in whose Room 412 he says he will be at four o'clock. I am to pay the desk clerk the fee plus $5 room rent before going up. I tell him that I like his attitude and without arguing further, agree to what he says.

The classified interests me more and more; there is a whole world out there that I have literally never touched. At one point I felt like an entrepreneur, above the whole thing, manipulative, so to speak, but now I am not so sure. By opening up the market for advertisements of this sort I have, in effect, created desires, made possibilities, and I must be faithful to them. At the proper hour I am in the lobby of the hotel, a small, smoky building in which, signs tell me, classes in karate and black pride are offered on Wednesday evenings as well as a ceramics workshop. The desk clerk, a round menacing man in Army fatigues, asks me my business and I tell him Room 412; he asks me for $25 and drops his hands below the counter to fondle something which I very well think might be a gun. I remove the money from my wallet, give it to him and am then asked to stand straight, arms by sides for a moment. I do so and the clerk emerges deftly from behind the counter through a swinging door and checks me out top to bottom for concealed weaponry. At last he says I may go up, not to Room 412 but to Room 216 just one flight above. He advises me that I must return at the end of half an hour or he will go up to check on me.

I climb the dangerous stairs, sliding a bit on the unsteady steps, clinging to the bannister, and walk down the hall of the second floor, past a few pans of lukewarm soapy liquid and an old man dozing inside an open elevator. Room 216 is at the end of the corridor, and I try to enter without knocking, find it locked, knock gently until the door is opened by a huge blond man bare to the waist. He asks me to state my business and I say that I have an appointment. He gives me a long, careful look and then takes me into the room and leaves, locking the door behind him. I feel no sense of apprehension; I am too suspended in admiration for technique to have any fears whatsoever. Besides, all advertisers in our newspaper, we give our readers to understand, have been pre-selected and may be assumed to have our Seal of Approval. Even the prophylactic creams.

A small, wiry man is on the bed, naked except for socks which are knee-length. He is wearing glasses which he removes when I come near him. "Please undress," he says. "If you don't mind, I'd rather not talk. I don't like conversation and if you have anything to say, you'd better say it now."

"I don't have anything to say."

"Good. Then please undress."

I undress except for my socks. "The socks off too, please," he says. "How can you leave those on?"

"You left yours."

The man shakes his head. "You don't understand," he says. "I'm very sensitive about my feet. No one sees my feet, do you follow that? No one."

"Why not?"

"You don't understand toe queens at all, do you?" the man says. "My feet are mine. They are the most private part of me. Take off your socks unless you want to leave the room at once."

I do not particularly want to leave the room at once. I remove my socks, looking out the window which has a fine view of Broadway; several people are gathered around a fruit stand which seems to have toppled; a perfect explosion of cucumbers, peppers and grapes lie on the asphalt, and the owner, tearing at his head, is trying to get some organization into the affair while passers-by snatch up the scattered fruits and vegetables and stuff them into large shopping bags which they appear to have brought for the purpose. I lie down on the bed next to the toe queen who instantly moves away, comes to his knees, looking at me with piercing eyes.

"Do you really want it?" he says. "Do you?"

"Yes," I say.

"Tell me. Tell me you really want it."

"I do. I really do."

"Tell me what you want me to do with your feet. Go on. Tell me."

I tell him, relying upon certain chance phrases which I recall from a couple of dimly remembered books. Also I rely upon an article on foot-fetishes which we had received for publication a year ago but which I rejected at that time as being wildly improbable and applying, at best, to a very small segment of the population. I had suggested that if the author tried to inject some humor into it and did it as a satire on normal sex practices it might be funny but I could hardly see it as a serious piece. It is hardly likely, but perhaps I am with the author of the article now.

"All right," the toe queen says, "I'll do it. I'll do everything you want. Just lie back."

I lie back and let him perform upon me. It is quite interesting although not particularly exciting. From the new angle I cannot see through the window; I wonder if the vegetable crisis has continued or whether the owner has somehow taken control over the situation. I am all on his side; it is no fun to see one's goods and produce shuffled away by small old people with brown paper bags.

"You're not concentrating. You've got to put your mind to it."

"My mind's right on it."

"No it isn't," he says, but continues. I observe him for a while and find, much to my surprise, that I have an erection. He observes it with satisfaction, reaches out to touch it, then continues. The sensations are mildly pleasant although nothing to write home about. They have everything and nothing to do with the act of screwing. I decide that I am not really a toe fetishist and at that moment, to my greater surprise, ejaculate. The toe queen makes a small approving noise, moves away from me and says, "Well, that's it."

"That's what?"

"That's it. You got what you came for. Now you've got to leave."

"So quickly?"

"Unless you want to pay again."

I decide that I do not and get up slowly; feeling vaguely disconnected; get into my clothes. The toe queen, of all things, curls himself on the bed, yawns, and goes to sleep. I dress; try the door, find that it is locked, suppress panic and knock lightly. The blond man opens it from the outside, comes in, checks the sleeping man on the bed and nods.

"Well," he says; "what are you staying around here for? You got what you came for, now get out."

So I get out. I do not know exactly how I feel, it is not precisely liberated but then, as my own articles in the newspaper have pointed out, too much liberation at a single time would undoubtedly kill us. It is better to take things in small doses. Unconsciously I have been limping, I realize. The desk clerk gives me a knowing, sideways look as I stagger past him and I push my stride into its usual free-form float as I hit the pavement, although unquestionably my toe *does* now ache a bit as I come into Greenwich Village.

The vegetable man is standing by his cart mumbling as I pass. No one is around him. All of his produce seems to be gone; all that remains on the cart are some wrinkled ears of corn, a few brown radishes and a rotting pumpkin, a face carved into it in an inept rotting grin which seems, eyeless, to wink at me as I pass.

My foot tingles unpleasantly for several days thereafter and I go in for epsom salt baths. They do no particular good but induce sufficient tenderness and sensitivity in the foot as a whole to make the toe no longer an object of special concern.

XXXIII

Tony from the Bronx has a new system. His brother has been fired from the racing sheet in a general shake-up and cutback maneuver which is part of the economic depression, and now Tony will play on his own hunches and inspiration. "He was never any good anyway, the lousy son of a bitch," he confides to me over the phone. "Every now and then he'd give you a little something but more often than not it would pay a low price or lose; and the real good stuff he was always holding back for himself. He was the same way when we were kids; I was a couple years younger than him, and I was always getting the girls that he dumped. By the time he ran through them, they wasn't good for nothing. I was running on seconds; until I was twenty years old I thought they was loose inside." Tony has an excellent hunch that Prophet's Bell in the feature will run in at 7–1 or more. He wants me to go out and play a $100 to win for him and apply the profits to his bill if he collects; otherwise I can carry it on for him. And he will, of course, pay my car expenses, admission and even a very small lunch.

"But listen," I point out to him, "I don't want to go there anymore. I don't want to run your bets, Tony. I'm a publisher; not a runner. I've got better things to do in the afternoon than run out to Aqueduct."

"It isn't Aqueduct any more, you dummy, it's Belmont. They run at Belmont until the middle of October and *then* they go to Aqueduct because that's the winter track. You don't keep up, do you?"

"I'm not a horseplayer. I really don't find that it interests me. If it's all the same to you, Tony, I'd just as soon not be a runner."

"Now you listen to me, kid," Tony says over the phone in a rather ugly tone of voice; although I have never seen him (this is a fact), I can picture the convolutions on his face as he gathers the mouthpiece close to his lips. "You listen to me; I been floating your lousy stinking little operation up here on the Concourse for two years. If it wasn't for me you wouldn't *have* a Bronx circulation. Everything you make out of the Bronx, every penny, you owe to me, and furthermore I got contacts in Brooklyn and Richmond Hill, too. I can cut you off just like that, you understand me?"

"I understand you."

"Listen, kid," Tony says, "I really don't like to talk to you like this. It breaks my heart. You seem to be a nice kid from our conversations and you got a nice little rag there; nothing sensational, you understand, but a lot of fun, and personally I enjoy reading it. I don't mind pushing it around. But you got to understand in this business exactly who your distributor is and what he means to you and what he can do, and you got to show a little common respect. Now I've taken it easy with you because you obviously ain't been around very much yet and a lot of these things you got to pick up by being in earshot. But sooner or later, you got to get the point across. It really hurts me to have to talk to you like I did. Make believe I didn't, huh? Just forget the whole thing."

"All right," I say. "It's forgotten."

"Just go out there and bet the horse for me and I'll finance a little bet for you, too. Say you put five on his nose and charge it on my account. Win *or* lose. If he comes in, you can get to keep everything, even the original five. All right?"

"All right, Tony," I say.

"That's a good kid. And you can call me from a luncheonette outside the track right after the race and tell me how it all worked out. I don't like to wait for the wire, it takes forty-five minutes and gets you all distracted. Okay?"

"Okay."

"What I think you ought to have in that sheet if you don't mind my saying so, is more young girls. I mean, a distributor just takes the stuff out, he doesn't have the expertness that you have and I don't want to presume because you probably got a hell of a lot more education than I do, but I got good taste and I know what really interests people. You ought to get some young girls in that sheet, like thirteen, fourteen years old, you know what I mean? Young stuff with just half-formed titties spreading it open for you. That's what the guys like to see. They don't like to look at a whole lot of hippie whores about forty years old."

"I appreciate that, Tony," I say, "but there are certain problems when you start printing pictures of kids. They can get you for corrupting the morals of minors and so on, even if you have signed releases. Of course we can try to get some models who *look* like kids and get them in there. I'll keep that in mind."

"Well, sure. Whatever you say. You're gonna make that bet for me now, are you?"

"Yes," I say, "I'll make the bet for you."

I hang up the phone after more courtesies and editorial comment and get my coat and go off to the track. At least the job as it has been developed leaves you with a certain mobility, there is no question of that. It is a long drive to Belmont — much longer than to Aqueduct — and I lose my way several times, but I manage to get there by the seventh race and put a hundred on Prophet's Bell for Tony, five on Prophet's Bell for myself. Then I stand in the garden, drinking beer under the toteboard, waiting for the call and hoping that the horse will lose. If it loses I can look forward to less Belmont errands in the future.

The horse wins and pays $9.60. A lot of people seem to have been in on the information. I apply the three hundred and eighty dollars profit to Tony's bill but it turns out that he still owes us several thousand dollars. I begin to have a vague understanding of how Tony plans to work that off and of who exactly is going to do the working for him.

XXXIV

New sales figures, tentative, but highly trustworthy, indicate that circulation has dropped off alarmingly within the past month; from 110,000 to 80,000 or perhaps even a little less. Everyone seems at a loss to understand this; the newspaper has remained in the same format for two years and the quality of the last issues did not vary from the standard we have established. It is true that the book reviewer quit, saying that he had run out of books to review, but this can hardly be called an outstanding feature and otherwise the mix has held to its previous level.

I have a series of conferences with myself — there is really no one ese to talk to about this, Virginia is nothing more than a secretary and the faggarts are purely mathematical types — and decide that I can do nothing but ride on as before. The basic soundness of the package has been proven, even if the District Attorney took some of the strength out of it at the beginning. Perhaps it is a reflection of the overall economic situation and people, cutting back on their purchases, are reusing materials to jerk off to. This is plausible and means that when the stock market and employment begin to curve upward again, masturbation will begin to occupy its role once again as a joyous release in the lives of our consumers and sales will move far beyond the initial curve.

Part of the problem could be solved by a sophisticated advertising campaign to upgrade masturbation; make it as status-mobile an activity as full-dress suits and new automobiles. There is no reason why a persuasive, well-researched advertising campaign could not accomplish this within a very few months — the potential is certainly there — but we simply lack any kind of a budget for promotion of this sort and will have to make do with our present standing.

The afternoon after my conference, I fuck Virginia savagely and she takes it all without making a sound.

XXXV

Virginia announces she is quitting. She has found an interesting job as promotional director of a magazine for college girls and in addition is beginning to become bored with her work here which, she now feels, never gave her a true creative outlet. "I'm just fortunate," she says when she breaks this news to me at the end of work one day, "that they didn't hold my experience here against me. I mean, I couldn't conceal it or anything; I had to tell them what I'd been doing for the last year and a half, I couldn't say I was traveling *all* that time. But you know something? They kind of liked it. They didn't think there was anything wrong with it at all. Of course I told them that I was the editor; I know you'll back me up if they check. I'm starting a week from Monday. They want to start a new campaign then, so I can only give you a week and half's notice. That'll be all right though, won't it? I mean, it's not as if you'll have trouble finding someone who can do the job just as well as I can."

All of this is said with such stunning casualness that it takes me aback, leaves me for one of the few times in my life without anything approximating an attitude. Furthermore, she has already put on her coat and is obviously in the process of leaving, casting distracted glances toward the door, chewing gum (a new habit). "But for God's sake, Virginia," I finally say, "what about us? What about what we have between us? Surely you can't walk out on — "

"Oh, listen, Walter," she says, "about that. I've been meaning to say something for quite a little while now but I thought you understood so I didn't have to. I mean, it doesn't matter, Walter. You go through certain things in life; they're all stages, you follow what I mean? First this stage and then that stage and then you wind up where you're going, or maybe you never do, you just keep on changing. Anyway, it was all part of a stage here: working for you, having sex with you and so on, but I'm kind of out of that bag now. I'm interested in like other things and I've got to move on."

"But Virginia — "

"Oh, look," she says, "for heaven's sake, Walter, it doesn't have anything to do with *that* if that's what's on your mind. We can go right on fucking until I leave. I'm not cutting you off or anything like that; even when I'm in the new place we can see each other now and then. We can ease out of it gradually if that's how you want it to be. But of course it's best that it end sooner or later."

"But you wanted to get married. I was even going to break up with my wife, we were — "

"Oh," she says, "oh, that part. Well, that's insecurity, Walter, that's all it was; I come out of this very rigid background full of guilt, you see, where sex was ugly and dirty and I could only enjoy it if I felt it was sanctified or something. Like if we were going to get married. But I'm getting over a lot of those hang-ups now, I really am. I'm just as glad you played me along the way you did because it would have been a really bad scene if you had gotten divorced; I don't want to get married now after all. I'm just beginning to live. I think that the whole thing worked out the best way, and anyway your wife must be a very nice girl."

"I can't spare you, Virginia."

"Oh, don't be ridiculous. You can spare me very nicely. You can get in some very pretty girl here who can do everything that I was doing and probably even better because she'd have less hang-ups. But I've got to move on. Stages, you know? It's time for a new thing."

"I know who it is," I say. "You've been talking to those two accounting bastards. I should have known it all along. They've filled you full of this crap, they've been whispering to you like old ladies — "

"They happen to be very nice people and I'm disgusted with you, Walter," she says; "and if you do anything to Don or Jim because you think that they're to blame I'm going to get very upset, I'm going to have to talk to a few people about you. They're very good friends of mine but that's all they are. There are all kinds of relationships between men and women, you know, and sex is just one part; there can be lots of other things, too. But they've had nothing to do with my trying to get this new job; I decided that all on my own."

"I'll call them," I said. "Tell me who you're going to work for, and I'll call them and kill you for the job. I'll tell them that you were our model. That we've published your cunt in every centerfold for two years, your cunt hanging out through your fingers."

"Don't be crude, Walter; it isn't like you at all. Anyway, they may really be calling you to check, and if you say a single thing like that to them it'll get back to me and I'll have to get very unpleasant, Walter. You listen to me, I'll have to get very unpleasant."

"You can't do this to me."

"Just cut it out, Walter. I've been working here for two years, don't you think I know what's been going on? I'm a college graduate, I keep my eyes open. I read a few files here and there, I keep up contacts. I know what you've been up to. Don't even make me say it. Don't even make me *hint* it. But you don't want to make any trouble for me at all, Walter. You really wouldn't be smart even thinking about it. Oh, dear, I really meant what I said; I wanted this to end pleasantly and I'd be happy to go on having sex with you, but I can see that you don't want it that way at all. You don't have to look at me that way you know, you haven't exactly been walking on water for the last couple of years."

"You bitch," I say. It is quite a rare lapse of control; this kind of thing is not my style at all. "You lousy bitch. How could you do this to me?"

"Good night, Walter," she says. "I'll be in tomorrow."

"No you won't. Get out of here. You're being fired. I never want to see you again."

"You don't have to act that way."

"I mean it. I really mean it. You ever come into this office again and I'll have you arrested."

"You owe me three days salary."

"I'll mail it to you."

"I don't trust you," she says and looks at me intently, pauses one beat, says. "Is there any reason, you know, why I should? Is there?"

I take out my wallet, remove five twenties and put it on the desk between us. "Go on," I say. "There it is. I'm not even docking taxes. Take it out of here. Get out of my life."

"You don't understand, do you," she says and takes the money, puts it in her handbag, goes to the door, "you really don't understand any of this, do you? That's why you get nasty and sometimes do the things that you do. Not because you want to be mean so much but because you think that you're the only sane one in the world and it's just because almost everyone understands something and you don't. You don't, Walter. Well," she says, "good bye." And she leaves the office. I hear her tapping past the desks for a last time and then the slam of the outer door.

Poking my head through the window, I can see her walking down the street. A fine bitch, self-contained, good implacable ass, fine bearing. Well-constructed. If I had the M-1 rifle I had in the army I could lay her out on the street, small bright flecks of blood disturbing her implacability, but they took the M-1 away when we finished infantry training and not for the next year and a half did I ever get to handle a weapon. Company clerks are not particularly strong on armament of the heavy kind.

She turns the corner and is gone but she is a hell of a lot longer than that getting out of my life. A hell of a lot longer than that.

I never realized until the bitch's leaving what she meant to me. And now, never again.

XXXVI

In the night, everything seems possible. Close the eyes, take the hand, take the long trip, make the pictures before the eyes. Moans, mingling, the wind, bodies amorphous then coalesced in the gaze. Make the pictures. Breasts from her, eyes from the other, hips from a third. A face. Perhaps a face glimpsed on the subway or on the street at noon many years ago. Touch the face, manipulate the breasts. Make the connection.

In the night all possibility, in the dawn, before awakening, in the half-broken sleep, shrieks, cries from under the earth, a feeling of distance, loss. Awakening then to the cold stone of the ceiling, the genitals shrunk like a flower, the hand curved skeletally underneath the cheek. The hand a reminder, a recrimination. Nevertheless, there will be other nights.

I never had such women as I had alone in bed in the nights, making all the changes. Never, never, never. Making all the lovely changes, up and down the scale, colors flashing in the night. Fist aflutter like a bird. Breath like diminished seventh chords to the ear. The ear a crackle on the pillow.

XXXVII

A member of a militant civil rights organization has been unjustly imprisoned on high bail and a protest rally is being held on the steps of the library to rally support and donations to his cause. I find myself invited to speak, as the representative of the new journalism, and because I wish to align myself with worthwhile libertarian causes, I go, but almost from the beginning of my speech, I am in trouble. The crowd does not want to listen.

It is raining for one thing — thick drops of hard water coming resonantly upon us — and for another the crowd has already heard too many speakers: a folk singer has led them in a thirty-two verse song against injustice, the dean of a large women's college has predicted the end of America in our time, a noted writer has called for the breaking of the state, a professional revolutionary has recommended the removal (but through legal means) of certain important public figures. Police ring the demonstration suddenly; perhaps half as many police as attendees, only five hundred of us in all and now the rain has become heavy. The crowd has had enough of injustice and calls for revolution, they would like some stronger meat or at least a cessation, but there are at least a half dozen speakers still to be heard and not one of them will stand aside while the militant leader is in jail. They want to stand as one with him even though the television trucks have trundled back to the studios long since with their reels to be edited for the eleven o'clock news. I decide to try a humorous approach, saying that we need to get a little life in the resistance and I know exactly where to put the juice, but the line falls flat, and something ugly and murmurous seems to drift up from the crowd and come over me. "Seriously," I say, "seriously, we have been trying now for two years at *Spread* to say the things that you people have been saying here tonight; we have been trying to open up people's heads and let a little sense in, make them understand that all the old shibboleths and myths are dying or dead." A couple of random boos and hisses come up from the crowd, circling me and finally falling with the rain. It is enough to break something inside, what with the problems I have had both professionally and personally, and I find myself screaming into the microphone, "What the hell is the matter with you anyway? Don't you understand that it's too late, too late for any of this nonsense, the whole goddamned thing is falling down around our heads and the only thing that we can do is to pick up a few of the pieces and make a run for it? Don't you see that? It's too damned late for any of this crap. The age of rallies is over. Unless you want to pick up the pieces all your life!"

"You do, you son of a bitch," someone shouts and it occurs to me, sweating in the rain, that my entire history as publisher of this newspaper seems to have come down to running bets to Belmont for a distributor and being heckled at rallies or panels. "You've been picking up the pieces for two years, that's all you are, a piece-picker, not a peacemaker, why the hell don't you get into the air and swing right? Yeah, swing right, swing right!" Other voices began to chant, and I lean toward the microphone and shout, "I believe in liberation! I believe in the sanctity of the human soul! I believe in the luxury of choices, don't you understand that you have to make choices?"

Apparently no one does. Someone is at my elbow now, speaking quietly, reasonably, suggesting that there are several speakers yet to follow and it would perhaps be best to speed up the rally by giving everyone a chance and sending everyone home; it is getting cold and dark and the matter of donations has not yet been raised. "Donations!" I shout, picking this right up (it is possible that I have blown my cool but even in this loss there is a horrid cunning; I am more alert to things than ever before, there seems to be a genuine sharpening of the senses, a gathering-together, a coming to head). "Donations, that's the ticket, everybody's out for the buck, America is a supermarket and the hell with you! Everybody's putting the knock on me because I'm making a few dollars, but who went out on the limb for you? Who's taking the chances? Who's actually down in the grit and the grime so that you folks can get a little piece of liberation, too, answer me that one! Answer me: do you think any of this is easy? Do you think that there isn't a better way to do things, but you've got to get down in the mud and take things on their level, swing right and if you come up with a little bit of the shit on you, so what the hell's the difference, it's their shit, not yours. Theirs, all of it."

"No, son, it's yours," someone shouts. The moderator of the rally, an energetic, very hip young evangelist in bell bottoms says to me. "That's it, you've had your say, now turn over the mike," and with a determined ecclesiastical hand, pulls me away. It is stunning how much force there is in that grip, for the first time I begin to sense the true mania that must exist in priests (even confused ones whose parishes are full of golden-agers in the West Village), and I try to fight my way past his grip but no hope, no hope for all of that. Several of the other speakers who have been ranged around the dais gather around me and with a series of yanks pull me all the way from the podium and assist me down the steps of the library and hurl me into the crowd. It seems that I have not been one of the major successes of the rally. The crowd, quite hostile at a distance, ignores me when I am thrust among them; no one looks at me. "For God's sake," I say, "what kind of shit is that? Don't you understand that we're all into the same bag altogether, the whole thing? Why must we make differences where there aren't any?" No one answers. No one pays any attention. It occurs to me that for all the effect I am having upon the crowd I might as well go. So I do, hands shoved into pockets against the cold, head hunched against the wind, strolling to the corner of Forty-second and Fifth where I get a taxicab and go home. It seems that I have not had one of my major publishing successes here, but I am unable to detect, at this instant, whether or not it is part of a pattern.

XXXVIII

At home I find a good portion of the apartment cleaned out and a long note from my wife on one of the end tables. It seems that she has decided to leave me, whether on a temporary or permanent basis she cannot tell at this time. The important thing is that there have been changes in her life and she feels that she cannot fight them but must continue groping toward the kind of person she is going to be, someday, if she can only continue to grow. She makes certain references to our sexual life which I cannot bear to read and thus skip over to find that her subsequent paragraphs have to do with how those elements of our sex life seemed to reinforce her own feeling of growth and change. She is going to live, at least temporarily, with Charles, the English teacher, but she will not leave his full name and address for me because she only knows that it will lead to a confrontation which she cannot handle psychologically at the present time. She might as well confess to me that she has not only been involved with women's lib but psychoanalysis as well during these recent months; she has been seeing a certain doctor three times a week and he has brought her to an understanding and self-awareness which she has never had before. This doctor has made her see certain things in me which were very painful for her at first and which she did not want to accept, but gently he led her through them and finally she was able to grant the value of the insights and could understand that what he was saying about me was very accurate and very painful. She then summarizes certain of the opinions the psychiatrist and she have settled on about my personality, but again I can hardly bear to read them and pass on to the next page. It is a very long letter, typed, single-spaced, full of cigarette marks and ashes, and the following pages seem to be pretty much more of the same although there is a tender passage toward the end about our engagement and early married life which I find brings tears to my eyes. She closes with best wishes for me always, says that she relinquishes any further income from me or share of the savings (she will soon be starting a job in the fashion industry but can tell me no more) and advises that she will get a lawyer who will be in touch with me to arrive at an amicable settlement sooner or later. She is taking those few goods from the apartment which she bought or which mean the most to her but is sure that I will have no objection to this since she relinquishes everything else. She is really sorry, but of course part of growing up is to understand that things go on and people change and one can only have faith that it is all for the best. She signs it with one of the intimate pet names I gave her early in our marriage which is really quite stupid of her because this endearment more than any other fills me with rage and opens up within me as cold a stone of remorseless as anything which I have ever known.

"I'll kill the bitch," I find myself saying. "I'll kill the lousy bitch for this when I find her." But I realize that I do not know which bitch I am talking about; Virginia as well has not been very nice to me recently. "Both of them," I say, appeasing the mad, logical inner voice, "if that's the way it has to be, I'll kill them all." But reason intervenes to point out that this would be difficult, would demand planning and execution and, in the bargain, happens to be illegal at the present time. "The hell with it then," I add. I want to wreck the apartment but wrecking is not quite my gig; I would have no idea of exactly where to start or how to do so in the most spectacular fashion and, anyway, I would only have to come back and clean it up later, which is discouraging.

There seems to be little enough that I can do. I pour myself a drink which is not satisfying since I am not a drinker, try to feel melodramatic as I sip it but this rather fails to work as well, and finally I decide to leave the apartment and strike out in the best way known to me. If she betrays me, I will betray her. (I have forgotten in this pose, my adulteries.) I will go to midtown and pick up a prostitute.

So I lock up the apartment and go to midtown and pick up a prostitute easily enough from one of the streets, but in the hotel it turns out that she recognizes my face; has, in fact, been reading the newspaper for years and years and for some reason this fills her with shrieks of whorish laughter. "They'll never believe this," she says underneath me, her breasts moving all over her abdominal wall as she giggles, as I try to pump her, "they'll never believe this if I ever tell them; isn't this the craziest thing? I mean, I was just so surprised when I recognized who you were; maybe I shouldn't have said anything but I was just so *surprised*." I huff and puff and try to discharge within her a mean, boiling load but there is absolutely nothing, and I slide off. "They won't believe this," she says again in a different tone of voice and then pats my prick and tells me not to worry, don't feel bad about it, she knows how these things are, she's been through it hundreds of times. I wouldn't believe the stories she could tell me and anyway this one time she will remit the fee. The hotel I will still have to pay; she has nothing to do with that part of it. They gave us the room space and anyway they give her protection and shield her from the cops.

XXXIX

We hire a new secretary, a blond machine from Northwestern University who says that she wants a job in publishing and is willing to break in any way she can, but if I get any ideas about her just because she is willing to work for me, I will find myself in a lot of difficulty. She is engaged to a physics graduate student who took physical education courses at New York University and can kill people with bare hands if necessary. She will do the work but she owes nothing beyond that single obligation and if I do not like her attitude, I am free not to hire her or, for that matter, to fire her at any time, take it or leave it. Oddly, I find that her approach excites me, and I tell her that she can have the job, no questions asked. Her first day of employment I make a desultory attempt to take her out for a drink after work but she says no, she will have none of that at all; she is meeting her fiancé right after work for drinks and then going to his apartment where she is half-shacked-up anyway and if I do not like this I am perfectly free to fire, etc. I tell her that this is perfectly all right. In fact, I feel a perverse sense of relief. It seems that for the moment at any rate, I am finished with involvements.

XL

Our lawyers report that matters are settled with the District Attorney who has decided to drop all charges against us and remove from wholesalers and distributors any covert sanctions heretofore imposed. This means that for the first time since we began, we are completely free of legal harassment, free of the threat of court-and-imprisonment, free to do our thing as it were, but rather than feeling elation there is a peculiar letdown which I communicate to the lawyers, a couple of bumbling bald men in the Wall Street district who have great contacts in the Municipal Courthouse and a ferociously prompt billing system. "I should think you'd be very pleased," they say. (They seem to talk in chorus.) "This is what we've been struggling for all this time."

"I suppose so. It's just a feeling of letdown. And you begin to wonder why he took the pressure off at this time. What does he have up his sleeve?"

"Oh, nothing," they say, "nothing at all. I just don't think he wants to fight it anymore, he knows that he'd lose on appeal."

"That never worried him before. Maybe they feel there's nothing to fight anymore. That we're no longer a menace."

"Oh, my, indeed," the lawyers say, "you simply do not understand. The pressures of the District Attorney's office. The turnover in personnel all the time. The political intervention, the harassment, the difficult line they have to walk, the newspapers. They have enormous problems. They simply don't choose to fight what they know they can't beat. When you've been around as long as we have you'll understand this. By the way, we're withdrawing from the case."

"What's that?"

"We're withdrawing from the case. The case is closed and our services are no longer needed. So we won't be representing you anymore. Our bills are due immediately upon being rendered; we'll get a final settlement."

"Now I really don't understand. Why are you dropping us?"

"It's not that we're *dropping* you," the lawyers say with a nervous giggle. "How could we do that? We've fought the good fight through the end and received, ah, a most satisfactory settlement. A total resolution as a matter of fact. Now we feel it's time to get into other areas, areas where our competence is, ah, more needed at the present time. Our bills are due when rendered and the final bill — "

"So if the case is won, there's nothing more to worry about. We aren't a problem anymore. Representing us would be easy. So why drop us?"

"It's a corporate decision," the lawyers say rather primly and fold their hands. "Internal pressures, a question of work load. You wouldn't be able to understand; it's not your field. I'm afraid this decision is final. The partners concur."

"You mean the partners ordered it."

"The partners concur. I'm afraid that this appointment is running somewhat, uh, overlong; if you'd be good enough — "

"You're dropping us," I say, "that's what you're doing. First the District Attorney and now you. No one cares about us anymore, is that it!"

"Why, I thought," our lawyers say, rubbing their palms and looking wisely at one another as the secretary comes in to usher me out, "why, I really thought that that was your prime objective from the beginning, wasn't it?"

XLI

A letter arrives registered mail from an attorney in the midwest. He represents one Norman Boggess of Joliet, Illinois, who incurred severe damages to a personal area of his body through the use of a product advertised in our pages. Mr. Boggess is now receiving competent medical treatment, but it is the opinion of the physicians that he sought and received said treatment too late. Mr. Norman Boggess and his wife have been irretrievably denied the pleasures and obligations of the marital act and in addition have been denied children. Accordingly he is instructing us that he is filing suit against us and the B&E Corporation of Santa Barbara, California, for five million dollars plus exemplary damages as of the date of the letter. If we wish to avoid legal action and its subsequent penalties and unpleasantness, we and B&E may jointly send a certified check in the amount of five million dollars to the attorney in full settlement of all claims; the attorney will then make disposition of the check to his clients. He will assume that if he does not hear from us within forty-eight hours of the date of receipt, we are uninterested in seeking a settlement and civil action will then continue.

I close the doors of my office and phone B&E. After some time the information operator tells me that there is no listing for such a company in California. I point out to her that I have been through this once before and that there must, simply must be a listing for the company whether filed or unlisted, and I will thank her to produce this information immediately. She connects me with her supervisor with whom I become exceedingly abusive, but there is no listing for a company such as B&E or any of their other listed names, and the supervisor is incapable of helping me further.

I send B&E a copy of the letter registered mail, special delivery, and tell them in a brief covering letter that the matter is entirely out of my hands. Two days later, I receive a phone call from my friend, the conveyor of information from the company.

"They told me to tell you," he says, "that they are canceling all advertising as of this minute. Every single bit. You pull out all the mechanicals, they ain't paying for no goddamned thing as of this minute."

"Did they receive my letter?"

"They didn't tell me nothing about no letter. They gave no messages about no letter. They just me to tell you that all the ads come out and they ain't never going in again. That's all."

"They had to receive my letter. I sent it registered mail. I have a receipt."

"They don't tell me nothing. I just work for them, I don't know what's going on and I don't want to know. You tell them about the letter."

"All right. I'll tell them about the letter. Connect me with someone."

"They're all out to lunch. They'll be out to lunch for a long time; it's a sales conference."

"Have one of them call me."

"They don't make no outgoing calls on sales conference days. They can't.

"So let them call me tomorrow."

"It's a sales conference *week*. The whole week, they're tied up with sales conferences."

"So they can call me next Monday."

"The week just started today. It don't end until next Thursday."

"So tell them to call me Friday. I'll hold off until Friday."

"They don't make no plans that far ahead. I'm sorry but that's the way they run the shop. Sometimes they got to go right into a sales conference week again. Then there's the matter of the conventions. They go to lots of conventions, these guys."

"We're being sued for five million dollars!"

"I don't know nothing about that. They didn't tell me about no five million dollars. I just deliver the messages."

"Tell them to forget it."

"I don't tell them nothing. I just take messages. You tell them what you want to tell them."

"Get me them."

"They're out to lunch."

"All right," I say. "All right. I get the picture by now. Forget it."

"The ads come out, you remember that now. They were very explicit about that; the ads, every single one of them, come out. If they don't come out they will be very unhappy and they are not going to pay you anyway."

"Good-bye," I say and hang up.

I go to the cabinet and remove another B&E product, a plastic inflatable doll with the female features of a cartoon character, the rubbery mass of it now odorous and clinging together. With gasping, arching breasts, I blow up the inflatable doll to its full expanse, four and a half feet of stiff rubber that has the warm, sticky feeling of a balloon. Painted on the balloon are nipples. The mouth, expanded, smiles down at me, the eyes wink. Armless, the balloon totters on an uneasy base, bangs against me as I touch it.

I put my arms around Lindy the Inflatable Companion, wonderful for home or trips, and think about many things for the remainder of the afternoon.

XLII

"Marry me," I said to my wife, three weeks before she said she would, already, she would. "Marry me and let this be the second chance in our lives. Everybody is entitled to another chance, that's America, that's fate; that's what the whole country believes in and I believe in it, too. I know that whatever we have suffered, whatever we have lost, whatever we feel has been denied us we can reach for again. Just say this: say that between the two of us we can make another beginning and what our history has denied us, we can make again." I was an extremely melodramatic young man, perhaps more melodramatic than is the style nowadays but this was the late 1950's, of course, and I had just become a college sophomore after two years in the army investigating the interior of northern Germany, and I was rather desperate. My wife — this is hard to believe — was a freshman who painted pictures and who wanted, at least once to sing art songs in a concert house in Europe. This is not ridiculous, it is the way that many people thought back in the 1950's, and for that matter I wanted to write novels.

"I don't know," she said, "it's too fast. The whole thing is too fast. I've just been on the campus for three months, the first time I've ever been away from home, the first time I've had to discover that there's a person there outside of my parents, and before I even have a chance to discover that person, I find that you want to get married. I mean, it isn't as if I'm not flattered and I do like you very much but I *am* only 18 — "

"Marry me," I said, "it's not a question of support; I have the assistance from the government for the tuition and I can get a job. And my parents have a little money for me anytime I want it. And somehow we can manage. We can live more cheaply than the two of us could separately. It will be like saving money. And you'll have a chance to do everything."

"I don't know, Walter," she said, "I don't know." And she kissed me langorously, even then she knew how to kiss, oh, God how she could kiss! and we began to neck, and in due course in my old car parked up at the cliffs, we began to pet and one thing led to another although of course that was the year when "nothing went on below the waist" unless you were engaged and we were not engaged until three weeks later when something did "go on below the waist" and she decided that this would be the best thing to do.

"Marry me and change my life," I said and so we were married and so my life was changed and so we lived happily ever after. For a time. For quite a time. It is surprising to realize how much time we had. More than we could have understood then. If not enough. But nothing is ever quite enough, to be sure, in the long run.

XLIII

There were almost no slush submissions all last week and more than half of the personal advertisers have pulled out. The loss of the B&E business has left a terrific hole in the paper, of course, and we have had to cut back to a sixteen-page format, something we have not been at since our fourth issue. I do not know if the personal advertisements have all made their connections or whether they have simply given up hope. In any event no one seems particularly interested.

I have made it a matter of pride from the first never to check the competition — the lousy parasites and thieves who jumped in when I had the courage to show the way was clear — but I broke policy to the extent of picking up a few issues yesterday, and they all seem to be having similar difficulties. B&E has moved over to one of them but the others are back at twelve pages and the B&E ads printed are not the lusty ones I remember.

Something seems to be terribly wrong but I do not know what it is and I lack the energy to investigate. Some terrible events are occurring in the public domain — I try to shut it out as much as possible but now and then it intrudes — having to do with the invasion of yet another country and the near-assassination of a powerful conservative congressional figure — and perhaps when these ease off and things return to "normal" sales will improve. On the other hand, perhaps they will not. It is difficult to say. In other times I would have been more interested, but a peculiar apathy seems to have overtaken me; a physical weakness in the limbs and joints which moves placidly enough throughout the body and which leaves me weak and submissive, feeling like a limb which has gone to sleep and knows too well the agony of being joggled awake, so remains crouched under the other limb, the arteries pressed tight, denying the pressure of the living heart.

XLIV

I have left the apartment and now live in a furnished room in a large, odorous rooming house near the offices. Subletting the apartment was easy enough, I threw in the furniture, kitchen equipment and a large sheaf of pornography spread over three closets in the bedroom which will be a pleasant and unexpected bonus to the young couple who rented it should they ever stumble across the goodies. Giving each other yearning looks across the coffee tables, accepting every figure I quoted with quick, mumbling nods of the head, I doubt that they will stumble across the pornography for a long time even though the spirit is known eventually to flag, one's true love to turn pale and the embers of desire to ash.

I live in this furnished room; it is far more convenient, contiguous with the offices, and having as it does only a bed, desk and chair, it imposes no housekeeping problems. Once a week the landlord, for a fee, sends up a chambermaid to clean out the refuse and put on fresh sheets; every third night or so a hasty bump and thump from the adjoining room, a cry of sheer passion, remind me that the tenants here, no less than anywhere else, are possessed by common desires. My wife's lawyer contacted me shortly before I left our apartment and worked out a rather equitable, generous settlement which provides that she get no settlement fee and nothing weekly in alimony for the rest of her life. I understand that a quick, uncontested divorce has been worked out somewhere or the other and this is for the best. My wife was always a highly moral type; it would be expected that she would seek a divorce to sever a marriage as quickly as a marriage to cement a relationship; there is something surgical and merciless about her, for all her talk of living flexibly toward the inconsonant future.

My single companion is Lindy the Inflatable Companion whom I took home from the offices last week and who now keeps me company in the room when I am home and not engaged in professional tasks. I can perch her atop the desk to witness me while I lie on the bed; I can place her on the bed to see me while I struggle with an article at the desk; I can put her between the bed and the desk to see me pace as I work out the details in my head. She is not lovable, but she makes few demands; she is hardly attractive either but there is something to be said about the solidity and sheer sanity of her presence: she engages in no dialogues, makes no arguments, has no sting to relationships, has no questions about the future. I still feel her faintly horrid to the touch and pity those men to whom she has been sold as a masturbatory object (and at the same time am perversely jealous of those men, thousands of them possessing copies of my Lindy in small rooms dotted throughout this and the other nations), but my interests go far beyond the blatantly sexual: I have not attempted sex since the night my wife left me. Desire seems to have been excised surgically too; something else burns within me in exchange but it is nothing which has to do with human beings or the huffings and heavings of ejaculation. Lindy knows of this and the other things quite well; she regards me with a smile as I work and sleep, she may, for all I know, be making up a set of observations for her memoirs. She has all the time in the world. Built to last at a rugged fifty-two inches out of solid latex with a tough inflatable base, Lindy will undoubtedly survive me and all of those who made her. In that sense alone, she is not to be dismissed out of hand.

I have, I understand now, been in a furnished room all my life. Sometimes the furnished room was occupied by another person, sometimes by fifty-two, sometimes by three or four in the special services division. But it was always the same furnished room and huddled under the covers nearby, observing everything, saying nothing, waiting until this moment to reveal the aspect of her presence was Lindy the Inflatable Companion.

XLV

The two faggarts announce that they are quitting. It is high time because I was on the verge of firing them. The most recent sales circulation figures have been more disastrous than ever; we are down to 40,000 copies and sinking. No one seems to know the answer although the cutback in the personals and the loss of the pulling power of the B&E ads is suspected to be part of the reason. The faggarts want to get out before things collapse underneath them and they become hopelessly identified with a disreputable enterprise that has failed. The disreputability is fine; it is the failure which is the problem. "I was about to fire you, you know," I say to them on their last day as they stand over their neat unoccupied desks, mournfully stuffing papers into identical briefcases.

They nod sadly. "I know," Donald says. "I know," Jim says. "It had to be that way. We did what we could but in the last analysis I guess we couldn't pull it through."

"I can't give you any notice, you know, or any severance pay. That's the way it is."

"That's all right," Donald says. "We understand We'll live on unemployment until things get straightened out a little bit. We'll work it out."

"How's Virginia?"

"What's that?"

"How's Virginia?"

They look at one another. "We don't see Virginia anymore," Donald says cautiously. "We haven't seen her for a long time. She stopped coming around soon after she quit. We hear she's all right though."

"Yes," Jim says, "she's all right. I think she's getting married or something. I don't know, though. It's just a word you hear around. It doesn't mean anything."

"You haven't seen her?"

"No," Donald says, "we never had that kind of relationship. It was just one of those office things. She'd bitch to us and we'd bitch to her. It was a fun thing but when the office goes it all goes."

"And I guess you were bitching about me, right? That was the subject of the bitching, huh?"

They look at one another and then at the floor. "I guess we'd better go," Jim says. "No point in hanging around. It's getting late and we really aren't needed."

"Yes," Donald says, "I guess we should get going. It's been great, Walter."

"Tell me," I say, "what is it like to have a cock in your mouth? What does it feel like to suck another man off? Does it really make you feel good when you see his balls start to quiver under your tongue? What is it like to open up an ass and stick it all the way in there and reach around to grip a nice sturdy prick?"

They back toward the door, their eyes round. "Tell me what a prick tastes like!" I shout. "Tell me what it's like when he comes in your mouth! Do you really feel like a man when you make another man come off? Is that the secret of the whole thing, having another man in your power makes you a man at last? What is it like when the two dicks rub together and they're hard and you're both about to come?"

They open the door and step outside. "Cocksuckers," I say. "Stinking, lousy, self-righteous, son of a bitching cocksuckers, that's all you are. Do you hear that? Cocksuckers!"

I hear their sounds on the steps and the slamming of a door. There seems little to think about so I return to my office where the blond machine has been sitting, hunched over a file cabinet, trying to get some of the back correspondence in shape. She looks up at me brightly, a pencil clutched between her teeth, as I come in.

"I heard that," she says. "I heard every word of it. I don't think I like you very much."

"It's none of your business."

"You're damned right it's none of my business. I don't *want* it to be my business. I don't think I want to work here anymore if it's all the same to you. I don't like your goddamned attitude."

"You don't know the background."

"I don't want to know the background." She stands, uses her calves to slam the cabinets, walks to the door. "Who do you think you are?" she says. "Just exactly who?"

I have never seen so much passion in her. "Forget it," I say. "Tough times here. It goes back before your time. It doesn't matter."

"I quit."

"You said that already."

"I mean it. I don't do anything for effect. I don't want my check or anything. You can keep the day's pay you owe. I just want out of here."

"So go," I say.

"This is a disgusting vile place. You've made it that way and you're a disgusting vile man. Not because it has to be but because you've made it turn out that way. You only feel happy if you've made it ugly because it's only the ugliness you can understand. The ugliness and cheapness of it. No, don't you turn away, you listen to me."

"I don't have to," I say. "You quit."

"You still have to listen to me."

"No I don't, you stinking, lesbian bitch," I say and seize her by her shoulders, push her toward the outer door, snatch her coat from the rack and hurl it over her as I fling the door open and shove her in the hall. "I don't have to listen to a fucking thing you say, not ever again, as long as you live. Get the fuck out of here." I slam the door on her, hard enough to make the glass buckle and then lock it. I am in the office alone, it seems, and the clutter overwhelms me. I sit at the blond machine's desk for a while, going through her drawers, but there is nothing personal in them; nothing I can learn about here to nail her. The faggarts' desks I don't even bother with; I know them too well.

I get up and go around the office throwing out files and inventory. Back correspondence is pointless, back advertisements are history, past bills have been paid or never will be, and the majority of the submissions are worthless. The mechanicals have no significance. All of it into the wastebasket. I find that I am shaking and spitting into the wastebaskets in a state somewhere between grief and laughter, so I say enough of this, a day's work is all that can be asked of any man, and lock the place the hell up and go home. At home, however, I find that there is nothing to do, and so, much later, on a couple of drinks, I come back to the offices and spend the rest of the night reconstituting the place, putting back all the materials I discarded, neat in blank rows in their separate drawers, making the office faceless again. Only then do I go home to sleep and when I wake up I realize that I have missed a whole day and what the hell is the difference?

XLVI

I call Virginia. The phone rings only once and she answers. "Hello, Virginia," I say, "this is Walter."

"Walter?"

"I wanted to find out how you were doing. What was going on. I miss you Virginia; I — "

"Walter? I don't know any Walter."

"Virginia, come on."

"I never heard of anyone called Walter in my life. Are you sure you have the right number?"

"Virginia? Virginia Nelson?"

"That's me, but I don't know any Walters. You have the wrong number, friend. You have the wrong number."

"Please, Virginia. I'm suffering. You have no idea. You just couldn't understand what's happening."

"I'm sorry that you're in such bad shape, friend, but you've got yourself the wrong ear here. I can't help you. I never heard of you."

"Virginia, please listen to me, I was all wrong. I see that now. I was wrong, I admit it. Listen, we'll get married."

"Once is a joke, mister, but now it's not so funny anymore. I'm going to hang up on you."

"I said we'll get *married*, Virginia."

"You are into the wrong switchboard, pal," she says and hangs up on me. A ringing, hollow sound in the ear. Clank. Total disconnect.

I dial her again but the phone is busy. I dial once more an hour later and the phone is not answered. I dial her at four in the morning and a male voice says that he is going to call the police. I do not dial again.

Lindy the Inflatable Companion. Lindy the Inflatable Companion knows. To Lindy, then. To Lindy.

XLVII

I receive a brief, handwritten letter from Tony in the Bronx. He is sorry but he is pulling out of the distribution chain. Business costs, change of retailers, other factors. He has enjoyed our relationship. He will be happy to do business with us in the future should we get into another branch of publishing. He does not mention the several thousand dollars still owed and unearned from horse bets but then, as the letter makes clear, Tony is something of a functional illiterate and cannot be expected to have any kind of precision about financial matters. The unschooled in our society must be protected from their own inadequacies; this is one of the functions of a democracy.

I phone Tony but find that he is out for the week. There is something to do with a change of office locations and also a matter of shifting personnel; in any event, he will be out of contact for a long time. The operator, who sounds vaguely sympathetic, says that she will leave any message which I care to drop off with her, and I say that this is not strictly necessary, I only want to convey to Tony my thanks for his assistance and his willingness to stand by me at a difficult time. She says that she knows that he will appreciate this.

XLVIII

I should hire more staff but inertia rules; there seems no reason to. The newspaper runs on momentum. I have been cutting out old pages for the mechanicals and am reprinting many of our best features. It is impossible that any of our readers will note that he has read something a year or two ago and is thus reconstituting his experience. I inform the freelancers that we will be cutting back on our use of material for a while, but they hardly seem to care. Almost no one comes by to see us any more. It is very lonely in these offices although somewhat airy.

In the afternoons I amuse myself by calling numbers at random in the phone directory and making indecent proposals. My favorites are those names which include only a first initial; this is a dead giveaway to be young girls living alone since the phone company and police advised several years ago that this was the best way to cover their identity. I tell J. Nichols that I have been watching her for a long time and will make my move at any instant; she will never know from whence it comes. E. Cohen and R. Peters seem to be at work for the afternoon but K.L. Scott picks up the phone herself and I tell her that the end is very close now; one of these evenings very soon I will crawl through her window and launch myself upon her like a hand grenade, all splinters and fragmentation within. K.L. Scott seems somewhat interested and asks me if she might know me from somewhere at which point I hang up and go for afternoon coffee, not wanting to make too much, so to speak, of a good thing. This approach must be saved for emergencies.

XLIX

I telephone Rona Milliken at her offices. She sounds embarrassed for a moment and even then seems to have a little difficulty recalling me. "Oh, yes," she says, "oh, yes. Look, I'm sorry that the piece didn't run with your interview. There was a change in policy upstairs. I didn't have anything to do with it. They decided they wanted to upgrade and have a look at the social issues in a quality way and they cut out almost all of the interviews. Listen, I have nothing to do with that at all."

"I didn't even know," I say. "I never read the magazine. That's okay."

"Oh," she says after a pause. "Oh, so it's okay. That's fine. Listen, I have to go out on a beat right away so if we could — "

"Do you want to go out with me?"

"What's that?"

"What's so complicated? Do you want to go out with me? On a date? We can go to the theater or to dinner or both or neither or something and come back to my place or to yours. How about it?"

"I'm afraid not," she says. "I'm engaged. I'm getting married in three weeks."

"Oh," I say. "I'm sure I wish you all happiness. We could still go out, though."

"I see the man all the time. We have to make, like, arrangements. It's going to be a pretty big wedding it turns out."

"Well for God's sake," I say, "what am I supposed to do? I've got to go out! Don't you have any consideration for me? Please, say you'll go out."

"I'm sorry," she says, "I really am, but I think you've got the wrong idea entirely."

I begin to rant into the phone. I tell her about my loneliness, my fear, my pain, my necessity, my desperate need to connect with a woman, my fear that all my contacts have disappeared and that I am losing control of myself. I talk floridly, passionately, and mix in one or two threats. After some time I understand that I am talking into an empty wire and she has hung up on me. That is probably all right because I am more than a little ashamed of myself and do not want to feel that anyone knows the extent of my vulnerability.

XLX

In the morning, when I report to the office, it is locked up. Shuttered. My key fails to work in the door and I am unable to smash the glass. Tacked to the door is a legal form which after a while I notice. It has something to do with the granting of a temporary injunction. In line with this temporary injunction, the premises are closed, etc. I notice a sheet of paper sticking under the door and find that it is an eviction notice from the landlord, dated two weeks earlier, an old trick. Further hangings and smashings on the glass fail to yield any results.

I walk downstairs and phone the landlord from a booth in a luncheonette. He says something about five million smackers and lawyers and complications with which he does not want to deal. The word *impounded* seems to come through along with something that sounds like *certiorari*. He includes his regrets but says that he is now attempting to sell the building to a large landscape redeveloping corporation which will convert it into a luxury-class apartment dwelling and he simply cannot afford to take any risks, such as attachments. He can only cooperate with things as they develop.

I hang up on him — it is a pleasure to break the pattern and hang up on somebody — and go home. There is very little, after all, to do. At home I find that I am very tired and I sleep all day. When I get up at eight in the evening everything seems pretty much the same. The fact that I have not been in the office appears to have made little difference to anyone. I discuss this with Lindy, along with certain ideas I have begun to develop of the Law of Universal Balance, and then I go back to sleep. Sleep is comfortable. I have been functioning without it for so long that it is stunning to understand how totally absorbing it can be, how necessitous, how nourishing to all the corridors of the body. Sometime during the night Lindy must stick to me, for I wake up to find her smashed in the bed beside me, thin strips of rubber sticking to my flesh a smile against my abdomen, a smell like glue pervading the room and nothing, nothing, absolutely nothing to hold on to. But there is no weeping. I went beyond that a long time ago and there is no going back, not in that direction, not ever.

I never thought it would happen this fast. I thought I had time, I thought that there was time enough to do many things. The culture accelerates madly; everything reaches beyond itself, the stunning accumulation of data and possibility makes calculation impossible. There was no time. There was never any time at all.

LI

The next week I take a walk through midtown. It is a gray day, wind in the air, much business being transacted in the Forty-second Street shops and in the theaters. I hunch against the cold, passing newsstand after newsstand. Whores and fags stand in the doorways of the arcades, wondering if the whole thing is worth it. Still trying to make that decision, I cannot help them.

Every newsstand I pass carries an issue of our newspaper. It is not the issue I last worked on, it is a new issue, one which I have never seen before. I buy four copies and they are all the same. The masthead contains my name and picture, below it are articles which I have never read although they are very similar, of course, to all the other articles.

The newspaper goes on. It goes on independent of me; kinetic energy of its own carrying it. This is a mystery. Nevertheless, it has happened. The paper exists. I was totally extraneous. Separate from me, it continues. What am I to make of this? What am I to make of any of it?

I fold the copies of the newspaper under my arm and go home. I will spend the afternoon with them. Perhaps there will be an answer. Perhaps even — and I feel a surge of anticipation at this — perhaps there will even be something worthwhile in the classified section that I can pursue.

THE END

Horizontal Woman

BARRY N. MALZBERG

I

1964. Bedford-Stuyvesant. Bedford-Stuyvesant, no less! She knows she
will never forget this, even when she finds her destiny in Mamaroneck
or Scarsdale; she will hold it to herself forever. In Massapequa. Perhaps
New Rochelle. Oh my! oh my! Lying on the Morales floor, limbs open
and locked at last to his necessity (how driven he), eyes fixated on the
ceiling which glows with sensually disadvantaged fire, Elizabeth Moore
groans, closes her eyes, feels the Morales dong wedge into her with
terrific force. Finally! Incredible! What an urge to breed still exists within
this simple Home Relief case: she had never been able to judge, until this
joyously unsprung moment, the pain, the greed, the sheer *social
dislocation* of the man ... but now, as she feels him working on the last
enjambment, crooning to her in his exotic native tongue, a flicker of real
feeling, even compassion (the compassion was the point) invades her
along with his member and she puts her arms around his neck, drags
him to her secluded breast muttering, "oh baby, baby, it's all right, just
come into me!" ... and Mr. Morales, whimpering, kicks in response,
grunts, reaches down and through the cloth of her sensible investigator's
dress and takes her left breast in his hand. He squeezes it absently, one
large Puerto Rican eye inclined upwards to regard her, a slow, socially
decompensated glare seems to infuse the pupil and she feels his elongated
genital, fired by longing and the generous allotment of Home Relief
surge into her. His mouth falls from her breast in this extremity. She
remembers from her reading that buccal play is negligible in the lower
and working classes and does not force the issue. His history has taught
him that playing at the breast is childish; Kinsey cleared this up as early
as 1948.

"*Ai,*" Mr. Morales mutters, "*si, si, si.*" The pressure against her is
suddenly hard, almost taxing, and she tries in that instant to slide apart
from him, gain some small space in which she can recover respiration
and insure her caseworker's detachment but two generations' worth of
moral debasement; alienation, that is to say, on the rolls of social
welfare have made Mr. Morales suspicious and insistent and so he only
holds her the more tightly, shaking his head, a fine, lunatic glare now
obscuring the deprived glaze of his pupils.

In the adjoining room children shout. They seem to be engaged in
moving furniture from one wall to the next and Elizabeth shakes with
discovered excitement: she is helping Mr. Morales perform the act of

creation almost in the presence of those who have come from such actions although in no way does she think she bears resemblance to the absent Mrs. Morales who, she knows, is far away, at some sub-level of the project, participating in the food surplus program. (At all costs Elizabeth wants to protect her from the pain of displacement: it will surely do no one any good if Mrs. Morales begins to project upon Elizabeth her feelings of inadequacy.)

"Please," she says, nevertheless, all of this conceptualization not quite emptying her of pain, "please not so fast, not so fast, take your time," afraid that she will go dry around him and increase his frustration and shame, raise her own resistance above tolerance level. But then she remembers, fortunately, that in his particular subculture, swift and earnest copulation is linked with the very idea of manhood. Only three or four generations removed from his barbaric natural state, Morales and his peers put the highest premium on those men able to copulate swiftly and effectively (because otherwise in no way at all) and her cries shift to submissive whimpers.

The thing is to comfort him, he has suffered so much, he has deserved so much better. She links her fingers into the Morales shoulder and urges him on, grunting, to higher, even excess speed. "Oh I know," she says, "I know how you feel, I really do: the confusion, the pain, the loss, do it then, do it, get it all out of you, every last bit, do it to me," wondering if any of these words, not to say the import of her sudden shift of emotional resistance (lability is inevitable under stress) can be understood by him. English is only his second language, after all, and although he has been on the mainland for ten years, he has steadfastly refused to attend courses for the foreign-born because he feels it to be, at least Elizabeth *suspects* that he feels it to be, a slur upon his intelligence and adequacy. Also, it would render even more questionable his failure to find a job.

"*Mira,*" the damaged Mr. Morales mutters. His motions increase, although staying within a small compass, his tiny mustaches twitch ferally in some aspect of light that bounces off the sheen of his face, his nostrils flare into a powerful if somewhat displeasing thrust and he heaves himself fully over her crying *mira, mira, I'm coming, madre dios* … and at this focus of ambivalence, dead-centered, the tortured thing between need and shame, he pours into Elizabeth the largest, fullest flower of sperm which she has yet contained. None of them have emitted the quantities produced by this five-foot four-inch Morales. She can feel herself pulsing with it, trembling to take the full impost of the

Morales burden and as she jerks reflexively, moans, squeezes her eyes against the light, runs a forefinger across the unemployable's forehead, she feels his thrusts subside to whimpers and then to full-fledged ethnic moans which, meant as they are, only for her, assault her with a kind of premature nostalgia. She knows she will not forget Mr. Morales. Close with her now, there is no future so impenetrable that he will not be close with her yet. It is one of the real satisfactions of her job although, to be sure, not the central issue.

My pesos he murmurs and slides his genitals from her. Disengaged, he clambers to his feet, murmuring private Island insights, tucks his shirt into his open pants and then, arranging himself deftly behind her, goes to the water faucet and brings Elizabeth a small glassful of opalescent Bedford-Stuyvesant water. *Public assistance water*, she thinks, sipping, and the taste to her, although cardboard, has an aspect of sacrament. Her limbs feel like glass as she slowly arranges them underneath. Now that she has been possessed, she feels shy against him and this can only be beneficial to his shattered self-image. She lets the shyness overtake her; feels her face turn rosy in the soft light. A part of this for him must have religious overtones.

She is shy before him. There is no way that it could be otherwise because her pattern with clients is invariably withdrawal after copulation and there is still no way that she can tell, looking at his impassive, culturally-deprived cheeks, the closed slit of his dependent parent's mouth, what he is truly thinking of her; whether she has been satisfactory to him or not; whether he has interpreted this sudden commitment to him as a gift or merely as an insane caseworker's reaction. Caseworkers, Mr. Morales would surely think, are able to do almost anything. There is too much ambiguity in her role. This is something, however, that is correctable.

"Good," she says, "I think you were very good," putting the glass down with a lurch and looking for her fieldbook and panties; the fieldbook still in her hand of all things (she must have gripped it convulsively) the panties, tossed by Mr. Morales somewhere in the distance at the first shock of contact. "I just want you to know that in terms of manhood you have nothing to be ashamed of," she says, trying to approach the client on his level, trying to build a sufficiently masculine self-image for Mr. Morales that he will be able, almost single-handed, to combat generations of neglect and despair. (She can see a revived Morales, at some time of apotheosis, tangling fiercely and with serious expression, with legions of exploiters, blown past his limitations at last and toward some high place of destiny.)

He scrambles to his knees when he sees what she is looking for, hobbles, staggers, mumbles, finds it and hands over the object. She curls them to deposit in the book's inner flap, noting the fine blush now coating the abused Morales cheeks. "Much pleased, terrific, well, thank you very much," he says. "Appreciate everything a lot, oh boy, really terrific." He is trying to talk her idiom. "Terrific," he says. "Terrific."

"Sure," Elizabeth agrees, "you were wonderful." She sees that her self-doubt — and this is an old problem, a *personal* problem, not to be so easily alleviated although she is certainly coming to grips with it — was far out of proportion and that in his own context, Mr. Morales cares for her enormously. He would have to, to be so moved. She has reached him. He appreciates — truly now — what she has brought to his need.

And gratified, she could kiss him for this (but no passion this time in the kiss, only a kind of searching-and-bestowal), kiss him for the knowledge that his feeling too can overrun articulation — but at the instant of impulse she retracts, shakes her head, comes back into herself and scrambles, not at all awkwardly, to her feet. There is no point, after all, in overstepping the bounds of a relationship which, barely initiated as it is, must remain clearly structured in order to aid him.

"Beautiful señorita," Morales mutters and supports her elbow. She totters, her eyes watering to a sudden glaze from the steaming pots on the burning stove in this cluttered welfare kitchen. She thinks of sociopathy.

Meanwhile, the door opens. Three of the Morales children (wards of the state and themselves locked deep into the grinding cycle of disuse and brutality, pity them, pity them) come in one by one and stand against the wall, regarding her sullenly from the depths of their anomie and alienation. These, she knows, would be the three *middle* children and a simple glance at her fieldbook would give their names and ages but to put up a barrier at this time against the children of this man with whom she has just performed the act of procreation, might well shame him and destroy some of the real, if tentative, good that she has done. So she only wipes a hand across her forehead, feeling the gentle Morales damp sift against her palm and stands there with a smile, waiting the moment out. How she handles it will be crucial in determining the long-range effects of the relationship. The children look at their father intently, turn and leave the room with shrugs. *"Fuck, fuck,"* one of them says and giggles. "Perhaps," says another, somewhat older. Elizabeth feels a flick of sympathy for a lifestyle, a culture so despised that the act of love can be reduced to simple scatology.

Morales closes the door again, turns an inconspicuous key and, coming back to her, puts a proprietary hand on her neck, runs it down the back, soothing, gives her an absent tap on the buttock (she feels the attack of possession; now she will be part of him) then moves the hand up again and rubs his face against her cheek. She has brought him, she sees, to some awareness of tenderness. Very possibly this is for the first time.

"The clothing," he says. "I must talk to you now about the clothing."

"The clothing?"

"Clothing, clothing. The *ropa. Ropa* for the kids, you understand, Miss Moore? I ask you about this ten times, twenty times even already how the kids are needing for going back to school. Clothing. They really have nothing to wear. We need, you understand, all kinds of things. My wife now for instance; she — "

"The grants can't be administered until September," she says with some confusion, "not until just before the opening of the school. Now it's still July, Mr. Morales, you've got to realize that there are, well, almost two whole months — "

"But my wife," the welfare client says, reflexive defensiveness easing toward projective hostility, "she needs time to investigate the shops, the sales, there are plenty of bargains and anyway," he says, putting his other hand on her shoulder and pressing her, not too gently, against the wall, "anyway if I could work I wouldn't put myself through all of this, my pride, she is so hurt, the welfare is no good but Miss Moore, my *heart* — "

It is hopeless. Really now (she reproves herself) she should have known this; it is quite hopeless. She has heard about the Morales heart from her initial home visit when she took over the caseload some seven months ago; other caseworkers have heard about the heart as well, twenty-five years of Morales history as recorded in the casebooks of the department contain the heart or at least some foreshadowing; it has flickered on the edges of discussions for decades but never, at least, never has it stopped going. Not quite. Then again, it has never gotten much better. And now, no more than on any given day, is the damaged Morales capable of understanding that his hypochondriacal symptoms are merely neurasthenic justification for the psychic lack. Of course they are. It is that evident. But he is not ready for this insight; simply not ready for it by a long margin. She had hoped that this planned infusion of sexuality into their relationship would pave the way toward insight …

but it is still too soon.

Too soon. A massive weariness overtakes Elizabeth; it is a weariness that she has felt before to be composed of nothing so much as despair at her insignificance and the dimensions of what she must combat. Alone. She is only one person but these needs are so manifest, the background chaotic. She can only take one step at a time in a limited way and it will never be enough; there is nothing that she can do to bring even a fiftieth of the Morales' of this world to their senses, blown past decompensation.

Still: how sure they are of themselves! How locked into their madness! He stands before her, stricken perhaps by some aspect of her own insight, his hands twitching slightly, the planes of his face falling into a kind of dismay. He is really (looking at this objectively now) quite a small and pitiful individual and the very ease and swiftness of his sexual functioning must be part of the problem since his actions in that area are so compulsive that he cannot yet be unblocked. Cannot open himself up to the full possibilities of the sexual spectrum. And as she allows herself to understand this, Elizabeth feels a slow relaxation beginning within her, one of the more blissful of the sensations she knows she will gain from him and his come still moving limpidly within her, the come seems to have congealed into a series of strings which pull her responsively across the room. It was not her fault after all. She has done what she can. She slaps her fieldbook on a chair with a sense of command, using her free hand to wave clouds of the Morales steam from her face.

"Oh we'll get into this," she says, "we'll get right into it at the time of my next visit. I have to be out here for a statutory home visit next month. We visit once every three months, you know. You're due in May, August, November and February. Those months. This July visit was just an extra. Not a statutory but what we call in the department a proprietary. We'll talk all this over when I come by on my regular visit in a couple of weeks and try to systematize your needs."

"This wasn't a regular visit? This was a extra? Well that may be all right for me but my wife isn't going to like this. The *ropa* — "

Post-coital *tristesse* seems to have turned Morales stupid as well. "You mean you come out to see me special?"

"I wanted to service your needs," she says and risks a quiet wink. There are disadvantages in explicitness: still, at this socio-economic level, how subtle can she be? She would like Mr. Morales to know that she desired him. It can only help his self-image.

"Needs," he says "but I have such needs. You could not understand these, Miss Moore, the needs of this family. I mean you a social worker but — "

"I know, Mr. Morales," she says, "I know that, I really do, but we can't solve all of this at first; we have to go at it piece by piece. By piece. Did anyone ever tell you by the way that you are an attractive man? You are, you know. I want you now to keep all of your appointments at the division of employment and rehabilitation."

"Employment? Rehabilitation?"

"That division"

"Oh. Division. Attractive? What do you mean by this attractive? Have you saying — "

"Oh we can't go into that now," she says, "just believe me; in your own way you are. You certainly are and you must report to the division every week and try to let them help you. Next month now we'll have a long talk. Mr. Morales."

Their new relationship is still unfixed. She cannot call him by his first name, she knows, until at least the next time because their relationship must be kept on a level of relative impersonality. Besides, although it is right in her fieldbook, penciled in by the previous worker, she is not sure that she *knows* his name. Felipe? Perhaps that was it: Felipe Morales. *Felipe*, she may mutter to him the next or third time. *My señor, Felipe.*

"I'll see you next month, Mr. Morales," she says now, keeping it within the professional context but tossing him a careful smile just in case and, tucking the fieldbook under her arm, feeling the restoration of their more formal relationship as she does so (above all she owes him a firmly structured situation, a central and authoritarian figure) she goes to the door and, opening it, finds herself in the lightless hallway. She pulls the door behind her to face the familiar investigatorial dark. With old skill (she has learned a few things in her time; one is the essential construction of these oldline tenements) she manages a flight of stairs in the more congenial hallway and then, increasing her pace, springs past the mailboxes (all of them broken) and comes onto the street. Boerum Street.

It is a splendid summer day on Boerum Street: the July heat not yet congealed toward madness, the disadvantaged still on their stoops or, from the very depths of the alienation effect, playing an educationally-disadvantaged poker at tables set up for them by the buildings department on the sidewalk. They nod at her. At Elizabeth Moore.

She nods back. There is no problem. It all comes down to the question of handling these people; she learned the secret early on. Professionalism is one kind of protection and there is always the Hidden Part. Only the despair remains, despair that she can move through painfully bit by bit and that long before she had even touched the surface of loss the spawn of Felipe Morales will have come to another generation. Dislocation and need multiplied past Malthusian proportions. And tumble at last into the Fire.

But she, Elizabeth Moore, is no apocalyptician. Not at this moment. Her tasks are simple, her own needs focused, her devices in connection. Chip away. One little bit at a time. Mountains from tiny kernels, great oaks from sprinkles of fallen rock. She can try to beat it. Piece by piece. By piece.

II

Walking briskly to Fulton Street, Elizabeth enjoys the momentary open space of Nostrand Avenue, feels the wind of the tenements blow against her face and her depression wafts away: she feels released, fulfilled, although there will certainly be some pain in her thighs for the next day or so, part of the price of effort. She has good thighs, good breasts, a striking if somewhat affected face — she knows all of this because she has been told so by clients and dates many times — but she knows what they can never tell her: that her best feature is her compassion and she wears it like armor through all the streets of Bedford-Stuyvesant, listening with amusement to some of the remarks which she hears drifting toward her from men muttering in storefronts, peddlers working under huge umbrellas near the bus stops. *Hey baby*, they are saying out of their ignorance and desire, *do you want to fuck? Dios, would I like to fuck that* and so on and so forth; so highly limited and they will never understand her compassion. From compassion she could reach out to them, from compassion she could gather them, even the ugliest to her and say, "If only fucking could solve your problems; if only I could fuck you right here and now to prove to you that the basic structure of your life is untenable and this cheap lust of yours merely an excuse against coming to grips with any of it," but she cannot; she knows that she cannot do this because she must save what she has for her caseload and so she only passes all of them down two blocks of Nostrand Avenue, a chastened, quiet smile on her face, a swing to her hips, a faint buoyancy to her behind which, she knows, must desperately inflame the poor things but there is nothing that she can do about it ... and in daylight, carrying her fieldbook, rape is impossible.

She waits for the bus and goes back to the welfare center. She is due for two more statutory visits these days and a pending application from an old Chinese woman … but they will have to wait. She has nothing more to give; she no less than anyone is entitled to respite. Back to the welfare center she will go and there perform paperwork, the least diverting but most necessary part of her job.

III

At the center, in mid-afternoon, her supervisor, James Oved, tries once again to put the make on her. Elizabeth has no interest in the man or in anyone at the center; her sexual energies, such as they are, are totally dedicated to her caseload … but Oved will have none of this. He has gotten into his mind the perverse idea that Elizabeth will not date him because he is a Negro and short of giving him facts, documentation, background on the many Negro clients she has laid (and she is too sensible to divulge any of this to anyone) she must put up with his advances and insults in the interests of her higher mission. She is still only a provisional worker; she will not have her full civil service status for another three months at which time she will apply to transfer to another case unit. For the moment, however, she must listen to Oved, accept what he has to say, come to terms with her own subtle revulsion which is not easy. "Listen here," Oved says in a high whine, motioning her over to his desk at three-thirty, pointing to the Morales case record which she has put through his incoming box along with a small grant for school clothing, "you can't do this kind of thing. It's not time for school clothing until September; this is months too early. And besides that, I already checked through this son of a bitch's case record. They had two hundred dollars for clothing last November; they're way above my level of approval."

"I'm sorry," Elizabeth says, putting her hands flatly, palms down on Oved's desk and trying to look away from him, down the vast, smoky surfaces of the loft over which, even at this late hour, several dozen people are scuttling from file drawers to doors or back again, "the needs are really evident — "

"What needs?" Oved says. "Now this man won't work. He simply won't work at all; he's been claiming a heart condition for fifteen years and the doctors can find nothing wrong with him, nothing *is* wrong with him except that he's a bum but he's got a nice, sweet new lady caseworker and he's going to take you through the mill. Now listen — "

"I don't think you understand, Mr. Oved," Elizabeth says quietly. "Mr. Morales is severely decompensated. He has no self-esteem whatsoever;

his asking for clothing is merely his way of asking for love. If we can *show* him — "

"Don't talk to me about love," Mr. Oved says. "I make one hundred and thirty dollars gross a week, take home about half of that and no one loves me." His face seems to slant, his eyes dilate. "Least of all you," he says. "Could I take you out to dinner tonight?"

"I'm busy."

"That's what I mean. You're always busy. How about tomorrow night?"

"I'm sorry, Mr. Oved," Elizabeth says, "I'm going steady with someone. And besides that, I would never go out with anyone in the office; I've told you that. I don't think it's fair; too many problems come into a relationship."

"I know about your relationship," Oved says sullenly. His face seems to inflate, his black cheeks glow, of a sudden he looks three or four shades darker, reminding Elizabeth of the intensity which Martin Luther King seemed to possess when he was speaking on television, "reason you won't go out with me is that you're one prejudiced chick. Afraid to lay it on the line and tell me the truth. Well, I don't care; I'm going to supervise you and make an investigator out of you no matter what tricks you pull."

"I'm not prejudiced. Mr. Oved, it isn't that at all," Elizabeth says. They have been this way before but there seems no end to the man's insistences. "You have no right to even *say* that. When the NAACP lunch was here two months ago I was on the serving line for two *hours* and besides that — " She stops, in some confusion. Despite her resolve, Elizabeth had been about to tell her supervisor that not three days ago she had copulated violently with William Buckingham III, the 18-year-old and home relief receiving son of Mille Perkins, a lifelong recipient of Aid to Dependent Children. "Oh God," Willie Buckingham III had said to her during and after intercourse, "we gone through hundreds of social workers but never one like you lady," and it had been good, she had been able to bring the young man to resolve to continue toward his high school diploma so that he would be able to socialize with people like Elizabeth. But she cannot tell this to James Oved; he is of a different circumstance altogether and in addition to reporting her instantly to his Case Supervisor for dismissal charges, he would somehow manage to take her action with Willie Buckingham personally, a slur on Oved's own sexuality. So she shakes her head, mumbles, says nothing at all and lets Oved continue.

"I don't care," he is saying, "don't care what kind of bullshit this Morales cat has been giving you, bullshit not being a very nice word but then I only went to a Southern Baptist college, I don't care what you say about his self-esteem. We are not social workers here. We are *investigators*. Our job is to protect the City of New York and taxpayer's funds and reduce the public assistance roles. Morales is a fraud. Three-quarters of your caseload are frauds. And besides that, you haven't made an entry on Morales' resource situation. This is the third time I've warned you that you have to update the folder every time and explain that you asked whether or not the client has found any new resources. You take this whole thing back, Miss Moore and you do it right and if you want to put through school clothing I want a complete memo for the case supervisor." He turns, looks heavily at the desk, rubs his hands over the frayed blotter. "The other stuff we'll just forget," he says. "I don't want to hear any more about that again."

"Yes," Elizabeth says, "yes," taking the huge Morales folder, spilling little halos and streamers of its contents behind her as she staggers back to her desk in the otherwise empty case unit, managing to keep tears from her eyes. It is so hard. It is so hard to be a social worker here and to try to do rehabilitative work. So hard to be able to take the job seriously. She wishes that she was with a good service agency like Catholic Charities or the Jewish Family Group where she could do serious counseling and devote herself wholly to her clients' needs but what can she do? … she has only a BA degree. Sitting at her desk, picking up pieces from the Morales folder, trying to put James Oved from her mind Elizabeth succumbs momentarily to the feeling that she would like to quit, put all of this behind her and give up the quest … but it is an old impulse, she discards it easily, she bites her lip and returns to work. Nothing was easy. Nothing was ever easy. Felipe Morales waits for her and behind him a thousand others and they need, need so greatly that if it were not for her, what would they do against all the Oveds?

IV

Elizabeth, alone, attends a college graduates & medical personnel mixer at the Hotel New Yorker. She feels that it is important to retain some connection to the social rituals of the outer society or so she has told herself but as she stands in a huge room, backed against a wall with a watered drink in her hand, watching the medical students & college graduates descend upon her like a group of slumlords … she realizes yet again that her dedication and interests must most truly lie in the area of social dislocation. "Come on up to my pad, you'll love it," a heavy, sweating medical student tells her, rubbing his palms together, "and anyway we're in a time of the complete destruction of the double standard, am I right? Am I right? am I right?" he says and puts his hands on her back. She feels their pressure like shells against her spine and tries to put down a flare of revulsion. "No," she says, "I'm just waiting to meet a girlfriend here, we have to go somewhere together," but that is no good for the medical student; he is insistent, he is desperate, his name, he says, is Harry and he is as much entitled to consideration as anyone in the room. Elizabeth considers all of this, then at some level gravely agrees: Harry too is one of the socially decompensated although at his socioeconomic level he could never admit this and she agrees to go to his pad. He takes her there on the IRT local, up to the 96th Street stop on the west side and by the time they have gotten there he has managed a hand on her thigh and a confession that he is not a medical student at all, not even a college graduate, but the committee at the door does not check credentials and anyway he is a creative writer which is more important. Elizabeth follows him out the subway doors, she follows him to his dismal one-room furnished apartment which reminds her of the Buckingham quarters in their dishevelment and high, hard smell, but it is not Willie Buckingham III who puts urgent hands on her in the dark and begs for intercourse.

"Please," Harry the creative writer says, "Please, I need you so much," and tries to part her dress. Willie Buckingham, even though just eighteen had worked her over with purpose and assurance; this one does not but the way to the door is too wearying and Elizabeth decides that she will let Harry have his way … she is more than passably attractive, she is the best girl he will ever have in his entire life, twenty years from now, lying in the dark, he may still be reconstructing her for masturbatory fantasies which would be (Elizabeth decides) a kind of immortality. He talks to her of his unpublished novels as he gets her clothes off, talks to her of his schemes and plans as he himself undresses, talks to her of his literary intentions as, stumbling through piles of books and clothing, they make their way to the studio couch. Moaning, he throws himself upon her and ejaculates immediately all over her thighs and waist, panting with disgust as he upends himself and Elizabeth decides, not for the first time, that she must save herself for her clients. Any other way is pointless. It is not as if even the men enjoyed it. At this socioeconomic level, sex must be the grubbiest and dirtiest relationship going on in all of New York City. "Let's get together again," Harry says as she puts on her clothes in silence, whisks her way out of the apartment and is gone.

V

Once, a long time ago, her father had taken her into synagogue for a service which had something to do with celebrating the Torah, the huge scrolls. Men of the congregation had carried these scrolls, unwieldy as blocks of wood, through the aisles of the temple and people had bent over to touch or at least gaze at them closely (Elizabeth had smelled talcum powder: something Hebraic and mysterious) but as religious experiences went (and for Elizabeth they did not go very far; she was not sure that in the post-technological culture ancient institutions could carry any weight at all) none of that had anything to match copulation with Rabbi Schnitzler.

Rabbi Schnitzler, his forelocks dancing across his damp forehead, his bearded face creased with a Talmudic concentration, approaches her hobbling, murmuring intricate orthodoxies in an undertone, his fine Chassidic hands already clasping as if in some apprehension of her breasts and even in this awkward position, collapsed on the orange couch with sheaves of hidden religious texts prickling her back, Elizabeth can feel a surge of reverence, call it *belief* if you will in those forces which move Schnitzler toward her.

She has never had a Rabbi, never conceived that she might be able to reach any of the *chassids* in this way but this merely will show you how you can never tell; how the primacy of certain forces may indeed be universal.

Despite the fact that he is a Rabbi, nothing in Schnitzler's background seems to have prepared him for what is happening now: either that or he is managing to dissemble in a way which would take him into unsuspected cunning. His face seems wiped clean of orthodoxy now, all traces of his heritage falling from him and in the dense light he looks literally Anglo-Saxon as he paces the room. "I don't believe it," Schnitzler is saying, "I don't believe it."

"Yes you do," Elizabeth says, lying back, opening her thighs, making herself inviting to him as she takes off the last piece of clothing, her shoes. "You can accept this gift. It's all right. All right." She wants his beard now against her breasts so that she can tell him in secrecy how deeply she accepts him.

"Incredible," Schnitzler says without an accent, "this is absolutely incredible but what is given, God knows, must be taken in that spirit, otherwise would be a sin." His eyes gleam. He begins, layer by layer, to divest himself of his rabbinical garb, flicking glances between Elizabeth and the closed door of the living room which he seems to fear might at any time fly open to disgorge his wife and thirteen children, all of them on their knees in some intricate prayer of release which they will then cry to him. The earlier Schnitzler assurance seems to have receded: maybe his wife and children are not, as he had insisted to Elizabeth, at the Synagogue consecration of the bath ceremonies after all.

"Ah," Schnitzler says, forgetting about the door as he grunts with the effort to enclose, "ah, you cannot imagine, you cannot, young lady, possibly imagine, but nevertheless I do not believe this," and now his robes are coming off, Elizabeth watches with fascination for she has never seen a *chassid* in less than full dress: first goes the outer coat, a long black construction with two prayerbooks dangling from a pocket, after that comes a belt which seems to hold religious implements and then the first robe which is of a pale blue shade with certain Hebraic characters stenciled on it. "Warm," Schnitzler says, running a hand across his forehead, "very warm all the time," as if explaining the benefits of his dress and then that robe falls to the floor.

Now there is a complicated arrangement of garments which Elizabeth decides, despite their greenish hue, are probably a suit, a suit for prayers and underneath that is a set of incontestably dirty but orthodox underwear which Schnitzler manages to take off easily. It is surprising how prosaic the elaborate chassidic costume is at the core but then what could she have expected? There are basics to the human pattern. Naked they are all the same: this is something she must teach them, that the devices, ornaments, prejudices and fears merely keep them apart. They are like everyone else. Schnitzler need have no feeling of dislocation.

"This is really strange," Schnitzler says, moving upon her then with an embarrassed chuckle, "really, really strange, are you sure that you want to do this, Miss Moore?"

"Yes. You know that."

"Because I wouldn't want to get into any trouble with the department or with you. I am a gentle man, I make no problems. We need the supplementary home relief because my small salary from the teaching is just not sufficient — "

"Yes," she says, motioning him to come against her, "yes, yes, I understand that, it's perfectly all right. I won't tell any one. I want you."

"I never thought that it would come to this," Schnitzler says musing, now poised before her, "to make an honest living in America in my own way, that was all I wanted. But in Williamsburg there are so many rabbis — "

"Please," Elizabeth says. She must break through his dissimulation, confront him with his own, aching lust. "No more of this — "

"Very well then," Schnitzler says with a strange, European air, a curious formality of expression. "If this is really what you wanted then all our instructions and teachings are that you cannot be denied. Is this not right?" His eyes become abstracted; perhaps he is thinking of his drab wife Rose Schnitzler, her grey complexion, her continuing state of pregnancy. "You are very attractive," Schnitzler says and then his mood changes, his expression becomes fierce, lust does indeed appear at the periphery of his eyeballs and he hurls himself upon her.

He is enormous, needful; it is all that she can do to take him in a single burst but Elizabeth wills herself to do so feeling his mouth on her breasts, his hands manipulating her pubis as if it were a portion of sacred texts. "God," Schnitzler says, going against her nipple, "oh my God," and she knows that she has won again; all Hebraic knowledge seems to be stripped from him, now he is moaning as Felipe Morales, Willie Buckingham, Jesse Culver, all of the others. At the root they are all the same. "Ah God," Schnitzler says, and righteously begins to fuck her.

It is strange: a strange and solemn experience this one. Of all those she has had she has never yet had a *chassid*, although her caseload is full of them. To now they have been grumbling and resistant, seemingly stupid — despite all of their children — about sex and all of her suggestions. But now at last she has one, the most procreative (imagine, thirteen children!) of them all ... and in addition she has never copulated in circumstances quite like this. They are in a huge living room which also serves as the Schnitzler dining room and library: the holy texts are scattered on the shelves and tables, a gigantic menorah, seemingly hoisted by invisible wire, dangling from a chandelier. At the far corner of the room, just within her line of sight, furthermore, is a small closed ark which can contain nothing other than the scrolls of Schnitzler's faith. In the presence of the ark he is fornicating: these orthodox have no sense of repression in the way that she has come to understand it.

Leaning back further on the couch, impacting her buttocks deep into the cushions, spreading her thighs even wider to receive the Schnitzler seed, Elizabeth thinks that she may hear a faint keening outside. It sounds like a police siren or the sound of children at play with weaponry until she remembers some fragment of her earlier interview with Schnitzler: this must be the sound of the afternoon services, the *Mincha*, coming from the Lubavitcher congregation down the street. Orthodox Jews pray three times a day: morning, afternoon and dusk and what is there to be said about Schnitzler who is missing one-third of his daily output of prayers to possess her? Maybe she will be able to convince him after all that his religion is an anachronism, that he must not hide his self-sufficiency and esteem behind it and can instead enter into the world. "Ah," Schnitzler says again, "God almighty," and she feels him come within her. Most of them she cannot feel but this one she definitely does: his orgasm is enormous, spilling and guttering into her and patiently she rides him out. She is anesthetized underneath which is too bad because in some intense way, with Schnitzler, she would like to come: a pity that she cannot.

He collapses across her, at length, groaning, burying his head into her neck, sniffing and snorting, his cheeks moving as if in laughter and then slowly, slowly moves upward from her, rises to his knees and looks around the room with a curiously abstracted expression. It is as if he is looking at everything for the first time. "Well," he says stupidly after a while, "I should be getting dressed."

"If you want to."

"So should you. They won't be at the baths all afternoon. Just to be safe."

"Whatever you say," she says. She flexes her arms, stretches, yawns in an affected way. "That was wonderful," she says, "it was really good."

"Well," Schnitzler says, making a tilting gesture with his hand, "well, you know how it is. Are you by any chance Jewish?"

"Does it matter?"

"Not really," Schnitzler says. "Not if you say so."

"Do you feel that it would be better for you if I were Jewish? Do you have any sense of guilt?"

"No," Schnitzler says, standing, groaning, looking for his clothing. "No, no guilt. I do not understand. I cannot talk so well in English. Do you perhaps speak Jewish?

"No."

"But you could be Jewish, is that what you say?"

"Look, Rabbi Schnitzler," Elizabeth says, at ease before him in her nudity. "Jewishness has nothing to do with it. You must stop this parochialism. You cannot live like that forever. There are larger meanings, possibilities — "

"Of course," Schnitzler says absently. "Of course, I understand that." His brow is creased, his face distracted, in no way does he seem to be the man with whom she has fornicated. Rather, with clumsy haste, he stumbles toward his clothing and begins to dress. "Many social workers we have had during our time in this country," he says. "Of course — "

"But you feel this is different."

"I feel you should get dressed."

"I will, Rabbi," Elizabeth says gently, realizing that Schnitzler for some reason is on the edge of panic. "I'll get dressed right away. I only thought we might talk for a moment."

"What is there to talk about?"

"Many things," she says, standing, looking for her clothes which as always do not seem to be in the spot she has left them. She must remember to make a more precise accounting of this; it would eliminate all kinds of awkwardness at the end of copulation. Elizabeth is willing to admit that things still are not working out quite the way they should; rather than being open and easy to counsel after fornication Schnitzler (like many of the others) seems to have gone away from her. "Why do you think that I had sex with you?"

"Sex?"

"Don't you know what that means? Why do you think that we made love together?"

"Oh," Schnitzler says, "sex. Made love. Now I understand. I do not speak English too well; I have many troubles with the language although I try. I do not know why you had sex with me, Miss Moore."

"Don't you? Are you sure you don't?"

"Miss Moore," Schnitzler says, reaching for his phylacteries and adjusting them around his belt, "believe me, I would like to tell you these many things but I cannot. I am not even sure that we should have done this. It may have been a grievous sin. There is an accounting — "

"You must stop," Elizabeth says, putting on her panties, reaching for a sweater, "with this incessant sense of guilt. Guilt follows you wherever you go; you will not permit yourself to function. Your whole religion is based on guilt."

"Are you an anti-Semite?"

"No," she says with exasperation, "I am *not* an anti-Semite; I'm only trying to help you." It is impossible, quite impossible. In a way she is sorry that she has gone to the couch with Schnitzler but then the only way, often, to deduce certain cases is to take chances with them. This will, probably, turn out to have been another one of her mistakes, yet she had to take the chance. She adjusts her skirt around her, suddenly anxious to be covered, anxious to end this. His shame and guilt have infected her; she is on the verge of losing her professional detachment. "Sometimes it's important to talk about the things that are bothering you," she says, "talking is very important, expressing your feeling, coming to grips with yourself. Don't you understand that?" but it is hopelessness which envelops her like a shroud, not her clothing as she stands, dressed, before him. "You can't go on this way," she says, "don't you realize that? You've got to take a stand, make a stand, cease this awful dependency. You must accept the fact of your own desires and act upon them without ambivalence; otherwise you'll be on public assistance for the rest of your life."

"I am sorry," Schnitzler says, "truly sorry, Miss Moore; I do not know what you are saying. I feel now that I must atone for a terrible sin. What I did I thought was right but now I see it was wrong. Forgiveness is what I need," he says and goes to a shelf at the corner, seizes a prayer shawl and with hurried gestures covers himself. "I must go to the temple."

"Oh forget that nonsense," she says, aware that she is losing her control and not even sure why this is the case but she is out of patience, thoroughly out of patience at the moment with the Schnitzlers and all they represent. "You just use that jargon to seal yourself off from reality, that's the whole point of this. And it's time for you to think of birth control. You must begin acting as a responsible adult; this breeding, this inconsiderate immature bearing of children into the world which you can neither support nor understand — "

"Sorry," Schnitzler says, "I am truly sorry. You do not understand. I do not understand. Forgive me, Miss Moore, I will have to leave. You believe? Good." He goes to the door, pulls it open abruptly and leaving Elizabeth to the emptiness of his apartment, stumbles into the street. Looking up through the cellar-level window she can see him scuttling on the sidewalk for a few paces, then he passes from view and is gone.

Elizabeth shakes her head, picks up her fieldbook, takes a look around the apartment. For the first time she feels some regret: regret not for her behavior-pattern (for, confronted by all this need and longing how could she have done otherwise?) but for cajoling Schnitzler into an act which obviously he cannot rationalize. He would need heavy support-therapy to accept the lustful side of his own nature; she does not have the time or experience for this kind of counseling. Then too, there are intricacies to the chassidic subculture which, somewhere along the line, must have evaded her: she did not think that Schnitzler was capable of moral complexities. Tired: she feels tired, that is the basic thing. She has been trying too much. She has been pushing too hard. Overwhelmed by her inadequacy and the needs which it must, almost by itself, satisfy she has failed to take herself into consideration and this has been the prime failing.

She puts her fieldbook under her arm, adjusts her pocketbook over her shoulder with the other hand. Tonight she will allow herself to rest. She will for the moment forget her burdens and put the job behind her. Oved himself had told her when she began in the case-unit, only two weeks at the training institute behind her, "You can't take this thing home with you. You have to leave it here and forget it. Otherwise it will tear you to pieces. Look at me: I haven't missed a night's sleep in five years because I learned. But a young girl like you, right out of college, sometimes has to learn the hard way. Don't learn the hard way. How would you like to go out for dinner tonight?" and so on, some of it good, some of it bad, but all of it to be considered.

The Oveds have their purposes too, their reasons, their motives. Because he is her supervisor and she does not like him is no reason to totally disregard everything he is saying. "Yes," Elizabeth mutters, adjusting a shelf of prayer books which, seemingly responsively, fall luminously over one another, sifting aisles of dust into the room, "yes, I will rest. I will relax, I will put all of this away from me," and slightly comforted walks out of the apartment, leaving the door open behind her, into the midday streets of Williamsburgh and this one time home … on voluntary sick-leave.

VI

In the early evening Oved calls her to check on her condition and she says she is fine, fine, feeling much better and he says that he is glad to hear this because she sounded a little upset, calling in from the field. The point is that if she feels better perhaps she would go out to dinner with him or at least he could come over to her apartment with some food and keep her company. When she says no, this is impossible; she has already told him what their situation must be and in any case she needs rest, Oved's tone again changes and his conversation becomes slightly incoherent.

"You just think I'm some kind of a fool, Miss Moore," he says, "always coming in and barking around and getting turned off by you and coming in again. Well, maybe I have my reasons. Maybe you ought to have more respect for James Oved than you do, maybe you ought to take me a little more seriously."

"I don't want to hurt you," she says, "I just think that we should — "

"Maybe you don't want to hurt me but you are hurting yourself, Miss Moore. Now, as long as I'm your supervisor and whatever you make of James Oved, you are going to do a job. You are going to meet the policies and procedures of this department and you are going to show some self-discipline. Now, you coming up for permanent status, Miss Moore, soon. I check over my workers' records because that's my responsibility. When you come up for certification you going to need your supervisor's approval, are you aware of that?"

"Well, yes — "

"And you aren't going to *get* my approval if you don't show a more professional attitude. Now this has nothing to do with your not going out with me; far as James Oved is concerned you can drop dead if that's the way it has to be, on the social level. But on the business level you will remain one of my workers and will be handled in a professional way and I am not pleased with your performance."

"All right," Elizabeth says, switching sides on the bed, trying to push the phone away from her although this is immature thinking. Trying to relax alone at home might have been the wrong idea, "I'm trying to do a job. I take my work very seriously."

"You may take it seriously," Oved says in a high bleat, "but that seriousness don't manifest itself in your case records and your performance. Your dictation is very weak, very skimpy and you letting those cats take you over the coals with a lot of lies and old bullshit. You be in the office tomorrow? I hope you be in the office tomorrow and we take a fresh start, look at this thing all over again. I am not happy, Miss Moore. This has nothing to do with sex. I am just not happy," Oved says and before she can say anything, point out, perhaps, that he is projecting his own frustration upon her in an unwarranted way, Oved hangs up with a clash which sends small reverberations through her head, momentarily making her dizzy. It is not fair. It is not fair that she should have a supervisor like this. Most of the supervisors at the welfare center are women in their fifties who are overweight and need heavy glasses to read the case records but it would be her luck — and with all the responsibilities she has — that she would come up with an Oved. Still, there is nothing to be done. It is part of the burden of the job; she knew, at the beginning, that nothing would be easy.

She replaces the phone, falls back on the bed and begins absently to read the *Saturday Review of Literature* again but it is difficult, with all the tragedy she has seen, to take any of its empty liberalism seriously and so after a time she drops it across her lap, looks up at the ceiling, begins idly to inspect her apartment. It is not a very nice apartment, only a studio on a bad block off Atlantic Avenue, but then she arrived in Brooklyn to take the job at the department with very little money and highly disorganized and possibly this is the best she could have gotten; she has no fair complaint. The rent is only eighty-three dollars including the utilities which means that she has sixty-two dollars of her weekly salary to carry herself on and even with the twenty a week which she is sending back to her parents in Chicago (her father has quit his job as a bookbinder to look for a "more meaningful set of opportunities in the interpersonal structure" and in the meantime has run out his unemployment benefits) she has enough to live adequately, certainly far more than she would have if she were paying some of the rents she hears about. Even the welfare clients, most of them, are paying more than eighty-three dollars a month and that for living in dreadful, rotting tenements in the heart of the subculture; she should be grateful. She should, in fact, be grateful for everything: she has enough money, she has her health and she has a job through which she can make her life meaningful. How many others have that at twenty-three? Sometimes she thinks of some of the girls with whom she went to Beloit University and shudders for their deprivation, their ignorance, their lost possibilities, trapped into pointless marriages and irrelevant pregnancies ... while she, Elizabeth Moore, is in the center of the urban dilemma, free to deal, if she will, with the world.

"I'm grateful," Elizabeth says quietly, as she has often said before; the habit of talking to oneself is a harmless piece of projection which she knows in her own case to be not at all schizoid, "I'm fortunate. I have a chance. I can *do* something," although what she has to do seems, as always, a little beyond her. Nevertheless, she succumbs to a moment of euphoria: things are not all that bad and if nothing else she has shown Schnitzler that ritual in itself is not the sufficient compensation for guilt. The phone rings. She knows it is Oved again. She will be firm and reasonable, quiet and contained. Above all, she will deal with him.

"Hello?" she says and then decides to be professional. "This is Elizabeth Moore."

"Hello there, Miss Moore," a voice drawls, "I did get your number you see? How you doing?"

"I don't know," she says. "Who is this?" although she knows already; it must be one of her clients. Sooner or later they would break through the cycle of resistance, attempt to call her at home. She is establishing a relationship. "Who did you say this was?" she continues when there is momentarily no answer.

"Well I thought you would knew. Would know, I mean. This is Willie Wallace Buckingham."

"Oh," she says, "Willie. How are you?"

"Well, I'm pretty fine, Miss Moore. I am pretty good, all things considered. I was just sitting in this old telephone booth down the corner because relief families you know ain't permitted no phones and we certainly do not *have* a phone, and I was thinking about you and I decided, I was going to call Miss Moore at home and find out how she was. And I called information and they gave me the number just like that and it was you. How are you, Miss Moore? You still ain't told me."

"I'm fine, Willie," Elizabeth says. She finds that she has drawn the sheet up above her waist, is clutching at her pubis: symbolic referent indeed! "What can I do for you?"

"Well," Willie says after a pause, "the thing is this and I don't quite know how to put it. You know, I been having a lot of trouble at the school. You know?"

"I know that. But I thought that we were helping you make an adjustment."

"Well, I'm making a fine adjustment but I'm still having trouble. Like they call me a truant and things like that just for missing a roll check. And I want to tell you, it's been making me very depressing Miss Moore. Because school is mighty important to me; I want to be a physician as you know and finish up my studies. I take that stuff seriously. Otherwise I would surely quit now at eighteen and get a job and help get my family off relief because I am *ashamed* that they are on relief but then so is everybody in the neighborhood. What can you do? Anyway, I've been sitting in this phone booth in this grocery store very depressing and I said to myself, maybe I'll call up Miss Moore. She cares about me; she knows what my problems are and how to fix them. I was thinking," Willie says in a different tone, his voice dropping an octave and assuming sudden alertness, "I was thinking that I could drop over to your place tonight. To talk to you a bit."

"I'm not feeling very well, Willie," Elizabeth says and realizes that this is the wrong tack; a social worker can never show personal weakness nor allow her own personality to extrude in a client relationship, "well, I'm feeling fine, but that's not it. I just don't know if you should come over. It would be better if we kept our relationship — "

"Now our relationship," the voice says, "our relationship Miss Moore is already a *very close one*, you know? You very important to me and I'd feel terrible, just terrible, if Miss Moore didn't want to see me. Because, you know, it would be like the whole world, the only person I could trust, turned away from me and what would happen then?

Anyway, I thought I could come over and talk over my troubles with you. Of course if you don't want that — "

It is not as if they have not established a relationship. Three times already she has had intercourse with Willie Buckingham III, breaking through various levels of resistance, sullenness, hostility and fear and in a way the fact that he has reached out to call her at home is one of the most moving things which has yet happened to her; it proves that she is coming through. And she cannot pretend that she doesn't feel well because the fact is that ever since she left Schnitzler she has been feeling better and better; it was only the momentary upheaval, looking at the scrolls, which must have unsettled her. "All right, Willie," she says, "if you want to come over."

"I don't know your address, Miss Moore. They gave me the number at information but they don't give no addresses."

"I'm on Henry Street," Elizabeth says. "Can you remember that? 270 Henry Street, on the third floor. It's a walkup and you'll have to ring but the bell is broken so the best thing to do is just to wait around until someone comes in with a key and just follow them. There's a lot of traffic in the building so you shouldn't have any trouble."

"Well, fine," Willie says. "That's just fine. You don't worry about me getting in; I get in and out at various places. I be along there in about forty minutes, I don't think you're too far at all. I'm going to bring a friend."

"What?"

"A friend of mine, my best friend; he standing right outside this booth right this minute looking at me except that it's soundproof in here and George can't read no lips. George Jones, he is my oldest and closest friend. We go to the high school together even though he live four blocks away. We take all the same classes. I been telling him about you, what a wonderful person you are and he very anxious to meet you. He being depressed too about a lot of things."

"Now I don't know," Elizabeth says, distracted, "I just don't know about that. He's not on my caseload — "

"That relief talk. I know exactly what you saying, Miss Moore; you saying that you ain't his social worker so you don't know if you should see him. But you're *my* social worker and he's my friend so it's like the same thing, right? By treating him, you treating me. Anyway, this cat and I run together and anything you say to him goes right to me and vice versa. We see you in about forty minutes, Miss Moore. I looking forward," Willie Buckingham says and puts down the phone so abruptly that Elizabeth leaps in the bed, tilts the *Saturday Review* and knocks it with a rasp to the floor.

For an instant, then (and it is only an instant but subjectively, like all stress reactions, it seems to go on for a very long time) Elizabeth has an impulse: the impulse is to phone information for the number of a James Oved and call him, "Listen, Mr. Oved," she will say, "maybe what you are saying was right; maybe I am not being professional, maybe I am getting too involved with the clients but it's all getting a little out of hand now. What should I do? What could I have done? I know that I'm right in the way I wanted to do this job but I seem to be having a little trouble now and you'll have to get me out of it," and go on to tell him what has been happening … but it is an impulse, that is all it is, a panicky reaction, conversion-hysteria probably and she puts it out of her mind. What would Oved do? Aside from bringing her up on charges — for she knows that no socialization is permitted with clients after working hours, much less at the investigator's own home — he would only become embittered because Willie Buckingham and not he was the recipient of her personal life.

No, it would not work. She is deeply in this; her course has been engaged, there is no alternative. Slowly, determinedly, Elizabeth pulls herself from her bed and prepares to dress, to order the apartment for the imminent arrival of her client, Willie Buckingham III and his good friend, George Jones.

VII

The closest she had ever come to being involved with someone, well, maybe it wasn't being involved at all, it was only that she talked to this one more than the others, was with Calvin Hunter, a Dartmouth graduate who had worked briefly in Unit T at the welfare center before quitting two months ago and going to California where, he said, he would pick oranges if necessary and go on relief himself rather than stay as a social investigator in New York. "Let me tell you," he said to her during one of the four or five intense dates they had before he phoned in his resignation one Monday morning and said he would never come in again, "let me tell you, there is a time limit to this job. With some people it is a month, with others it is three or four but with no person is it really more than a year and if you don't get out of here in a year you'll never be the same person again. You see, in order to survive, you've got to seal off all your feeling. You've got to convince yourself that all the clients are cheats and frauds and don't need the money anyway because if you don't you'll go crazy trying to get clothing grants through or worrying about Mrs. Rodriguez getting evicted. Now the fact is that most of them *are* cheats and frauds because that's the way the system works and ninety-five percent of them have some kind of income which they aren't declaring but that isn't the point. The point is that you've got to convince yourself that all of these people are down-and-out bastards and loathsome sons of bitches or you won't be able to function at all. But if you convince yourself of that — and if you stay for more than a year you believe it deep down — you'll never be a compassionate human being again, toward anyone. You'll lose something of yourself which may be useless but is kind of nice to have, at least until it's gone. So that's why I'm getting out. Why don't you come with me, Elizabeth? You aren't like most of the girls here; you really care about this job and it's going to wreck you. Come out to the coast with me. We don't have to get married or even shack up together; just travel out together and go our own ways. It will be better. Believe me it will be better."

"No," she said, turning in the bed to run her breasts over his stomach, gently touching his genitals (most of their conversations were in bed, it turned out, and anyway she had to admit it, she was genuinely attracted to him, she liked to fuck him; if she could put her Mission out of her mind there was a very serious possibility that she might have taken him up on the offer), "I don't believe that. I believe that you can be sensitive and compassionate and caring all the time and that you can make some kind of a difference as well. I *care* about these people and it isn't hurting me at all. And I'll keep on caring."

"No," Calvin said, small groans interrupting his conversation as he responded to the pressure of her fingers, slid around so that he could bite her shoulder as he murmured the rest of this directly into her ear, "no, that isn't so, Elizabeth. You don't care about these people at all; you just care about something in yourself which finds it attractive to get involved but that won't last forever and anyway it's hopeless. Really hopeless. I came here because I needed to raise a few dollars between graduation and getting to the coast but I'd rather die than say I'd be here a year from now and that's because I care. Oh do that, do that," he said, abandoning all conversation whatsoever as she opened against him, slid her breasts into his mouth, enveloped him with her hands to drag him down and in a long, nerveless moment he entered her, moving more quickly until all thoughts of public assistance were blasted from her mind (and probably his as well) and when he fell away from her, gasping, he said nothing for a long time, while he played in the surfaces of her vagina and then delicately wiped his hand dry on her hip.

"Okay," he said, "okay, have it your way, but you'll find out what it gets you," and she had cared for him so much at that moment that she almost wanted to tell him the truth of what was going on, the mechanics of her insight: but Calvin would have been shocked. He would not have believed that she was actually laying the male clients and if he did he would have been appalled, might have been righteous enough to report her for what he would feel to be her "own good" and in the interests of binding her into a relationship. She couldn't have that. There was no way, with his middle-class background and talk of compassion, that he could even understand.

So she let it go, let the moment pass, and eventually Calvin Hunter went out of her bed and out of her life. It has been two months now since he has gone; occasionally she thinks of him, wandering the coastal spaces of California, moving through orange groves or used car lots, doing odd jobs with which he would pass through his life until he "found out what I want to do because frantically I don't have any idea and don't even feel guilty about it. I went through eight years of public school and four years of high school and four years of the best men's college in the country, most of them with straight A's and wonderful reports until it occurred to me last March that I had absolutely no idea what I wanted to *do* with all this crap and I had walked through sixteen years doing well mostly because I didn't want anybody to bother me and I didn't want to make any waves. That's going to stop right now; I don't know if I'll know what I want to do for years but I can tell you one thing," he had said, poising again, quite ready to enter her as he almost always was, "I don't want to investigate cases for the New York Department of Welfare and I don't think I ever want to see New York City again because at the rate things are going, in fifteen years everybody in here is either going to be on relief or working for the department, so the hell with that." She thinks of him; it would be interesting to know what he is doing, it would be even more interesting in a way to tell him what *she* has been doing but it is just an opportunity which will have to be considered lost. She was then, is now, dedicated to her purpose and there is no way that she could work Calvin Hunter into her fabric.

Nevertheless he had told her, "as far as I can see, that supervisor of yours isn't crazy. You'll miss a lot of bets if you think of him as being out of his mind; as near as I can judge he is a fairly typical long-term employee of the Department of Welfare and unless you want to wind up that way, dear Elizabeth, you had better be making some plans now, whether or not they have anything to do with me."

He had not understood that whatever happened to her, she would never be a James Oved. She *cared*. Calvin had qualities but no perception. If he *had* been told, in a bad moment, what she was doing, he would have called *her* crazy, and their relationship, so delicate and fine in its unfinished way, would have collapsed without dignity.

"You'd better see a psychiatrist, Elizabeth," he surely would have said, "before you get yourself into some real trouble," and there is no way, no way whatsoever, that she would have been able to leave work on Boerum Street and go to California with someone who would say *that*.

VIII

George Jones turns out to be even more decompensated than Willie Buckingham III; he is a thin, intense youth perhaps three or four years older (she is sure that Willie lied about their going to the same high school) with nervous tics and a fractured self-image and sexually he is barely able to function in a credible way. With Willie watching intently from her bed as she lies back on the blanket on the floor which George had insisted upon ("can't do no fucking in a bed," George had said, "bed gives me all kinds of bad vibrations") the boy moves above her, enters at once and instantly comes, a deflating groan pouring out of him as he realizes his failure and furiously twists her breasts. Elizabeth lies passive-submissive above him, allowing him to act out his fantasies, a flush of humiliation — and she will accept this; she is willing to come to grips with her own dysfunctional emotions — overtaking her.

"Get off her, George," Willie says, slapping the bed. "You are done, man. You just playing around now."

"I'm not finished," George says, continuing to work on her breasts. "Not until I say I am. She is really built, you were right. She is some built chick."

"You can talk to me, George," Elizabeth says, trying not to wince at a flare of pain from her right nipple. "You can have a relationship with me. Your friend has nothing to do with what happens between us."

"Sure I do," Willie says. "I introduced the two of you and I set you up and I was watching and I am your client, Miss Moore. What you do, you do for me." He winks, slaps the bed again. She must admit that he is a rather repulsive youth; it is difficult for her to love Willie Buckingham and yet of all her caseload with whom she has fornicated he is the one with whom she has come closest to a breakthrough. The time before last he had said, without irony, that he loved her and only wanted to please her and from then they had moved into an interesting motivational discussion during which he had definitely promised to stay with school and make good so that he could be worthy someday of a woman like her. But now his mood has changed; he has become arrogant and insulting. She has counseled herself time and again to expect setbacks, revisions in their functioning, sudden deadspots when all will have seemed futile — generations of decompensation, after all, are not to be solved in an afternoon by Elizabeth Moore — but it is painful to see how he is posturing now in an attempt to build up his ego as well as enact a subconscious homosexual attachment to his friend. "Off, Jones," Willie says, "I want her now."

"I don't care about you, Willie. You take your piece and shove off."

"I'll take my piece," Willie says. He has undressed and now settles himself between Elizabeth's thighs. "I don't need none of your jive to help me take that nor none of your looks either. Go into the other room."

"*Ain't* no other room," George says, settling on the bed. "Got to stay here. Come on, Willie; time's a-wasting; we got people to see."

"All right," Willie says. He leans close to Elizabeth, puts his cheek against hers. "You don't mind George watching us, do you?"

"No," she says, biting her lip, closing her eyes. "If it's something you really want, your friend — "

"Because I can chase him if you want but he feel better if he see there ain't nothing to it."

"I don't mind," she says. Willie will have to work out his repressed homosexuality, his unconscious need to enter his friend and this is as credible a way as any, she supposes. Nevertheless, she finds it difficult to maintain her professional detachment and Willie must see this in her face.

"What's wrong?" he says, in mid-thrust, taking his hand off her breast for a moment, "I hurt you?"

"Not you. No, you didn't hurt me. I'm still a little sore down there," she says motioning, "from something before." She considers mentioning Schnitzler to him and then realizes that this would be madness. "It's nothing really."

"Old George hurt you?"

"Not George."

"I didn't hurt her," Jones says. "I wasn't in long enough to hurt her. Don't make trouble for me now, man. I got enough as it is."

"He didn't," Elizabeth whispers, "he really didn't," and Willie relaxes. Even in these circumstances she can see the old easeful peace of fornication descend around him: fucking literally takes him out of his world and this she can understand and appreciate. She wills George Jones out of her mind, wills herself to an intense one-to-one relationship with Willie Buckingham who is, after all, her client and her concern and as she puts her arms around him she feels him relax, begin to whine with pleasure. "Ah," Willie says, "ah, this is wonderful," and bends her toward him so that he can suckle her breasts: remarkable how he has survived his socioeconomic strata to engage in buccal play. He works over her breasts singlemindedly and with passion; she feels him trembling with maternal yearning and she reciprocates this, feels some of it herself. Behind them she hears George Jones cackling, making obscene comments which she knows only come from his profound envy and she turns him off, throws him utterly out of her consciousness to immerse herself with Willie. She hopes that George will not suddenly join them on the floor. She has read about multiple intercourse, knows that it exists but she knows she cannot confront the issue at this time.

"Ah!" Willie says emphatically moving his head up from her breasts, "ah, ah!" and discharges; the third time today that a man has come into her and this, despite Schnitzler, is the most intense and copious of all. She almost feels a reciprocal wave of passion, almost yields herself to it before she reminds herself of her role and then she is cold, cold, as Willie finishes. He leaps off her quickly, shrugging, nodding, shaking his head, working his tongue over his lips.

"You see?" he says to George who has not moved from his position on the bed. "Did you see? Did I tell you true?"

"You told me true," George says. "You really did."

"Maybe now you keep your mouth shut when I tell you something and you believe."

"And maybe I open my mouth and you learn something," George says without anger. He sounds good-humored, so for that matter does Willie as he always is in the aftermath of intercourse and now, chuckling, they move toward their clothes and dress themselves quickly. Elizabeth lies back on the blanket, thinking of getting up but deciding that she will remain out of the situation in their own interest.

"We have to be going, Miss Moore," Willie says. "We have another appointment. We like to stay, we really do, but we got business downtown which can't wait."

"Important business," George says, adjusting his collar, finding the hideous hat in which he entered. "Very indispensable business."

"I hope it's nothing bad, Willie," Elizabeth says, sitting and reaching for a sheet to cover herself. Willie is her client; her concern is for him. "Nothing that you'd want to keep secret from me."

"Oh no," Willie says, his eyes dilating, "no such thing, Miss Moore. I ain't involved in nothing but the good things from now on."

"Because I'd be very disappointed," Elizabeth says, adjusting the sheet around her, trying to look as aseptic as possible so that she can augment the session with an insight, "after all we've done I'd be very hurt if — "

"No chance," George Jones says. He twirls his hat, walks to the door in an uneven, posturing stride. Possibly he has aphasia or then again it may be more ominous cerebral damage. "C'mon now, Willie, we got business to transact."

"Goodbye now, Miss Moore," Willie says and he follows George (who has, obviously, the basic power position of the relationship) and they go out the door, nodding at her, turn at the threshold to give identical waves and then, closing the door with a clatter they are gone. She thinks she may hear giggling on the steps but then again this could well be her imagination.

And in any event: if it is giggling, so what? If they compensate for an excess of feeling, a breakdown of the authoritarian structure through nervous laughter, what does she care? Their laughter only shows how deeply she has touched them; what dislocation she has accomplished in the otherwise unending cycle of greed and pain in their lives.

No, Elizabeth decides, standing wearily (there is so much to do, now; the apartment is in disarray) it does not matter what they think. What she accomplishes is important; this is the measure by which she will have to live. At the moment he came she had seen tenderness in Willie's eyes and this for the moment is enough: more may happen later and in any case she does not have to deal with the elusive and tormenting George … unless he or his family is transferred onto her caseload.

IX

Her caseload covers Boerum Street from Nostrand to Bedford Avenues; on these two avenues she handles two hotels as well, residence hotels filled with old men who must comprise, in their drunkenness and stupidity, almost half her caseload. At the very least she does not have to deal with them: the alcoholics and senile dementia cases are utterly beyond any of her efforts to deal with them and besides that (she is free to admit this) she finds the old men repulsive and frightening, is just as glad to know from her professional point of view that fornication would not help them at all, most of them long since having sunk into impotence, stagnation and regret. Some of the old men have tried to be friendly with her; a few have even attempted staggering, lecherous advances, but she has had no difficulty at all in repulsing them.

"I'm sorry, Mr. Stark," she has said to a particularly and peculiarly repellent old alcoholic, one whose case record indicated that he had been receiving public assistance since 1952 or the utter failure of his area of the garment business in Brooklyn, "but there's no way you can do that. If you keep on doing that," she had added, pulling his wizened, trembling hand from under her short skirt, depositing it firmly in his lap where, for all she cared, the disgusting old man could masturbate himself in front of her, "we'll have to close your case. You can't do that to a welfare investigator, I'm a representative of the city of New York."

"Of course," the old man had said helplessly, picking fibers from his pants, "of course, of course," and so much for Mr. Stark and the rest of them in the *Homeways Residence for Gentlemen:* despite all of her dedication Elizabeth had to draw the line someplace and it would have to be in cases like this. If it had somehow, by a disembodied agency or individual, been proven to her that fornicating with the old men in the greasy, fluorescent lobby (no one except residents was ever permitted in the rooms) would have helped them she would have had a dilemma to confront, a dilemma which (for all she knew) she might have resolved in favor of tentative advances and caresses (because she wanted to be thorough) but there was no way that Elizabeth was going to accept the fact that nothing she could do would aid these old men at all. They were utterly beyond redemption; working out their Old Age Assistance and Aid to the Disabled in the small and intoxicated expanse of the recreation room, lobby and their cells, they were beyond concern. Her services, her dedication would have to be reserved for the younger ones living, to some extent anyway, in the world: for Felipe Morales, Willie Buckingham, Rabbi Schnitzler she could go a long way but not for Mr. Stark in the *Homeway Residence.* Perhaps this was unfair but it was part of the generalized unfairness in the world which all of her clients would have to confront some day; better now than never and she could not do everything.

So much for the clients in the hotels but the management problem was a different question. She handled two hotels; the *Homeway Residence* and *Happy Hour Twilight Home* just three numbers up and across the street and there was no problem with the *Happy Hour* because the manager there was one of the alcoholics himself, a relief client in fact who worked behind the desk and collected the rents to mail on to a disembodied corporation which paid him seven dollars a week, deducted from his check. The *Homeway Residence*, however, was a different situation.

The manager of the *Homeway Residence* was a fat fortyish man named Mel who wore religious insignia underneath his sports shirts and the first time he had met Elizabeth he had been overcome by enthusiasm. "Listen," he had said, coming from behind the desk to squeeze her shoulders and knee her gently, affectionately in the thigh, "listen, I've watched investigators come and go for twenty-five years here and you are really something. You are really magnificent. You are the best. I think that you and I could really go somewhere together. In the meantime, would you take this?" he had said and pressed into her hand a five dollar bill.

Elizabeth, who had heard vaguely of departmental corruption but had seen no evidence of it until then on her own caseload wanted to know what Mel had in mind and Mel said nothing at all, absolutely nothing, this was just the routine gratuity which he gave every investigator every time they visited, "just so that we stay friends, to show my respect for you and your position." Since she was new, however, and this was her first visit to the Homeway, Mel felt that the least he could do was to give her a "little extra right here" he said and gave her a ten dollar bill with an air of curious intimacy, looking at her sideways then and murmuring that she was a lovely girl. "Listen," Mel said, "don't worry about a thing; the guy who had your caseload before you, Salant? was that the name? we worked together for six years here and we had a terrific relationship and I'm sure that I can do the same with you. What the hell," Mel said, "there doesn't have to be anything personal in this at all; just a way of showing my appreciation," and had then taken her by the elbow to lead her through the vast lobby of the Homeway, pointing out the various drunks seated in stuporous postures by palms and television sets, giving a little bit of the personal biography of each. According to Mel, all of them were homosexuals who had found themselves in such a condition because they were unable to have a normal relationship with a woman. "And you see?" Mel said, when he had escorted her back behind the desk and insisted that she sit on his high, awkward stool, looking out upon all of this, "there's nothing that you can do with a one of them. But they're all perfectly happy: we get along fine here, nine-tenths of this hotel is welfare and I'm always advancing them money. Everything goes right out for drink you understand except what I take right off the top for the rent and by the fourteenth and twenty-eighth of each month they're desperate. Starving. So I give them an advance right out of the petty cash box, at no interest at all and that keeps them all happy. You see? You see how happy they are here, how we get along?" He stood, waved in the general direction of two alcoholics swaddled together in a single chair, making drunken, groping gestures at the air. "How you doing, Tommy and Mart?" he asked, "how you doing?" The drunks said they were doing just fine, never felt better, as a matter of fact, and hoped he was the same. "This is your new investigator," Mel called, "her name is Elizabeth Moore."

"How are you? how are you?" the drunks muttered and settled back on the chairs again. Mel made a brisk gesture of dismissal and turned toward her, his eyes fixed, this time on her breasts. "So you see," he said, "it's really quite hopeless, but we manage to keep them happy and do the best we can. I hope you'll take the fifteen. And there'll be a little something else for you every time you visit. The only thing and I want to say this frankly is that I hope you don't turn out like Salant. Always asking for something, always needing a little extra. I think he was a horse player; he was always talking about making payments to the finance companies. Tell you the truth, I wasn't sorry to see him go even though I never thought we'd get a lovely young girl like you at Homeway. That's wonderful. How about it?" Mel said, putting his hands on her shoulders, "would you like to have a date?"

"No," Elizabeth said. She had been holding the fifteen dollars all during the lobby walk, now she crumpled the bills and put them back into Mel's hands, "no I don't want to go out on a date. No, I don't want your fifteen dollars. That's graft. That's absolutely unspeakable."

"You see," Mel said, casually, taking the money and putting it back in his pocket, addressing the ceiling as if it were an auditor, "that's the trouble with the department. The turnover. The turnover is terrible and everybody thinks they're going to save the world. Salant thought he could too at the beginning. Okay," Mel said, inclining his head back toward her, "if that's the way you feel about it fine. It doesn't make any difference at all to me what you do. The checks come in on the first and the sixteenth and we cash them and take the rent off the top. Still, would you like to go out with me?"

"No," Elizabeth said turning from him in some disgust, "I don't want to have a date."

"I'm an unmarried man," Mel said, hooking his thumbs into his belt, shoving his stomach subtly toward her. "This is perfectly legitimate. No graft. I find you very attractive. You look a little bit like Lauren Bacall."

"No," Elizabeth said, moving from the desk. "No and no again. I don't want to have anything to do with you at all," and had, in some confusion, opened her fieldbook, trying to locate the names of the cases she had come to visit. The alcoholics looked at her in vague interest for a moment, then subsided again into their coma. Elizabeth wondered exactly how far along in her work she would have to get in order to consider the *Homeway Residence* merely another stop in her afternoon's work.

"I could show you a good time," Mel said, coming from behind the desk and pursuing her. "You may not think I'm much to look at but this is a responsible job and I make a good salary. Also I'm a college graduate. Being an investigator isn't the greatest thing in the world you know; you could show a little manners."

"I won't," Elizabeth said, "I won't do anything for you; I don't want to deal with you," and her control had snapped, she had turned then and guessed that she had done some screaming at Mel (although this was hard to verify and her memory of that is gone) and he had retreated, apologetically, showing her his palms while the alcoholics twitched like fish in their chairs and looked at her with large, solemn eyes. Whatever went on in front of them seemed to make no impression at all. Elizabeth had found who she was looking for eventually and had taken the three of them off to a corner of the lobby for a confidential talk about their situation (respecting, as she must, the right of the recipient of public assistance to privacy and continued confidentiality about his condition) and as she looked at the three of them, Stark and two others seated like animals in a circus act, their dull, stupid beaten eyes radiating disinterest and fatigue she understood that there were limits to her dedication, she had found them right now and she was never, never going to be able to deal with the tenants of this hotel in the manner she wanted. It was the one small respite she had allowed herself, the one dead spot in her dedication but she felt that she was entitled to this. Later on, when she had found out that fully 50% of her cases by number were domiciled in those two hotels she had felt guilty about it — it was as if she had cut down her potential for achievement by exactly that much — but there was no way whatsoever in which she was going to be able to switch caseloads (no provisional worker could) and there was certainly no way in which she was going to be persuaded to fuck those disgusting old men so that was that.

Mel had pushed the issue of going out with her the next few times she had visited — and the nature of her statutory visits brought her in there twice a month — and then with disgust had dropped it. "The trouble with you," he said the very last time they talked when she had turned down a fifty dollar bill and an offer to go with him to a clubhouse box at Belmont racetrack the following weekend, "the trouble with you is that you're a cold bitch, that's your problem. You have no sense of life. You bitches come out of Vassar and put in your six months in the Department of Welfare and then go off to marry and have no idea ever of what kind of place this is, not that I want you to take my calling you a bitch personally," and then had abandoned her forever, only sitting at the desk to sullenly peep from newspapers at her subsequent visits.

Elizabeth had thought of laughing and telling Mel exactly how much of life she knew, how seriously she took her job … but she knew that this could only lead to complications and difficulties later on and so she had said nothing whatsoever.

X

She feels, the next day, that she should return to Felipe Morales and try to augment their new-found relationship as quickly as possible but she is unable to get there. Oved has her seated at his desk for an hour, going over entries in her case-records and proving that she has no idea of verification procedures, then there is a full staff meeting called in the welfare center and Elizabeth, surrounded by two middle-aged men in her case unit, finds herself seated on a row of chairs set up in the front where they are lectured by a Mr. Grey, dispatched from Central Office to fill them in on the latest policies and procedures.

"The latest policies and procedures are classically simple," Mr. Grey says in a high bleat, rubbing his hands together and running through some memoranda on the desk set up before the rows. He is an extraordinarily fat man in his fifties who Elizabeth envisions as a welfare case himself: Home Relief probably or maybe aid to the disabled for a psychological condition, but he is highly possessed of procedures and necessities and does not seem aware of his disastrous limitations. "Classically simple," Mr. Grey says, "we are going to come to grips with the root problem for the first time and eliminate the causes of the public assistance problem at the point of origin. You are all aware that the relief recipient is a sick person, socially unintegrated and in a state of psychic background: now we will resolve this. The procedures which you will be handed today will explicate the method of attack but briefly stated it is this: we have a three month program. Next month we will diagnose the condition of the various clients; you will go out into the field and interview all of your recipients and identify exactly those reasons and that psychological disability which put him on relief. This should be simple; the case records have ample background information. The month after that you shall initiate efforts at rehabilitation, drawing upon the diagnoses and working in conjunction with the Medical Social Worker who is standing by to assist you in these coordinated efforts. And the third month you shall totally rehabilitate the client and put him in contact with the social mores and imperatives of the larger culture. Is that clear?" Grey says and stands before them, still rubbing his hands, his eyes dazzled by the fluorescence, the sound of flush toilets working in the rear of the loft. "Are there any questions?"

"Lot of bullshit," Oved says, turning from the row ahead and muttering to his case unit and the two middle-aged men surrounding Elizabeth dig their elbows into her and yelp enthusiastically but when Oved turns back toward Grey his face must be quite bland once again for he does not move in his seat. "Are there *any* questions?" Grey asks but there seems to be no question whatsoever. Grey begins to look pained, struggles in his place. "This is a complicated procedure," he says desperately, "there have got to be some questions. Aren't there any professionally-oriented social work objectives in this room?"

"I have a question," Elizabeth says as those surrounding her look at her with hatred. Phones squall in the background; there is a murmur which can only be the clients in Intake below conferring among one another, preparing a murderous assault upstairs. "Assuming that we can effectuate rehabilitation and put them in contact with the mores of the outer culture, they're going to need a middle-class income to sustain that new compensation, aren't they? But most of them because of their psychic deficiencies, are capable only of finding lower-class employment and very few will be able to descend to the middle-class. I mean *ascend* to the middle-class of course. So renewed decompensation may begin as they find that their goals are irretrievably beyond their means. What would you suggest that we do then?" Elizabeth says, running a hand across her forehead, clearing the itch from her eyes. "This is something we must enter into at the point of rehabilitation," she adds.

"That's an interesting question," Grey says. He begins to rub his hands once more, his eyes dancing up and down the procedures. "That is a very interesting question. Would anybody have any answers?"

"My worker has been with us less than six months," Mr. Oved says, not standing. "She doesn't understand departmental procedures too well as of yet. She'll learn."

"Well," Grey says, "of course. Of course that's true, still our, uh, new workers often can give us a fresh insight into our problems. I'd say that the answer to those questions young lady will be found right in the procedures. Wouldn't you think so?"

"I don't know. I haven't read them."

"Well, then that's the answer. You'll find that the procedure contains a complete explanation of possible complications," Grey says happily and bounces away from the desk, merges into one of the doorways and nods to them from there. "I have to hit several other offices in Brooklyn," he says, "to go into this procedure with them as I have with you. I'd love to stay and discuss this further but we'll have to adjourn."

"Adjourn," the administrator, a stolid, heavy woman in a flowered dress says, standing from the front row and clapping her hands. "Meeting is adjourned. Clerks to the phones, please. Workers back to your case units. Intake, find out who's been waiting downstairs the longest and get those clients in touch with the case unit immediately." She moves away slowly, staggering back toward her office and Elizabeth, stretching, finds that the two middle-aged men — they are really quite indistinguishable, one might be fifty and the other forty, one might have a brown suit and the other a blue one but they have been in the case unit together for two months for reasons, they have said, of business failure — are nudging her and looking at her with triumphant grins. "That's putting it to them," one of them says, "that shows them."

"Shows them what?" Elizabeth says with some confusion.

"Shows them what fools they are, of course!" the other one says and nudges her harder, nothing sexual in the touch but it suddenly irritates her. "Rehabilitation! Diagnosis! This department is full of craziness. It's going to be this way until the day they die and they won't even admit to it. But you showed them."

"But I meant it," Elizabeth says, "it was a serious question. I think that diagnosis and rehabilitation is a very good idea, it's the only way to solve the problem of social decompensation; I'm just worried about the attendant problems as a rise in socioeconomic status is not accompanied by one in the lifestyle. That's what I wanted to ask," she says and swings ahead of them, trying to put them out of her mind, noting that they are looking at her strangely and beginning to mutter between themselves but she can barely be concerned with this, so much is she occupied with the news of the new procedure (which so well dovetails with her own recent thought and experience as to be astonishing; the department and she are really as one) and the events of the past couple of days.

Oved is already waiting for her at his desk; he has many things he wants to discuss he says "and diagnosis and rehabilitation are none of them; you put that bullshit out of your mind, Miss Moore, because as long as you and I are here it's going to be a matter of getting out a good W664 and W532, you listen to me, Miss Moore" but before he can get fully launched the unit clerk says that she has a call for her, her caseload number, *340P*, and Elizabeth, nodding in a conciliating way at Oved — he is a frustrated man, after all; she must have some tolerance for his projectivity — picks up the phone and finds Willie Buckingham on the other end.

"I got to see you," he says when she has identified herself, "no, don't tell me *no* Miss Moore, I got to see you, it's really important but I can't leave the house. Mama is downtown doing some shopping and I'm stuck here babysitting so you've got to come out here. You *have* to come out, Miss Moore," he says, "that is, if I mean anything to you at all," and there is nothing, in terms of the investment she has made in their relationship, to say in protest.

"All right, Willie," she says, "I'll be out." She hangs up the phone and turns to Oved. "I have to go to the field," she says.

"Field? On what?

"The Buckingham case."

"Buckingham? You leave that pack of phonies stew in their own juices. They been collecting relief three generations of them for twenty-five years; they can hold out a little longer this time. What did the old bitch want now?"

"It wasn't Sadie. It was the boy."

"Which boy? They got a lot of boys. They got eight dependent children in that house."

"It's none of the children. It's the home relief case. That Willie."

"Willie? Willie? That bastard? What does he want?"

"I don't know," Elizabeth says. "He said that something was wrong. I've got to go and see."

"You aren't going nowhere, Miss Moore," Oved says, laying a heavy, sexless hand on her shoulder. "You are staying in the office. Don't you remember that you're the emergency worker today?"

"I have to go," Elizabeth says. "He says that it's important."

"Who you listen to? You listen to some eighteen-year-old teenage pimp or you listen to your supervisor? Who you taking instructions from anyway?"

"I have to, Mr. Oved," Elizabeth says. She adjusts her handbag, looks toward her coat which is slung, ready for use at any time, across her chair. "It's my caseload and my case. He needs me and I'm going."

"You're the emergency worker!"

"I can't stay in the office all day and take phone calls when someone on my caseload needs me," Elizabeth says. She moves away from Oved, adjusting her glasses, reaching for her coat, balancing her fieldbook. "I'll be back in just a couple of hours."

"You are pushing me. You are pushing me very far, Miss Moore."

"I'm sorry."

"You are pushing me *very* far, Miss Moore. You are the emergency worker today. You have responsibility today. You are to stay in."

"No," Elizabeth says, "no." She is already in retreat. "I'll be back in a couple of hours," she says. "Even less than that. I have to go. I'm going."

"I'll be damned," she hears Oved say behind her as she moves past all of the desks in the loft, heading quickly toward the stairs, "I'll be damned; I bet she's fucking that coon," but what Oved says about her does not matter (or matters as little as anything else outside the center of her caseload). She moves down stairs, past Intake, through corridors, into the street and toward the Fulton Street bus imagining that she hears telephones still shrilling in the distance and she would not be surprised, in fact she is convinced that this must be the case, if all of the telephone calls were from Felipe Morales and all of them were for her. She has failed him. Their relationship has not even begun and yet she has failed him already. One in an endless succession of exploiters who have misused poor Felipe, brought him to feeling, and quit him but she vows that she will break the pattern: tomorrow she will have Willie settled down and will have somehow made her peace with Oved and will have read all of the new procedures and the very first thing she will do will be to call Felipe Morales herself, reach him through the candystore downstairs from his apartment and *mi señor* she shall say and *Felipo, Felipo* she shall say and *Felipo amor* until she has overwhelmed him with her need and then she shall head toward his apartment and see him. Just the two of them together, the wife and children displaced. She shall do that.

The trouble is that so many people need her.

XI

Her first sight of the five houses on Boerum Street which held all of her family units was shattering, almost too overwhelming for her to take: to this day she can only recall a dim impression of moldering filth, heat, noise, disintegration, the tenements seeming to engorge her as she walked in and to carry her up like bile from one level to the other, rats and children scurrying in the halls, piles of dog filth … but as bad as that had been, her encounter with the landlord, Mandleman, on that same day had been worse. Mandleman had come up beaming to the fifth floor apartment in which she was trying to interview Callie Simmons and four of her six dependent children and had taken her down. "I just wanted to welcome the new investigator," he had said as he led her, groping, lighting matches on the stairwells, laughing as the screams of the Simmons children floated down the well. "I thought on the first day — "

"Disgusting," she said when they finally got to the first floor and into the light; up until that point she had been wordless and appalled, shaking with the rage of it, "disgusting, how can you do this to people? Are these your buildings? Are you the landlord? How can people live this way? How can you do this to people?" and Mandleman had laughed, laughed and chuckled, held her elbow in a friendly way and escorted her to his office next door, a small real-estate and tax accounting office occupying a storefront and had sat her in a straight chair and brought her a drink of water. "Here," he said, giving it to her. "You're a lovely young girl, you're a new investigator. It's always a bit of a shock to come into these neighborhoods for the first time."

"Are these *your buildings?*" Elizabeth said, thrusting the water from her and trying to get back a sense of orientation. "You are the owner of these? You have people living — "

"I am the owner," Mandleman said and shrugged. Standing above her he looked wizened, kindly, small shards and puffs of grey hair streaming from an otherwise bald scalp, his large eyebrows also white to say nothing of the stubble on his plump cheeks. He put his hands informally in the pockets of his oversize suit and said, "I have a sense of compassion and therefore I own these buildings. Anyone else would have sold them or run away from them three years ago. But I care. And so I see do you."

"I'll report you," Elizabeth said. She had learned about building violations in the training institute. "You have insecure stairwells, filth in the halls, a fire hazard through the lobbies and stairways of all those buildings, cracks in the floor, signs of rodent infestation, complaints of no heat or hot water, torn linoleum — ”

"Ah Miss Moore," Mandleman said, still shrugging and going for a straight chair to bring over to sit beside her, "you see, I like to meet every new investigator in these buildings. That is how much I care. Not just to take, to take money from the department which is not enough even to cover my bills, but also having some kind of relationship. That is why I went upstairs to greet you. It's a bit of a shock — ”

"This is disgusting!"

"Salant was a good man," Mandleman said, shaking his head. "He was a little bit stupid, Mr. Salant, but essentially he was very sound. He had a good sense of situation and he was a realist. I was sorry to see him go but, of course, time moves on and nothing can remain forever. He became a parole officer, do you know that? That's a very good job."

"I don't care what he became," Elizabeth says. Surprisingly, she finds herself near crying. "Whatever he was doesn't interest me. I'm the investigator and it's my responsibility to help these people and I won't, I won't have my clients living in filth like this."

"You see, Miss Moore," Mandleman says, "let me, if I may, explain to you a few basic facts and so on and then your mind will be set at ease and there will be no difficulty. It is impossible to maintain these buildings properly. These people are pigs; the way they live is indescribable. They are not like you and me but are rather totally undisciplined and on a level of savagery. This is not a situation I caused but merely one which exists. I do not want it this way." With curious formality, Mandleman lit a cigarette and put the match neatly on the floor underneath his foot, pressed his foot against it a few times. "I would far rather it would be otherwise. But this is the situation. Now, who wants to house these people?"

"They deserve decent — ”

"They deserve everything, Miss Moore, like you and me and all people everywhere they deserve only the best but unfortunately we do not get in this world exactly what we deserve. I spent three years in a concentration camp of which I will not speak. No one cares for these people, Miss Moore. The Fifth Avenue management company does not care for them. The Mayor's office is not populated with people who would take them into their homes for bed and board. The liberal politicians are for relief only because giving them relief will keep them at a distance and keep the society from crumbling. I have thought of this often, I am a deep-thinking man. So it is left for people like Irving Mandleman to care for them. It is Irving Mandleman who gives them a place to live, who collects their rents from the Department of Welfare, who allows them to exist. Is this so reprehensible? Who else would want to look at them? No one in the entire city of New York except the welfare investigators and Mandleman ever have to deal with these people. Actually we are on the same side of the fence, Miss Moore. You and I are two of the last people left who will deal with them. So that is my explanation," Mandleman said, putting out the cigarette with a flourish and pulling the chair, groaning, back from the desk. "Sometimes it is good to have a talk with an investigator when he or she begins. It makes things much easier. And there are a few orthodox Jews in these tenements which, I agree, somewhat lifts the level of tenancy. So all in all things are not so bad, eh?"

"You've got to do something," Elizabeth said. "This can't be permitted to exist. You have violations — "

"Ah, Miss Moore," Mandleman said with a chuckle, "you are so industrious and so dedicated but the fact is that you are only reacting to your own disgust. You have no more feeling for these people than the office of the Mayor, believe me. They mean nothing to you and very soon, when you become less frightened and less tolerant of your sensitivity you will understand that too." He leaned toward her, suddenly a twenty-dollar bill appeared in his hands. He eased it toward her like a blessing. "Here," Mandleman said. "I give this to you as a gift, not a bribe, merely as a little gift of greeting because you are a very lovely young girl, a girl who reminds me in certain ways of my daughter. With it you can go to the hairdresser, perhaps buy something to wear or a little perfume. Consider it as a gift. Mandleman's gift, given freely and without strings. You will not be with this department long. Soon, perhaps even now, you will meet or are going with a fine young man and he will take you out of all of this and you will go to Queens Village or the Island and you will never see any of this again. In one year it will be unbelievable, in five years, you will not even remember it. You will live your life and enjoy it. Here. Take. It means nothing."

"I won't," Elizabeth said standing, bolting from the chair, backing into the wall clutching her fieldbook, "I won't take it. I won't take your bribe! That's graft. That's — "

"Ah Miss Moore — "

"I *do* care," she found herself saying rather hysterically. "I don't know what you are or how you feel but I know about myself. I care about these people and I won't let them live this way! I'll help them! I'll help them get out of this! If you don't put that money away I'll report you to the central office; they have a form to report bribe attempts, don't you know that?" she said and before Mandleman could say anything further or she could even get a look at his expression (she never wanted to see his face again) she had turned: now she was running, running from his office and up the four steps and onto Boerum Street; on Boerum Street people were sitting on the stoops drinking, throwing garbage against the walls, setting up card tables for a midday game and looking at her with strange, taunting looks but it did not matter, nothing that these people could say to her would matter because they were *hers*, unlike Mandleman they were already a part of her and she would, somehow, stand between his corruption and their own miserable lives to change the direction of their history.

"I *do* care," she said, grasping her fieldbook, "I do, I *do*," and as Mandleman came up the stairs to look at her, she turned from him and went quickly down the street but she could not get out of her mind the feeling (and she still has it to this moment) that Mandleman was not looking at her with sadness or remonstrance, Mandleman was not trying, somehow, to reason her back to him: no, Mandleman was laughing, he was filling the street with cries of hysteria and if she were ever to turn and confront him wholly she would see this and somehow she would not be able to take it, she could take everything that Boerum Street could give but there was no way in which she could accept that.

"I *do* care," she said, "I do, I do," and went off to make her visits and it must have been that very afternoon (she is pretty sure that it was that afternoon) that she had inaugurated her policy; fucked Washington Williams, unemployed father of three in his kitchen in the empty spaces of the apartment, drawing Washington Williams into her, easing his tortured cries, stroking his agonized head and knowing, *knowing*, that whatever Mandleman would say, she was doing the right thing.

XII

Elizabeth finds that the Buckingham apartment is jammed with youths: five or six of them, maybe seven or eight (it is difficult to count) in various positions around the living room and kitchen, some of them smoking, others looking sullenly at their nails, all of them regarding her with vast and hungry interest as Willie opens the door and moves her in. She thinks that she can recognize George Jones as one of the youths but then again it is difficult to tell; all of them look the same in this light and she is under a great deal of nervous strain. She wonders if Oved will really put her up on charges for running out on emergency duty and is already thinking about how she can get back to the welfare center as quickly as possible, maybe with apologies. "It was an emergency, didn't I tell you?" she will say to Oved, "but I was able to settle things right down and now I'm back." She is not exactly sure what she will describe the emergency as *being*. Maybe Willie will give her some ideas.

But Willie does not seem in that capacity now: she has never seen him so tense nor, for that matter, so detached from the situational fix as he appears now. It must be a neurasthenic block of some kind; he mutters and talks to himself as he leads her back to the living room. "Miss Moore, Miss Moore," he is saying, "I knew you would come," and the youths all look at her intently as she is led into the living room and there motioned to the sofa which is empty. She sits uneasily, clutching her fieldbook, holding it tightly against her groin as Willie stands above her and the others circle in. "Yes?" she says finally when she is aware that none of them will speak, "what is it, Willie? What can I do for you? What's the problem?" Her voice seems high-pitched and nervous; Elizabeth tries to work herself into a professional calm. "There's no problem I can see."

"Well, Miss Moore," Willie says, "Miss Moore, the reason I brought you up here — "

"Don't jive her," one of the youths says. He comes over to the couch, looks at Elizabeth with murderous eyes, stretches out a hand suddenly and runs his fingers insultingly down her sleeve, staring at her. "Take it nice and slow and easy. Willie been telling us — we, by the way, a group of his very best friends — Willie been telling us that you been making love to him and a certain George Jones."

"It's the truth, Miss Moore," Willie says, jumping nervously. He is in a highly agitated state; in some detached way Elizabeth wonders what could possibly be bothering him, how superficial her connection with him must have been if he can be so emotionally blocked, "now you know it's the truth; you tell them."

"Our relationship is confidential," Elizabeth says. "I am Willie's caseworker; he is part of my caseload that is to say and whatever occurs in that relationship is privileged. There's no emergency at all, was there Willie?"

"Well," the murderous youth says, "in a way there's an emergency, sure. You see, we friends of Willie but we don't believe him. We think he giving us a line of bullshit."

"That's a lady, man," someone in the back says. "Keep your mouth clean for a lady."

"Well, then," the youth says, "we feel that what Willie been telling us is some falsehoods, hypocrisies and lies. We do not find this possible to believe, even if the very honorable George Jones who is not here today also says that Willie is telling the truth. All of us here are very interested in finding out the truth from your own lips so to speak or as evidence in fact."

"I'm sorry," Elizabeth says, crossing her legs. "I can't talk about anything of that nature. You must be aware of that fact. Social work is a privileged position."

"But you are no social worker, Miss Moore. You are a social investigator."

"Please, Miss Moore," Willie says. He seems to be in some obscure but real distress. "Please tell them. It's important to me; I can't go into explanations — "

"Willie — "

"Please," he says. His eyes become soft, luminescent; sensitivity overtakes Willie's face, he leans more closely toward her. "It would mean a great deal to me. And I'm not feeling so well, Miss Moore; didn't you say you would do everything to make me feel better? This would make me feel better."

"All right," Elizabeth says, playing with her fieldbook and then looking up to confront the youth squarely in the eye. "If that's the way you want it. Willie and I have had some sexual contact, yes."

"Sexual contact?"

"Yes."

"Sexual contact," the youth says, musing. "You mean fucking, is that right?"

"I don't know what you want to call it. And frankly," Elizabeth says, not liking the situation at all and deciding that she is going to bring it to an end, "frankly," she says then standing, "I am very upset at having been brought all the way out from the welfare center where I was on emergency duty just for something like this. I'm leaving now. You are not my responsibility. Willie is my responsibility but I'm very disappointed in him."

"I'm sorry you're disappointed," the youth says softly. He seems to give a quiet signal and suddenly the others are around her. There is a juxtaposition of faces, forms, urgency. She feels heat in the room as they form a loose circle, all of them looking the same, cutting off her view of the walls, moving in more closely. Their faces are less threatening than curious; bland, unmoving eyes focusing on her. "Disappointment is a very bad emotion to have. But I am happy to know that Willie Buckingham was telling the truth. Now and then he has a lying problem."

"You can't intimidate me," Elizabeth says. "You are not my cases. None of you are my responsibility. I'm going to leave now. Willie, I don't like your attitude. I don't like it; you're abusing our relationship."

"Miss Moore," Willie says, showing his palms, "I couldn't do nothing. These cats wouldn't believe me, that's all. I couldn't lose face with my friends now, could I? It would have hurt my self-image, just like you were telling me. You got to build up my self-image."

"Cut it out, Willie," the apparent leader says. He turns back toward Elizabeth and gives her an enormous wink. "Bet you think that you got a right to be afraid now," he says, "isn't that so?"

"I'm not afraid of anything."

"Bet you think that we got you up here to have a party and that you are going to be raped by a bunch of niggers, isn't that the truth?"

"I don't like that word. I've never used that word in my life."

"Well that's fine; that proves you're real liberal and I'm pleased. But that's the thought in your mind."

"No it isn't," Elizabeth says. She makes a space for herself in the line, eases her way through. They do not resist. She walks toward the door. They do not come for her. At the door she turns. "You don't understand at all, any of you. I'm not afraid of that because if I thought that it would do any of us any good it wouldn't have to be rape. There's no such thing as rape. But that isn't going to happen because none of you except Willie are on my caseload and there's nothing at all I can do for you." She is vaguely aware that she does not seem to be making sense; nevertheless, they are at bay. Furthermore, she has no fear at all. This is one of the interesting aspects of this encounter; tensional elements are utterly lacking. If anything did happen in here it would, in the long run, probably be cathartic anyway. "Willie," Elizabeth says, "I am ashamed of you," and she walks through the door, closes it behind her and heads down the steps.

Whether or not there are sounds behind her means nothing. She does not even try to listen. Her primary feeling as she comes out onto the street is rage: rage that Willie would break the confidentiality of their relationship, rage that Willie would so misapprehend her motives as to hold her up for contempt and ridicule. But the rage wafts away like smoke as she walks toward the bus; wafts away in the realization that

Willie is still sick, her efforts to the contrary he is a very sick boy and if he is still capable of behavior of this sort … then she must accept the fact that somehow she has failed him. She has failed them all. She has too much in opposition; there is too much to overcome, she was wrong in feeling that it would be easy. Nevertheless, she must try.

She must try: sitting on the bus now she can only hope that what she has done has been for Willie and that it has, in whatever way built up his self-esteem. For an instant, looking out the back window, she thinks that they may be pursuing her but it is merely a clump of high school boys on the street running from the yards (they all look the same to her, still: she acknowledges this) and her thoughts shift onto other terrain; she wonders, then, what she will manage to say to Oved.

XIII

One of the things Calvin Hunter had complained about most in New York was the social alienation, the "fragmentation of the personal function into institutions" was the way he put it, the dating services, singles parties, moonlight matches and so on arranged through newspapers or box numbers that "took everything away from people and just made it part of the machinery; it is impossible to find any state of connection in this city" but despite everything that he said and despite all his good advice (and the fact that in her own way she supposed she had had some real feeling for him) Elizabeth had persisted in using dating matches, singles parties and so on even after he had left for the coast.

It was not that she had any interest whatsoever in meeting men — with Calvin gone she was now totally wrapped up with her caseload and her emotions and sexual energies would be devoted totally to them — but she realized that to a certain extent she would have to live by forms and rote and it would be better to play by the rules of the single girl in New York than not. It would really be in her clients' interests to do so because she could juxtapose her middle-class experiences against their alienation and, anyway, every time there was a failure of feeling in those middle-class experiences it would be a justification of the essential rightness of what she was doing. She could, in short, by contrasting the bankruptcy of the young single middle-class with the richness of her own professional experiences, reaffirm them. Reaffirmation. That was the important thing, that and helping her clients to get better so that they could recover their self esteem and get off relief and assume a higher socio-economic level and begin to lead normal middle-class lives.

So she had gone to a singles party advertised in one of the weekly newspapers; the party taking place in what was supposed to be a luxurious townhouse on the East Side but turned out to be a small, painful walkup in the mid-fifties off Second Avenue. There she had paid one dollar at the door ("ladies free until eight, one dollar thereafter; men fifteen dollars at the door at all times;" the surest indication of her relative worth, she knew) and had gone into a crowded room in which thirty to forty men were pursuing three or four rather ugly girls with painful indecision, casting occasional bewildered glances upward at the monstrous chandelier or over to the bar, which was closed. The men seemed to be puzzled more than angry; most of them looked as if they had been in situations like this so often that they were merely part of the expected fabric of their lives and the girls, only barely responsive to the men seemed obsessed more than anything else with their appearances: they touched their hair, readjusted their makeup at every opportunity and, one by one, made whole series of expeditions to the bathroom in which, presumably, they put themselves back together again for another series of advances by the men. Elizabeth had found it quite depressing, of course — in its staticity and posturing it was so far from the rich, free life of the relief subculture; there people were in contact with their impulses all the time and able to act on them without guilt; here people could only deny their impulses and circle around them in a way which would make them seem infinitely poisonous — but it had been interesting as well, all of the reaffirmation she could have asked and as the only remotely attractive girl in the room she had, of course, immediately been advanced upon by the men, most of whom, however, stood on the outskirts, wiping their faces and adjusting their glasses, looking with longing while three or four of the least decompensated types attempted to talk her straight out of the apartment and into their homes. It was depressing to think that a man would pay fifteen dollars to enter an apartment precisely so that he could leave it as quickly as possible but she guessed that this was the system. It seemed to be perfectly all right with the host and hostess, middle aged people who backed against the wall with expressions of fear, constantly counting their receipts and muttering to one another about unimaginable things while they kept their eyes on the food trays to make sure that too much was not taken by any of the men at any given time. It never was.

Elizabeth found herself in intense conversation with a thirtyish overweight man who said that he was a copywriter for the fourth or fifth largest advertising agency in the city and had personally been responsible for major campaigns for a ballpoint pen and a vaginal deodorant, both of which, due to his copywriting, had escalated some forty to fifty percent in sales in less than six months although there was no way that he could keep his group head from getting all the credit. "And the thing about writing copy on a vaginal deodorant," the heavy man whose name was Milton said, "the thing about it is that it isn't sexy, it isn't dirty, it isn't anything at all; people make a lot of jokes about you when you get into a business like that but it's all just words, just work and it comes out the same way. No matter what you're writing about or who you're supposed to sell it to it's exactly the same thing that you've always been doing. So I don't even think about it too much any more. I wonder if people who write novels feel the same way; someday I'd like to write a novel and really blow the roof off the advertising business. It's never been done you know and it would be sensational but somehow I can't seem to get the handle on it. What I want to do is to get a writing fellowship and go up to one of those places with log cabins and really let the whole thing roll out. I know that if I could only get out of this city everything would be fine. I was engaged until recently to a beautiful girl but we just couldn't make it which is why I'm at one of these things. I've never gone to one before in my whole life and let me tell you I never will again: it's pitiful, it's disgusting. Just a bunch of losers. Shall we get out of here?" Milton said, "shall we go and have a drink and go over to my place, maybe?" and actually Elizabeth had no desire at all to get out of there; it was interesting, very interesting and her insights were being confirmed rapidly; the longer she sat there the better she felt about what she was doing in her own life but Milton was sweating, putting the issue hard to her now, leaning forward with insistence chasing fear across his face and in the interest of salvaging his feelings — because he too was important, as important a person as any of her clients for the moment — she said she would.

"That's great," Milton said with a sigh, "that's really great," and under the loathing glances of all the men in the room the two of them left together, scuttling for their coats and passing by the host and hostess who gave them limp waves of farewell. "Hope you've enjoyed this," the hostess said, "and that you'll come back to see us often."

"That's right," said the host. "It's an important and healthy thing to do in New York, to meet new people," and they went into the hall, Milton murmuring to himself and took the elevator down. "Never," Milton said, "I'll never go again: why these things are terrible, it's just so exploitative and naked up there and so full of sadness. Those men must live sad lives; I just had to drop by once to see the way it was but never again. I never, incidentally, go to any of these things, I was engaged to a beautiful girl. What do you do for work?" he said to her but this was somewhat later, when they were leaving the bar, in fact, where he had put two Gibsons into her, talking intensely all the time of the power-relations within the agency and how, some way, he was going to be able to cut through it to produce good work, sensible work, because advertising too *mattered*, it was just a question of getting people into the field who had more respect for it and weren't all of them failed poets or bookkeepers on the make.

"I work for the welfare department," Elizabeth said, on the way to the subway, heading up to his apartment. "At the Lower Greenpoint welfare center but actually my cases are in Bedford Stuyvesant and Williamsburgh."

"That's interesting," Milton said, taking her arm briskly, leading her around a backed-up sewer, "but what is it really like? They're all cheats and frauds, aren't they? It's just disgraceful. Of course it's interesting experience, sometimes I envy the experience you can get there but the money is so bad. All civil service pays so badly. And it must be a very depressing job, don't you think? To come in contact with all that poverty and misery every day and know that there's nothing you can do to combat it and that most of them are laughing at you anyway. And isn't it dangerous? I don't know if a young girl should be walking through those sections. I was reading some very bad things about Bedford-Stuyvesant in the New York *Times* last week as a matter of fact; they had an interesting article about it. What is it like there? Is it really filthy and dangerous? A few friends of mine have worked for the welfare department but that's been in the projects in New York City and they don't have much to say about it. All of them get out fast. Are you going to be leaving soon? I hear the average term of an investigator there is about six months but most of them leave in three and only the old hacks hang on for fifty years to bring up the average. It must be a bad place to work. I'm really curious to know what it's like to work for the department, why don't you fill me in? According to this article in the *Times* over fifty percent of Bedford-Stuyvesant is on relief already. What would happen to the place if they took all the relief out, that's what I ask myself. Think about that! All of the profiteering, why it must be incredible, relentless. Do you know any of the landlords? The landlords must be the worst but then consider what they have to contend with, dealing with animals. I think that the real truth of the matter is that most of these people are animals. You can use all the social work terms like relevant or urban structure but what it comes down to is that they just aren't like you and me. Are they? The thing is that I'd really like to know something about the department if you'd tell me. Most people who work there just won't talk about it. According to this *Times* article eighty percent of the people in Bedford-Stuyvesant weren't born in New York City and came in in the last five years. That's frightening, don't you think? Just frightening. I was thinking — "

"Oh, I don't know. I guess it's not too bad," Elizabeth said but this was much later, considerably later, after they had gotten off the subway as a matter of fact and had walked the three crosstown and two uptown blocks to Milton's "pad" which was somewhere in the vicinity of Columbia University. "I mean it has its points," she added much later when they were in his apartment, having taken the old, dangerous elevator up sixteen deadly flights and gone into his three and a half room, two rooms of which Milton said were "indescribably filthy" and which he could not "show a respectable girl under any circumstances at all."

"I guess," she said as they were undressing, "I guess that it all depends," and then said and thought no more about welfare for the moment. She had made the decision at the bar that she would go to bed with him: she wondered exactly how bad he would be. This was perhaps not the right reason to go to bed with a man, there was, as a matter of fact, practically no justification for it but that was the way it had to be. With the possible exception of Calvin Hunter no man had ever attracted her until she became involved with welfare clients; now, she figured, the worse that Milton turned out to be the better she would feel, the more justified in the series of difficult decisions which she had made about her life.

"Oh my God," he said when they were naked and they had placed themselves against one another almost solemnly, silence descending for just a moment in the spaces surrounding Milton, "my God, it's beautiful, I've never seen anything like it," and then he had gone to work; his copywriting experience with the vaginal deodorant had apparently affected him (despite his disclaimers) he had, in fact, a seeming obsession and dove immediately between her legs where with ferocity and singlemindedness he had proceeded to work his tongue, his lips and then, it seemed, his entire head up her cunt, moaning and babbling all the time, his hands grasping her thighs like a dead man. She felt pain, slow pulses of desire which devoured the pain, mixed with it to produce an absent feeling of need and began to work against him slowly, he rose, seeming enormous in the darkness and groaning came to mount her. "Oh it's wonderful, wonderful," he said, "it was worth everything," and she wondered vaguely what he was talking about; what could possibly be worth this? but no time to think, Milton began to sing, babble deeply in his throat and entered her quickly. She thought that he would come like a rabbit (most of the clients did, why should he be any different?) but surprisingly he did not; he held out for an impossibly long time, pumping and squeezing her buttocks until she felt all desire drain from her and was overcome only by the need for him to finish and at that instant when she was most convinced that it would never happen, that she would be locked on this bed forever fucking this copywriter who seemed to have a case of *ejaculata delayed* (she is not sure of her Latin) he did come, so silently and with so little semen that she could barely believe it. He rolled away from her silently, silently rubbed his forehead into the sheets, silently caressed her arm and then he began again, as he leapt from the bed, to inexhaustibly talk.

"Wonderful," he said, "that was wonderful; you're really good, I don't know if this is the right way to put it or the exact time that I should but what the heck? I've never been graceful with words except in the professional context so let me ask you something; would you live with me? Would you like to move in? You can't be very happy living alone, I assume you live alone, and we're very convenient to the University here and the subway to the welfare center would be easy. Or you could even, I understand, get a transfer of welfare centers, what do you say? We could really make something come of this. I mean I don't want to force things and things should just be allowed to grow and develop on their own but who knows? we might even get married, well, we can think about that but you must tell me about your work now, I'd be very interested in hearing, you know what else the *Times* said about Bedford-Stuyvesant?" and so on and so forth, rubbing his genitals as if in congratulation, winking in delight, putting on his clothes, flicking on lights, making coffee or something else in the kitchen as he talked. Milton went on and on, went on as Elizabeth put on her own clothes and took her handbag, went on even as she decided to forego coffee and slip out for the night. Through the door she went and into the elevator and as it slowly creaked all the way down she thought that she could still hear him and out into the lobby, onto the dangerous streets near Riverside Drive and it had been terrible, absolutely terrible, the whole thing had been awful! and the best thing, therefore, that could have possibly happened to her. Elizabeth walked to the subway almost jauntily, repressing a witch's impulse to sing. It had been a wonderful evening. It proved. It just proved and to go and show you that she was right. Because Milton had been terrible and everything about him was awful and if this was what the single life in New York offered then she wanted nothing more than to stay with her caseload and rehabilitate them one by one carefully, bring them to a full acceptance of their condition and need.

Because you could do something with the caseload. Very definitely, you could do something with them and what was done mattered. For one thing sex with her seemed to affect them and they were different when, shaking, they came off her. And in the second place, Elizabeth decided, bounding into the subway in an almost unladylike way, in the second place and she was now willing to admit this, she enjoyed what she was doing, found it rewarding and was going to keep on doing it as long as she could, without any need, ever again for the verifying experience.

XIV

At the welfare center, coming back in quickly after noon she finds Oved in a silent, ominous mood. He seems almost unaware of her presence. "I see you're back, Miss Moore," he says to her at some later point and then, mysteriously, goes off to what he says is an "emergency conference" with the case supervisor. Elizabeth wonders vaguely if it has to do with her and whether he is really going to bring her up on charges but decides that it does not matter. If the worst should happen and she should be denied certification she will merely resign, take all the tests again and start anew in the department, at a different welfare center. They are chronically understaffed, they are desperate for people, let alone dedicated, competent people like Elizabeth Moore. As emergency worker, alone in the case unit, she works her way through the afternoon's crises almost casually, dealing with a threatened eviction, an aged applicant in Intake who claims that if he does not get emergency relief he will use some safety matches to burn the center down, a phone call from a landlord (not Mandleman) who says that he suspects one of the clients of attempted arson. It has so little to do with the realities of her job that she can almost enjoy it, finding it a relaxing break. She does not have to deal with the painful, interpersonal relationship established in client therapy.

At about four o'clock, with Oved still gone in his emergency conference (maybe it is his own job which is in jeopardy) she receives a call from Schnitzler. He begins to talk the moment she has picked up the phone, before she has even identified herself, and she understands — as she has already suspected of the *chassids* — that their monomania is so great and their view of the outside world so threatening that Schnitzler simply assumes she would be there to take his call when he placed it. "Miss Moore," he says in a quiet, frantic voice. "There is some trouble."

"What's wrong?"

"It is hard to explain. Yet I must explain it. Maybe I will not explain it. But then again I must try. Are you sure you don't speak Jewish?"

"I don't."

"If you spoke Jewish it would be so much easier. I cannot, as you say, express myself properly in English. It is so difficult. But I will try. There is difficulty."

"What is it?" she says sharply. "What's wrong?" She tries to put down a thrust of irritation: she reminds herself that their relationship is brand-new, uncemented and that she must expect ambivalence and tension. Still, the *chassids* are all so obscure; that is the basic problem in relating to them, they do not seem to admit connection and turn stupid and shy at the wrong moments. Only at the question of money do they seem to come into focus.

"Is it your check?" she says, "did you lose your check?" It is a foolish question; it is not even checkday — this is the twenty-eighth, checkday is three days from now or looking at it another way, twelve days ago — but she is momentarily at a loss and it has been a difficult afternoon for her. "What *is* it?"

"It has nothing to do with my check. All is fine. Only — " there is a sickening pause; she hears Schnitzler snuffling and sniffing in the background. "Only I must tell you — "

"So tell me," she says. "I'm very busy today, Rabbi Schnitzler." She does not want to be short with him; there is so much to be accomplished and she badly needs his trust … but the man can be maddening. "If you won't tell me — "

"My wife," Schnitzler says and then begins to talk quickly, disjointedly, "what came between us yesterday was sacrimonial is that your word? and made me feel very good but it also made me feel very bad as well and I could not sleep, the higher consciousness, the law of the sacred texts and the Talmud which regard so much as an abomination — "

"Guilt," she says shortly. "We've already spoken about guilt. We'll talk some more. You have no reason — "

"But I can't talk like that now, Miss Moore!" Schnitzler says with a whine. "It is too late, I feel guilty. Maybe the guilt is not right and what you say is interesting but you do not understand our tradition. *I* do not understand much of our tradition. The guilt was so much that I told my wife — "

"That," Elizabeth says tightly, clenching the phone, "that was really not necessary."

"Well yes. No. Of course. But I tell her — "

"Our relationship is privileged and exists only between the two of us."

"I know. I know. Nevertheless this tormenting feel of guilt, need. I have lived with my wife so many years. Also thirteen children. Also she is, you know, pregnant with the fourteenth? You know? I should have told you. So I felt that I had to tell her but the woman did not understand — "

"Why should she understand?" Elizabeth says. She wills herself toward a social worker's calm. The Schnitzler problem is a family rather than an agency issue. It will have to be resolved on those grounds. Part of the ensuing familial conflict would be cathartic, she supposes. It is not, in any event, her immediate responsibility. "We will talk more about this Rabbi Schnitzler," Elizabeth says. "I'm due out there for a visit next month anyway. But we can make it earlier. Perhaps I will be out there next week. We will try to resolve some of the tensions — "

"Tensions!" Schnitzler says sobbing, "tensions! My wife, she went to the Lubavitcher congregation. She went there with all thirteen of the children, two of them in arms, one of which she is still suckling. Thirteen children and my wife on the streets, leaving my house! Now she is in the congregation itself, in one of the emergency rooms. She told them everything."

"She — "

"Tension, Miss Moore! It is too late to talk of tension! Do you understand? She has told them everything and this very day there is a meeting being held right at this moment to discuss my fate and the fate of my family. I cannot bear this! This is not my fault."

"You should not have told her."

"I should not have told her but I did tell her. I appeal to you, Miss Moore," Schnitzler says out of the depths of his dependency. "I am frantic. Come down. Come down here at once and the two of us will go to the congregation and you will meet before the elders. You will explain what has happened. You will tell my side of the story."

"I'm sorry," Elizabeth says. Behind her she notes that Oved has at last returned, he is carrying a pencil in his grip as if it were a suitcase and seems filled with purpose. "That is impossible. You do not understand the functioning of the agency."

"Of course I do not understand!" Schnitzler says frantically, "I am a stupid man and now I am the shame of the community. Who is to say what the congregation will do to me? Who is to say what may happen if this reaches the level of the rabbi himself? I may be exiled in disgrace. You must tell them, Miss Moore! Tell them!"

"Tell them what?"

"You better get off that phone," Oved says to her quietly. "Trouble brewing in Intake."

"That it was an affair of madness. That you, what is your word, *verfluehren* — "

"*Ver* what?"

"That you how I can put this, that you enticed me against my will, that it was you who caused — "

"Big things brewing in Intake," Oved says cheerfully. "Off that phone, emergency worker." He seems to be a man at peace, an Oved reconstituted, but Elizabeth is under so much pressure that she is unable to become involved with it as she might have otherwise. "Come on, have a heart — "

"You must," Schnitzler says feebly. His tones have dropped an octave; some conviction of disaster seems already present. "You won't. I know you won't. But the congregation — "

"I'm sorry, Rabbi Schnitzler," Elizabeth says. "The workings of the department, the relationship between an investigator and the client are confidential and I couldn't get involved. I couldn't possibly get involved."

"This is so easy to say!"

"I'm sorry."

"Criminal! You are a criminal, Miss Moore!" Schnitzler ways weakly and then hangs on the phone. She can tell that he wants to hang it up on her but some frail, mad thread of hope still holds him on. "Please," he gasps, "please."

"We'll discuss this later," she says and puts the phone down, feeling some consternation — this is, after all, the second time that her relationships' confidentiality has been broken and it has been done so, it would seem, in bad circumstances. She turns, sees Oved smiling at her and feels an insane blush coming over her cheeks. She wonders what Oved would say if he got wind of the doings at the Lubavitcher congregation.

"Big problems in Intake," Oved says once again, benignly. "Got a lady down there who has been evicted and about seventeen kids. Not your case but that's life. We'll be working here until eleven o'clock to get that bitch resettled. Just the two of us and case consultation hand in hand." Oved winks, his features relax further, he beams at her as Elizabeth, trembling, backs from the desk holding her fieldbook. "It's tough, real tough," Oved says, "but it looks like one way or the other you'll be spending the evening with the black man, huh?" And winks and winks and winks at her, cheerful and confident, Oved transmogrified then, and nothing for Elizabeth to do but to stumble downstairs, thinking abstract thoughts of the doings at the Lubavitcher congregation, and take the case.

XV

They work together until past nine in the evening: the evicted mother is monstrously fat (she has been receiving a supplementary grant for special stockings and varicose veins for several years) and the children nasty and whining, the air in the welfare center after the power has been cut and all but one of the superintendent staff have gone home, becomes oppressively foul and Elizabeth, staggering from telephone to Intake to Oved to typewriter to give Case Consultation the maddening additional information it says it needs before it can authorize a hotel ("don't worry about that shit," Oved tells her happily, "them bastards put the approval on their desks and went home at five o'clock but left order that it ain't going to be released until they make you dance for four hours and that's the way it going to be; I got no plans for this evening and neither do you I hope so that's that") feels at odd intervals that she might faint but she forces herself through these neurasthenic moments, finding herself at last in a high, hard arena of sensation where everything is very distant and easy and she is able to accomplish what she has to do without thought. "You got nice legs, honey," the evicted mother tells her at one point, "real nice legs, I sure would like to have legs like that or even get a feel of them" and Elizabeth realizes that there is probably a lesbian undertone to this but this does not bother her. She has never gone to bed with a female welfare client and she will never do so; the therapeutic relationship has its definite limits and this is one for her. "I just feel so bad, so guilty about everything," the evictee had told her later, "it makes me feel that I'm worthless," and Elizabeth, who at a different moment would have tried a casework approach, shown the woman that what she felt was not guilt but hostility, the desire to strike out at the world by being evicted, found that she had no impulse to say any of it. The woman would have to take care of herself. Casework, like everything else, had its limits. At nine o'clock the approval came through and the check which the Head Clerk had left sealed in his desk all the time was released on phoned instructions from the clerk as to its whereabouts. "Somebody have to take those fools up to the hotel," Oved says musing, tapping the envelope in his hands. "The money has to be turned over to the manager by procedure. Actually I'd rather give it to the bitch and let her find it on her own. Maybe we'd never see her again. The trouble is that the cunt would probably drop off the kiddies in the nearest subway station and bug out of everybody's life forever so we'd still be stuck with them."

"I'm the caseworker," Elizabeth says. "I'll go with them and turn over the check."

"Well that's not strictly fair," Oved says, "you're a young girl and that upper west side turns out to be kind of a mean section this time of night. What I think I'll do is that the two of us will go together."

"That's not necessary."

"Oh come on, Miss Moore," Oved says with a contented little laugh. "You and the black man can take the subway uptown with these bastards and drop them off. I got an appointment in that neighborhood anyway. I have given up on you. I have no more interest in you. I am not trying to put any make on you ever again and you got nothing to worry about in that direction. You ain't even that pretty if you want to know the truth or at least I don't consider you pretty. The black man has had better than you in his time, just remember that."

"Please stop it, Mr. Oved," Elizabeth says, "it isn't prejudice — "

"Of course it isn't prejudice honey; it's common sense. We got nothing good to come out of us, I do accept that," Oved says. "Come on," he adds, reaching for his coat which has been at the ready for three hours, slung over his clerk's chair, "let's get going; we'll get out of here. I'd do it myself, carry the check and all but that wouldn't strictly speaking be right. It's the worker's responsibility but being the supervisor as I am, I'll share it."

There is nothing that Elizabeth can do; the situation is cast and Oved, remarkably, seems to be in control. She makes one effort saying, "Well, if you're going up that way anyway, if you have an appointment then couldn't *you* assume the whole responsibility?" but this new Oved merely laughs lightly, says that this would be completely beside the fact of procedures since the worker herself must be responsible for delivery of the check and case consultation would be in a fury the next morning, a complete fury, if they found that Elizabeth had dropped her responsibilities. "Them sons of bitches got lines into everywhere, they in contact with all the hotel managers and they'll check," Oved says to her cheerfully and so they go, all of them go: the evictee and her children and Oved and Elizabeth silently ride the empty subway to the upper west side and there Elizabeth takes the envelope from her pocket in the hotel lobby and hands it to the manager who, he says, has been waiting there for just this for several hours. "Ordinarily I go home at five, Miss Moore," the manager says, "but we were very concerned about this family, very concerned indeed. And so I made a special point of staying late. Thank you," he says, taking the check, "what I'll do is to cash this and return the food money to them after we've deducted our week's rent," and with a graceful bow and wink he leaves Elizabeth's life forever along with the evictee and children. The evictee clutches her and Oved's hands, thanks them for everything that they have done despite her irresponsibility, her ignorance, her poor care of her children. Tomorrow morning at nine A.M. her case will be transferred far from them and to the Amsterdam Welfare Center; it will be their problem.

"Well," Oved says, when they are back on West 95th Street, "it's been a long day, hasn't it?"

"Yes, it has. I want to go home."

"Well you can surely go home," Oved says. "Might I buy you some dinner first, though? We get a food allowance you know; you don't have to pay for dinner."

"Mr. Oved," Elizabeth says, "I appreciate what you're saying and what you've done but I just don't want to have dinner with you. I'm very tired and think I'll do better just to go home."

"To Henry Street? You don't want to go to Henry Street," Oved says with a chuckle. "Look, you got the wrong idea about me. You think that I trying to put the make on you still and again and you don't understand that I wouldn't touch you now for anything. I have absolutely no desire for you, Elizabeth Moore, because you are a racist."

"I'm not a racist," Elizabeth says, clutching her hands furiously as two enormous trucks go by making Broadway shake, as old people, stumbling with canes down Broadway seem to be blown like leaves in the truck exhaust. "That is not the situation at all. You have no right — "

"Of course you're a racist," Oved says happily, "and besides that, I'm not going to have to worry about you much more. Things are being worked through, things will come to their conclusion. I had a good meeting about you with the Case Supervisor, Miss Moore, and you will no longer be in my case unit. Effective very soon. Are you surprised to hear me say that?"

"I have to stay in the unit. I'm entitled to a hearing. I have clients — "

"Clients all over the city, suffering and needing. Maybe you find some others. No, Miss Moore, we have arranged a transfer for you. You are not being discharged because I have seen the error of my vengeful ways. Instead I feel that you can make some other supervisor's life miserable but I wouldn't do it to anybody I know in this welfare center. So effective next week you are moving uptown. Way uptown. You are going to the Fordham Welfare Center in the Bronx where you will be a home economics advisor."

"You can't do this to me. You can't — "

"Oh yes I can," Oved says beaming under a movie marquee; his face taking on the hues of red and green, lights dancing across it and here they pause while he grips her hands dramatically. "I may make only six thousand and fifty dollars a year with increments and have to jump to every case consultation clerk in Manhattan but I have a few prerogatives as a unit supervisor and I have used them. I have indeed used them. You are leaving the field, Miss Moore and going to a welfare center which is short a good home economics advisor. You can figure out a sweater allowance for the little bastards and special diets for their mamas. And furthermore, Miss Moore — " Oved says, starting to walk again and ironically it is now Elizabeth who has to pursue him to hear what he is saying, "furthermore, there is no way that you can protest because you are merely a provisional worker and are covered by none of the rights and privileges of the civil service. You will obtain your certification at Fordham and be able to make waves then for some other people but as far as I am concerned you are going to go. Of course," Oved says, "you can always quit. If you don't find the transfer to your liking, nobody is making you stay."

"That's not fair," Elizabeth says. She is crying. Fatigue, hunger, dismay, the interview with Schnitzler have all unsettled her, otherwise she would never show emotion. "I have responsibilities to my clients. I have a caseload. I have established certain relationships — "

"You've fouled up everything, you dirty little Jewish cunt," Oved says, all of the good humor suddenly fleeing from him, his face threatening, his eyes tortured, "you've fucked up your whole caseload with your social worker bullshit and you've treated me like a dog and now you are getting yours," and in mid-sentence he has already left her. He has darted into a subway kiosk and still talking, apparently to himself, is moving rapidly down the stairs. He passes out of eye view and there is nothing Elizabeth can see but slush in the pavements, pedestrians staring at her, a filthy newspaper with men's magazines hanging by clothespins to wire draped above.

"I can't stand it anymore," Elizabeth says and thinks she might cry but this would not be professional, it would be terribly undignified — and in any event, the welfare institute reminded you to be on your best behavior at all times; you could never tell when you might be in the presence of a client or a client's friend who would talk about you — and she would not give Oved the satisfaction. She walks, instead, down ten blocks of Broadway, blinking her eyes and keeping a rein on herself; at 96th Street she goes into the subway herself and waits for a long time for the local to come in, the local that will take her back to Henry Street, the local that will leave her at the door shattered and yet, somehow, she must manage to carry on.

Things seem to be closing in on her and yet she cannot get over the unfairness of it all: what she was trying to do was her job in accordance with the policies and procedures of the welfare training institute. Still, things seem to be closing in. To be closing in. Closing. In.

XVI

At home she finds a letter from her father and after eating and showering and taking her phone off the hook (she will not, she will *not* have Willie Buckingham intruding in her life this night) she feels that she is ready to face it. The letter, as is the case with all by her father, is long and somewhat convoluted, filled with strikeovers, erasures, and strange paragraphing on the typewriter which as he has often said is his attempt to find a definite and unique style in which he can break out of formal expression and into some apprehension of reality. Much of the letter seems to be the same old stuff: his unemployment has run out but he still does not feel an urgency to find a job, he believes that after fifty-one years he is just beginning to find himself, he has been doing a lot of reading in the Impressionist school over the past few months and does not agree by a longshot that Dadaism is dead but believes that it is merely waiting, albeit somewhat incoherently for a revival … but toward the end of the letter is something interesting, something relatively new to his correspondence and to the best of her ability she pays attention to it while letting the other parts run out and filter past her mind.

"What I often felt after we lost your mother," (the letter points out) "was a clear and terrible sense of inadequacy, that I would fail you, that I could not both be mother and father and instill in

you those qualities which I feel so important to a young girl and a human being in today's culture which is rapidly becoming the Assassination Age. But I can see from your letters and sense from their meaning that the guilt was misplaced and truly you are a fine young lady. I am moved by your sense of compassion for your 'clients' and agree with you one hundred percent that they are 'poor sick vestiges of post-technological American life which must somehow be put back into the machinery or die' and find that a beautiful way of putting things. You seem very involved with your clients and yet I sense somehow that you are 'holding back' that you are trying to say things which you are not ready to say and it is here perhaps where I can help you.

"I believe that you can no longer detach yourself from these people and agree with you that it is pointless to try. I do not think, dear Elizabeth, that you can truly 'help' them in the position of being an investigator because of the nature of the system as you have explained it and as I understand it from my reading in 'modern public assistance.'

"What should be done I think is for you to drop 'out of the system' and actually live with these people, no longer have the role of 'investigator' standing between you and them, holding you off from contact. In order to 'help' them as you want to it will probably be necessary for you to actually live with them, live in their neighborhoods, intermingle with them socially, even — who knows? — have a love affair or three. In that way I think you will be able to get close to them in a way which will not be 'strangled by the system.'

"Of course I need the money you are sending me and of course I am a selfish man: I realize that if you did adopt this suggestion there would be very little 'weekly presents' to look forward to. But I am willing to make the sacrifice for your sake if this is what you truly want. Ponder your heart long and your conscience.

"Remember, the last hope and energy of our culture may lie within these 'pitiful' people and who knows to what uses this energy might be put if directed by the right person in the right way? I hope there will be no further lateness in the checks; I realize that 'last week's little problem' was due to the mails and not you but I was half-frantic as you might have gathered from my collect phone call as well as dead broke."

She puts the letter away, quietly hangs up the phone, thinks of the letter as she lies back on the bed, opening her body up for the first time that day to the fatigue she must truly feel. She has given so much, cared so much, paid so much and what has she gotten? How far has it taken her? What is — and she must face this now — the *justice* of all of this?

XVII

Nevertheless, she has a life to live. She has a caseload to service. She has things to do. She will be on her desk through the end of the week and in that time there is so incredibly much to do that she is appalled.

She must somehow explain her transfer to her clients. (For she knows she must accept the transfer, at least for the moment: her father's suggestion bears much thought and she may even do it soon but for the instant she needs time to think and she also needs the money.) She must, in the case of those with whom she has fornicated, bring their insights and epiphanies to fruition within a matter of minutes rather than weeks and months. She must tie up loose ends, try to be in touch with each and every one of her clients to explain what has happened to her and help them find the strength to lose her. Even the disgusting old men in the Homeway Residence deserve to be told. She will have to work sixteen hours a day in and out of the field to even come close.

So she comes in at 8:30, by 9:00 is already finished with her paperwork for the day and ready to go to the field. Oved looks through and around her, restored to the cheerfulness which seems to be his new mood, the outburst of the evening far away from him. "Going to the field, Miss Moore?" he says.

"Yes, I'm going to the field."

"Going to say goodbye to all of your caseload, is that it? Go ahead Miss Moore; go ahead. Let them know that you're leaving. They may break down and all kill themselves. That would be nice."

"I don't like your sarcasm." She will be cold with Oved: cold and deliberate. She will show him that he is no longer worthy of the respect given by emotion. This is the only way that a man like this can be treated; she will refuse to acknowledge his humanity. "Not at all," she says. "And I don't appreciate your liberties."

"Liberties, liberties," Oved says, "I don't take no liberties at all; I make six thousand and fifty dollars a year breaking my ass while worthless bastards like the one you're so worried about knock down twice that in free money and off the books bartending and mail-order screwing. As far as I can see I lost my liberty when I applied for a job here instead of getting on the line down at the other end of the center."

"You're a bitter man, Mr. Oved," she says, "a very bitter, hurt man. I think you need psychotherapy."

"Well I'll be damned," Oved says smiling broadly, "I don't think I need psycho*therapy*. Of course a little relief might be good and then if I could get a little of that social worker therapy you're giving out I might do better. But you go on your way, Miss Moore. Don't you worry about me. You got clients to see, needs to service. You got to say goodbye to all your whores and pimps."

"That's right," she says, without emotion. "I do." She will no longer give the Oveds of this world the satisfaction of lapsed control. With dignity she takes her fieldbook, puts it under her arm and walks down the steps of the center to the timeclock, punches out and waits on the corner for the Fulton Street bus. She will be in the field until ten o'clock tonight tidying up, she knows. Already she is exhausted and why shouldn't she be?

The first one she will see, she decides, is Felipe Morales. Their relationship is hardly begun and now it is ended; perhaps she can hasten things along, give him something which will carry him through all of the alienation and pain to come. After Felipe she will have to see Willie of course; even though Willie has hurt her a great deal in the last couple of days he is still her most promising case and she must see what can be done there. And there are others to see as well, of course, many others, and somewhere toward the end of the day (or at the very latest by the end of the week) she will have to see Schnitzler. It is impossible to imagine what may have gone on in the Lubavitcher congregation. What shame and dislocation the man must feel! Maybe she will be able to yield him a little supportive therapy, grant him some measure of accomplishment and dignity to carry forth. In order to do this she will probably have to go to bed with him again but Schnitzler, she decides, will be the only one. The rest she must cut off immediately. Otherwise, they would find it too painful.

Musing, humming, looking through her fieldbook she takes the bus, sits in it, going through the entries by family and family member. Already she feels a premonitory nostalgia; she knows how she felt when she looked at these pages for the first time — Salant's fieldbook, all in his tight, repressed hand — and how impossible it seemed to her that she would even be able to sort these people out much less do anything for them. And now she knows all of them, knows all of them well: even to the grubbiest and dingiest alcoholic in the Homeway these are her people and she has done for them all that she can. She knows that she will miss them. She will miss them terribly; in a very real sense they have given her as much as she has tried to give them and any social worker can make this admission without shame. She loves them. Yes. Even the worst of them she loves. They are all little bits and pieces of her, scattered through the nightmare of Bedford-Stuyvesant. Although she will never see any of them again (her professionalism dictates the complete severing of all such relationships when the worker leaves the case) she will think of them always.

At Nostrand Avenue she exits, walks toward Boerum Street, abstracted and for the first time in several days optimistic. What has happened to her, the outcome of Oved's bitterness and jealousy, is unfortunate but she knows that she has a legacy and the legacy will live. Five of the Morales children are playing by the garbage cans outside and they nod to her, call her *Miss Moore ficci* as she smiles and bounds into the building. They know who she is. Even to the children she has managed a meaningful relationship. They care.

She walks upstairs and knocks on the Morales door, then enters without waiting for it to open. Once again she is assaulted by steam; little Mrs. Morales sits in the corner, smashing roaches into the floor with a newspaper and beaming at her with idiotic, mono-lingual good cheer as she passes by, seeing Felipe sitting in the bedroom, putting on his shoes. "Felipe," she says, risking it, "Felipe, how are you? I have something to tell you."

"Ah, Miss Moore," Morales says. He beams up at her, his face glowing with cheer and happiness. "I see you again. So soon. It is wonderful. I have been thinking about you so much." He stands, moves behind her to the door, kicks it closed with a bare foot and winks. "My wife know nothing," he says. "She very stupid and this just an interview between us, she thinks. I'm so glad to see you." He reaches toward her, grasps her breasts. She feels her breasts twist in his hand and with a yelp of pain drops the fieldbook. Embarrassed, blushing, he retrieves it and tosses it against a wall.

"We make love," Morales says. "Right now. *Magnifico*. Wonderful what we make in this room."

"Felipe," Elizabeth says, "Felipe, you don't understand; I came here to tell you something" — but she is unable to finish the sentence; she is in the Morales grasp, twirled in his grip, falling to the bed. She lands in the filthy sheets with a smash, feeling herself bouncing and colliding off children's toys seemingly buried within. Morales appears above her, already in a sexual position, his palms at the side of her head, smiling. He prods her panties with an enormous erection, smiling. "See," he says, "this is how I am for you. This is how I am for you now always. You are my lover. My *amor*. No?"

"Felipe," Elizabeth says, "I'm glad, glad to see that you believe yourself worthy now. It's a big step, an important step, Felipe, but I did come here to tell you — "

"Ah," Morales says, "you have to tell me nothing; it is only a feeling. Like you told me, a feeling." His mustaches flare, his little eyes glint. "Let me show you," he says, reaching down, pulling his pants free with a yank, exposing and holding himself. "This," he says, "this is — "

"No," she says, "you don't understand. We've got to talk, Felipe. Your wife — "

"My wife know nothing. What she know is the best for her. Ah," Morales says, and puts his organ against the sheen of her panties, reaches inside to stroke her thigh and fumble for her pubis, "this is beautiful. This is what I want."

"Felipe," she says, "Felipe," and then, dreadfully, she realizes that he is already poised for entrance, his fingers now digging into her crotch, her panties coming apart seamlessly in his palm, his prick now ready to slide in and she cannot take this, nothing is working out at all; this is not the way she imagined it. She begins to struggle and thrash on the bed. *"Felipe!"* she screams, *"Mr. Morales!"* and finally then he stops, stops in mid-stroke, his little face looking at her angrily and somehow in this light as well (can she believe this?) whimsically.

"You no hold out on me," he says. "You tell me you make love; then we make love. Now you come the second time and you tell me making love no good, you bitch? You tell me that." His mustaches move ferally; something within him, she sees, has been broken but she is more afraid of his rage, at the moment, than a new psychic block. "You must listen to me," she says. "I'm leaving, Felipe. Mr. Morales. Leaving."

"Leaving? Leaving who? For what?"

"I've been transferred. Out of the welfare center."

"I don't understand," he says, hunching above her. He reaches once again toward her pubis, then thinks better of it and drops a hand down along her leg. "What is transfers? What do you want? You come to close my case, you bitch?"

His rage is merely the hopeless cover for fear; she is not frightened. "Out of the center, Felipe," she says patiently, hauling herself up on her elbows. "I mean, I'm no longer going to be your investigator next week.

You'll have a new investigator."

"Who?"

"I don't know."

"Mr. Salant again?"

"I don't think so. He's a parole officer now."

"He always say he send me to jail," Morales says, musing. He looks down at her with regret. "You really not want to make love?" he says. Emotional liability is present; now he swings toward pathos. "That what you come to tell me?"

"I came to tell you that I won't be your investigator anymore. I came to say goodbye."

"Son of a bitch," Morales says. He clambers off her, cursing in Spanish. "Bitches, capons. They send you from the special investigations section I know. They send you to get Morales off relief. Now you say Morales raped you and you go."

"It isn't that way," she says, "it isn't that way at all." She reaches up to touch his cheek, then thinks better of it as his breath immediately quickens and he seems to poise to leap again, and she withdraws her hand. "Nobody's going to report you. Nobody's from special investigations. These things happen. I'm going to a new welfare center."

"You no be my investigator?"

"No. Not as of next week."

"I never had an investigator like you. There never been an investigator like you."

"I'm pleased. I'm pleased, Felipe."

"Salant was no investigator like you. That bitch, Miss Ames, before him long time ago, she not like you. You like no one else we ever had, Miss Moore. Why you leaving?"

"Procedures," she says and then realizing that the word will be meaningless to him. "Because that's the way it has to be," she says instead. "Things move on. People change. The department has its reasons."

"There never any investigator like you in the whole history. I no believe it."

"It's true, Felipe," she says. She must restore his confidence now, build him up piece by piece so that he will be able to accept this but then she has no time. She has already wasted too much time converting from the sexual reaction. "But I'll miss you very much. You are my most important client. I will miss you a great deal."

"Then why you go?"

"It isn't in my hands, Felipe. The department makes these decisions. I would like to stay."

"So you tell them you want to stay. You tell them you want to stay with Felipe Morales."

"They wouldn't listen."

"It's sad," Morales says, nodding. He seems to have accepted now the fact of her leaving. "Sad that you are leaving, Miss Moore." His eyes brighten. "Still, there is something. You will come back and see me?"

"No, Felipe."

"No? Why no?"

"Because I won't be your social worker any more and it wouldn't be fair to either of us to continue the relationship. You'll have someone else to be your investigator and I'll have other — clients."

"I don't want no other investigator."

"I don't want any other clients," Elizabeth says. "But that's the way it is. That's the way the department works. Also the world. You must accept this, Felipe. You must accept these facts."

"Accept what facts?"

Perhaps she has gone too fast. "That the world doesn't work for either of us, Felipe. That we have to make our own way and carry our own responsibilities. This can be a great lesson to you. But haven't we learned something from each other? Don't we mean something to each other?"

"I don't understand nothing," Morales says sullenly. He backs into a corner, kicks off his pants, shows her his erection which is still enormous. "I think it's all bullshit. I think you from special investigations section and now you cry rape. You say Morales, he fucks girl workers."

"I am *not*."

"Then why you leaving?"

Maddening. It is maddening. "I already explained that, Felipe," she says, patiently. "I explained it twice. Because that's the way it has to be."

"I don't want any more explain. You know what I want?" Morales says, tearing off his shirt and moving in one mad gesture atop her on the bed, "you know what? I want to fuck, that's what I want. You no hold out on me you bitch. I been waiting for this. You lead me on and then you tell me no more. Morales is a man. Morales not a pig or a chicken, he a man. He no laughing at. He no fool." Groaning he inserts himself into her, frantically begins to pump. "I show you, bitch," he says. "You scream, you get my wife and I slam your mouth."

She closes her eyes. The pain is intense. She knows that she should not permit this, yet short of total decompensation or violence she cannot get out of it. "All right," she says, gathering his head to her, "all right, all right." He eases all the way into her, she feels his width.

"Now," he says, "now," and begins to work on her avidly. From a distance Elizabeth hears pots steaming, children crying, the sound of bottles shattering on Boerum Street but they are far away. What can she do? Trapped outside him she allows Morales his last moments with her. Nothing she has done with him has been understood. He is not up to the supportive level yet. All of it has been wasted because she started too late, had too little time. And then it must be that this is her fault.

Nothing to do. Morales fucks her grunting, Elizabeth closes her eyes and lets him have his will. She deserves it. It is her penalty. If she had been a better social worker, this could not have happened. Morales comes and his sperm is like electricity shot through her, reminding her that never again, as long as she lives, will she ever be so smug or self-confident or faulty again. She has deserved this darkness.

XVIII

How she leaves the Morales apartment and in exactly what state their relationship is when she leaves and what she says to Mrs. Morales and what the Morales children say to her never quite comes clear in Elizabeth's mind; she only knows that after a certain sensation of struggling passage she finds herself once again on Boerum Street and her clothes seem uncomfortably heavy on her although she is not sweating. From a window way upstairs Morales is waving to her, at least he is gesturing toward the street in her direction but she cannot deduce his cries which may be in Spanish or merely poorly transmitted. "Yes," she says, raising her hand, "yes, goodbye," knowing that Morales will be one of her irretrievable failures (she has always been willing to express total internal self-honesty: she has failed utterly with Morales, nothing has worked out, she will have to live with this) and walks down Boerum Street, turns down Nostrand Avenue, decides that her next stop will be the Homeway Hotel where, at least, her goodbyes can be brief and not nearly so therapeutic in intention. There in the lobby she sees her clients once again, sitting in stifled, embryonic shapes in the huge chairs, gnarled and twisted in postures of agony, not one of them looking at her as she comes by them and to the desk. Mel is there, rubbing his hands, cheerful and efficient. He knows her caseload. "Let's see," he says, "this is July. That means that you have statutories still to complete with George, Jimmy, Jack H. and Willis K. I'll have them out here in just a second if you want to take a rest."

"No," she says, "that's all right. I'm not making any statutories today."

"Oh? Then what brings you by?" Mel fishes in his pocket, takes out a twenty dollar bill, looks at it. "If you've changed your mind," he says, "this is waiting for you. Anytime at all. Maybe — "

"No. It wasn't for that."

"Then I'm busy," Mel says and turns. "Got to manage this hotel; keep my boys happy. Unless," he says, turning, "unless maybe you dropped by hoping I'd ask you for a date. Okay. I'm asking you for a date. Want to go out tonight?"

"No," she says, "I don't go out with anyone. I just came by to say goodbye. I wanted to say goodbye to my cases and to you too I guess. I'm being transferred."

"Transferred?" Mel says, looking at her quizzically. "You mean, you're resigning."

"No, I'm not resigning. I'm being sent to another welfare center."

"You mean, you're not actually quitting. You're just taking another job with the department?"

"That's right."

"Why are you being transferred? You sick of Bedford-Stuyvesant. Wanted an inside job?"

"No," Elizabeth says. "It wasn't voluntary. I love my job. I was reassigned to be a home economist in the Bronx."

Mel shrugs. His eyes narrow. "All right," he says, "you'll be a home economist in the Bronx. That's okay with me. I've seen them come and go for ten years here and I guess I'll see some more. It's my loss but what can you do? Salant was a nice fellow but the trouble is they all want to improve themselves; they can't see a soft spot when they fall into it. So go to the Bronx." He extends a soft hand, touches her palm. "Shake," he says, "and good luck. No advances, that's not my ticket. If you don't want to shake, don't. Up to you."

"It isn't that," Elizabeth says vaguely, withdrawing from the clasp after a moment. "I mean, of course I wanted to say goodbye to you. You're part of the social work context of this hotel. But I wanted to say goodbye to my clients as well."

"So good," Mel says, raising a hand. "There they are, those that are able to sit up. Some of the others are in their rooms but you wouldn't be able to rouse them anyway. Say goodbye and godspeed and that's it. They'll never know the difference."

"You make it sound so disgusting," Elizabeth says after a pause. "It isn't. It doesn't have to be."

"It doesn't have to be? Well, that all depends. Excuse me," Mel says. With some finesse he hoists himself up onto the counter, stands there blinking for a moment until he gets his balance and then cups his hands to his mouth. "Boys!" he says, "I mean gentlemen. Our investigator is leaving us. She'd like to say goodbye. May we have your attention? May we have all of your attention please? Your investigator would like to say goodbye. I will repeat that; your investigator would like to say goodbye. I am talking about your welfare investigator. Attention please. She would like to say goodbye."

The men stir in their chairs, wink, groan, wipe their mouths with the backs of their hands, then one by one, like fish on a counter, look up at her beadily, without interest, their dead eyes popping. Some spit on the floor, others lean forward to mumble. "There they are," Mel says, presenting the lobby with a flourish. "Ready to say goodbye. Do you want to get up with me on the counter?"

"No," Elizabeth says. Abruptly she feels like a fool; she has no business wasting her time here when there are so many live cases, so many possibilities outside. She turns, looks at the men. "I hope that I've been able to help you," she says. "I'm going to miss you."

There is more generalized spitting, small conferrals between the men. She waits for them to say something but realizes after a time that they will not. "Well," she says, "I guess that that's all. God be with you." It sounds curiously formal; in fact it sounds stupid but she does not know what else to say to them. Most of them, despite their senile and alcoholic dementia, still hold childishly onto the institutions with which they were born; invoking the name of God is to reassure them of some continuity in their lives and this is as close as she can come with any of them to social work. "God be with you again," she says awkwardly and backs away.

"That was your investigator," Mel says with some enthusiasm, "that was your investigator addressing all of you. Your ex-investigator; she's leaving today."

"Well, not today, but *soon*. I mean this is the last day — "

"Enough," Mel says grandly, dropping an arm, "if this is your last time here then it's the last day for all of the boys and me here. I'm sure we all want to wish our ex-investigator the best. Don't we John? How about it, Bobby boy? Want to say goodbye to her?"

Two of the men detach themselves from their chairs, stumble, stagger against the walls and then begin, slowly, to advance upon Elizabeth. Their mouths are distended into grotesque smiles, their clawlike hands gesture wildly as they close the distance. Rotting teeth in their mouths seem to ooze liquids and suddenly Elizabeth finds that her control has broken. It is not professional; it is an unspeakable, inexcusable lapse, she does not in fact know what is happening to her but she finds that she is caught in a thrall of fear. She feels nausea, racking sobs. The men advance upon her, the distance narrowing.

"Oh my God!" Elizabeth says, "oh my God, I can't stand it!" and it is as if she sees the Homeway Residence for the first time, these clients for the first time, Mel himself for the first time and she pivots, in mid-scream, grasping her fieldbook and then, to her shame (and she knows that she will never forgive herself for this as long as she lives) Elizabeth runs. She runs from the Homeway Residence in dread, hearing the cackling behind her, her skin frozen against what she feels at any instant will be a terrible puncturing contact which will drop her.

"Goodbye," Mel calls after her, "goodbye, goodbye!" and she hears his laughter, hears the mumbles of the men as well, hears all of the activity in the Homeway Residence but as she stands under the enormous decaying sign, little bits of smashed fluorescence around her on the street, her control already returning, Elizabeth knows that what she should do if she had any professionalism at all is to go back to the lobby and beg the forgiveness of those men for running from them.

But she cannot. She cannot do this. She will have to accept this part of herself, that she is totally blocked. What it will lead to she does not know; what implications it will have upon her career she cannot understand.

Humbled, shaking, Elizabeth grasps her fieldbook to her chest and carries it like a shield against her on the dreadful streets as she moves away from the Residence and thinks of what she must do during the rest of this day.

XIX

For she must see Willie Buckingham now. She does not know why she feels she must wrap up everything on this one day, why she cannot use the remainder of the week to close down her relationships or at least the important ones but she has the feeling now, some insane compulsion to act, that if she does not do her work *now* she may never do it. For all she knows, Oved is lying in wait for her at the center, ready to laugh in her face and fire her the instant she walks in. Perhaps her transfer orders have come through already (the department is a paramilitary organization in certain respects) and she will be sent to the Bronx early. Perhaps her pain and dislocation are so great that if she does not drive herself blindly through the necessary tasks she will not be able to accomplish them at all. Perhaps perhaps. Who knows? She does not know. She knows that she must go now to Willie Buckingham.

She turns the corner again, wanders past the Morales apartment with her head down, forces herself toward Willie's building. Mandleman's office is closed today, a cardboard sign dangling in the window informing police and fire authorities of the emergency number to call in case of disaster and for some reason she is sorry that this is so; it would be nice to know that Mandleman was around. He is a terrible man, wholly misguided and corrupt in the bargain, his insights about the clients are twisted and grotesque, nevertheless it would be nice to know that he were within earshot if something bad were to happen in one of these buildings. Why is she thinking this way? What has happened to her? Maybe it is the Felipe Morales come now stiff and dry on her thighs, chafing her as she walks ... but then she has never been one to shape her attitudes around merely physical details. Morales' come is an annoyance, her relationship with Felipe has been a waste ... but why should this depress her so or make her fearful of simple Willie Buckingham?

She does not know. She climbs four flights and knocks on the Buckingham door. Mrs. Buckingham opens it and her face deadens and becomes cold as she sees Elizabeth; gentle Sadie Buckingham, mother of five out-of-wedlock children who to the best of Elizabeth's knowledge has never been anything other than totally obsequious. (She has been unable to break through to the woman.)

"Get out of here," Mrs. Buckingham says. "I don't want to see you."

"You don't understand, Mrs. Buckingham. I — "

"I understand everything. I don't want you around now, Mrs. — "

"Miss. Miss Moore."

"Miss Moore, whatever your name. We scheduled for no visit this month. You out here just last month and you ask a million questions and I tell you everything you want to know." Mrs. Buckingham is a huge woman, her breasts overhanging her waistline; staring at her Elizabeth can again understand Willie's obvious Oedipal block. "You want to know the rent and the maintenance and all that crap and I told you everything. You come back in two more months and ask more questions."

"This is kind of a special visit, Mrs. Buckingham. Is Willie around?" The thing to do is to barrel on through; jauntily, looking toward the purposes in mind. Nothing else matters. She will not stop. She eases her way into the apartment, the woman sniffing and coughing around her, little sparks of coughs lying around Elizabeth like flowers and inhales the deep, menstrual odors of a welfare apartment. "Is he?"

"Willie in the bedroom," Mrs. Buckingham says sullenly. "What you done with that boy is a disgrace. I tried to raise them proper. They say you on welfare they say you ain't no good at all but I had concerns. I care for these children; they don't live like pigs. A lot you care, Miss Moore."

"Willie told you — " Elizabeth says delicately. She stifles a little sneeze. "He told you — "

"Willie a good boy. You don't think so; you think he trash just like you think all of us but Willie have manners and he tell me everything."

Elizabeth puts her fieldbook under her arm and uses both hands to grasp Mrs. Buckingham's. "Oh," she says, "if I could only tell you, if I could only make you understand — "

"Like I say, I understand everything. I ought to report you. Miss Moore, I never heard of an investigator doing something like that. I know my boy a good boy; he never force the issue." Mrs. Buckingham sobs; obviously her hostility has been a thin, defensive cover for pain. "He never make you do nothing you don't want to do. How can you — "

"It just happened," Elizabeth says softly, still holding the woman's hand. "It's one of those things. Willie's a wonderful boy and you ought to be proud of him."

"Proud of him? I ought to report you!"

"That wouldn't do any good, Mrs. Buckingham," Elizabeth says. She has no time for casework and yet, instinctively, she persists. "If you're disturbed, you've got to think of the reasons you're so upset. What did this really mean to you? Can you let him go — "

"You smart white bitch," Mrs. Buckingham says, flinging her hands away, "you lucky I don't take a *knife* to you. Get out of my house. You get away from my boy, you hear?"

"I am," Elizabeth says softly. "I'm not going to be your worker any more. I've been transferred; this is the last time I'll ever see you. Next time you'll have a new investigator. Could I see Willie? Could I say goodbye to him?"

"Willie in the other room there. I don't think he want to talk to you.

I know he don't. You really leaving?"

"Yes I am. I've been transferred out."

"That's a break," Mrs. Buckingham says. "That's a blessing from God. You'd have all those other kids inside you in about two weeks, I figure."

"That's not *fair*," Elizabeth says, angered, her control lapsing with this woman for the first time. "You have no right to say that. I had reasons."

"I bet you had reasons."

"And they weren't for me; they were for your son. I wanted to do my best for him, don't you understand that?"

"What I understand," Mrs. Buckingham says, shaking her head, "and I been on relief twenty years so maybe this ain't worth understanding too much but as far as I can see you are crazy. You are a crazy one, Miss Moore. I never heard of no investigator pulling tricks like that. Some of the men with the girls, yes, men investigators; you know how they are. But a woman — "

"I want to see Willie," Elizabeth says. "I won't be up here any more and I want to say goodbye to him. I don't care if you think I'm crazy or not because you'll never understand and you're blocked anyway."

"He in the bedroom Miss Moore," Mrs. Buckingham says, seizing a broom and sweeping the floor violently, using the back end to administer small, directing pats to Elizabeth's buttocks. "But I don't think he want to see you."

"Sure I want to see Miss Moore," Willie says, opening the bedroom door, standing before them wearing dungarees and socks. "I like Miss Moore. You got no right, ma, to say those things — "

"No good," Mrs. Buckingham says, "this is all no good. You want to talk to each other, you go in there and you leave the door *open*. I hear any sounds, I see any sights and I gonna lay in there with this broom."

"I'm sorry, Miss Moore," Willie says, touching her gently on the shoulder, leading her into the bedroom. It is the first time she has ever seen it: a modified dormitory this is with five or six bunks heaped to the ceiling, all of them empty now except for one sleeping child in the rear. "I was listening at the door and I heard those things she was saying and they're all wrong. I don't agree. I didn't mean to make fun of you or anything. George Jones *is* a friend of mine and those other cats wouldn't believe. They just wouldn't *believe* — "

It is a changed Willie; Elizabeth can understand some of the reasons for this. His mother's aggression has stripped him down; to a real extent he will never be able to escape it. Also, she can see the neurasthenic signs in the wrist, palpitations of the neck: undoubtedly his friends have given him a bad time. "It's all right, Willie," Elizabeth says softly, taking his hand, looking at him. "It's all right."

"Leave that door open!" Mrs. Buckingham shouts. "Ain't nobody gonna close that door."

"It's open, damn it, ma! I wouldn't close no door — "

"I'm leaving, Willie," Elizabeth says. "I won't be your worker any more."

"I know. I heard that."

"I'll miss you."

"Well, I guess I'll miss you too. Can we see each other you think?"

"No, Willie," Elizabeth says. She feels maternal; reacts to her own drives and manages to suppress a desire to bring him against her. His dependency is so great. "Now that I'm no longer on your case it wouldn't be fair to either of us. Your next worker will try to help you too."

"There ain't never been a worker like you, Miss Moore."

"I'm glad to hear that."

"We seen a whole lot of workers in this house through the years and there never been one like Miss Moore."

"That means something to me Willie," Elizabeth says. She holds his hand still, bends over, scrabbles for her fieldbook which she has dropped. She must, somehow, terminate the interview before the emotional blocks loosen or Mrs. Buckingham comes in with the broom. In some tentative way she feels that she has reached Willie: Willie at least, may be her legacy. "I've got to be going now," she says gently. "You understand."

"Sure, sure I understand Miss Moore."

"But I had to come up and say goodbye to you. It was something I very much wanted to do."

"I'm glad, Miss Moore. You sure we can't ever see each other again?"

"No Willie. It wouldn't be right."

"Miss Moore," Willie says, dropping her hand, standing, turning around and looking out the window, "I got something I got to tell you. I mean I have to."

"Yes Willie," she says, looking at the panes of his back. He is, from this view, almost beautiful; she can understand how a woman might feel desire grasping him there. Of course *she* has never felt desire; her passions in fornication with the clients have been purely on the professional level but looking at him in this light she sees that one *could*, if one were motivated in that way, find Willie intensely physically attractive.

"I been wanting to tell it to you for a while now but I never somehow got up the guts. But I guess since you're leaving and all I'd better tell you."

"Yes," she says, looking over his shoulder and out at the sunlight; in this aspect Boerum Street could be Fifth Avenue or the Lower East Side: it is beautiful, everything is beautiful; it is only a question of perspective. "Do you want to say something about the way you feel for me? You may, you know. You have a right to these feelings. All of these feelings are beautiful and you have a right to express them without shame."

"I don't hear no door closing," Mrs. Buckingham calls, "but I got my ears at the ready. I don't hear no sounds either but I waiting to hear them. I give you young folk two more minutes in there and then I clean out the whole place with a broom. What's to be done is done."

"Well, it's not about feelings exactly, Miss Moore," Willie says. He turns, aspects of light cast shadows on his face; he looks solemn and aged now and she sees some intimation of the man that Willie will be some day if he finds the supportive therapy and casework he needs. Maturity and intelligence seem locked into his features, heaviness and great comprehension of pain. "Not feelings, except maybe in a way because I ain't been feeling too good."

"You can tell me, Willie. You can tell me anything."

"I know I can tell you everything but this one kind of hard Miss Moore."

"Don't worry. Try."

"Well," Willie says, swallowing; she can see his adams apple descend and bob up in his neck and finds herself thinking before she can cut off the thought *all of them have that trick* and then at this vestige of prejudice which she has not, somehow, managed to cancel from herself she blushes, feeling roseate and vulnerable on the bed. What if Willie says that he loves her? Somehow she will have to show them that these feelings can be converted to self-love.

"Well," Willie says again, running a hand across his forehead, "I make it short and sweet is the best, right? They got this free checkup, you know? Where they bring in the trucks from around the city and they park down by Fulton Street and everybody in the neighborhood can run in and have tests made. They advertise it over the radio and so on that everybody can come in for a free checkup. So my mama, she made me go." He tousles his hair, looks more vulnerable and boyish than ever standing before her. Elizabeth reminds herself of what she should always have been aware; that Willie really has the mind of a twelve-year-old. That is all he is, all that most of them are: not only sick but retarded. She must hone the edge of her tolerance.

"Go on, Willie," she says. "It's all right. I'm listening. Short and sweet."

"Short and sweet," Willie says, "that's right. That's the ticket." He gulps. "Anyway, I went down to one of those trucks last week and had this free checkup which they give you. I been meaning to tell you ever since then but even up to now I didn't have the strength. I told George Jones and he laughed and said I'd better tell you and I told the other guys but they said they didn't care. I been trying to tell you."

"What is it Willie?" Elizabeth says quietly. It must be a conversion hysteria of some kind; perhaps the boy has a heart condition or some form of diabetes. Then again, is it possible that he has lung cancer? The trucks, some of them she recalls vaguely, have X-ray machines. "What did you find out about yourself? It's all right," she says. "You'll be okay. They have wonderful medical facilities for welfare clients and you'll get the best of care — "

"I already being treated," Willie says. "I cured. I mean, I going to be cured, very soon. But I have to tell you. I don't know how to. I guess I'd just better."

"That's it," Mrs. Buckingham says from the next room. "That is the end of the line. I am coming in there with this broom and clean out the mess. Break it up in there. Break it up!"

"Well, Willie?" Elizabeth says softly, standing. She tries to maintain continued professional calm but strictly speaking this is not easy; she feels at any moment the broom of Mrs. Buckingham may fall across her shoulders and what then. What then? "Are you going to tell me or not," she says with the beginnings of irritation. "I don't have to put up with this forever, you know."

"All right," Willie says. He inhales. "I tell you but you're not going to like it very much Miss Moore. I don't like it myself. But I'll tell you and that's that. Miss Moore, it turned out that I got the clap."

XX

Sometime later, in slightly different circumstances, Elizabeth finds that she is riding the Fulton Street bus once again, heading back toward the welfare center. Her fieldbook is in her handbag now, her handbag gripped desperately between her thighs. Exactly how she got on the

Fulton Street bus and what has happened later in the Buckingham apartment and what the nature of her thoughts were as she walked to the bus she has no idea. There seems to be no sense of transition: for the moment she is living the life that she has understood relief clients to live: time working only in terms of impulses, all chronologically subdued to emotion, the concept of normal time destroyed by energy and from the moment when Willie gave her, finally, his secret, up until this moment on the bus Elizabeth has no clear recollection. Obviously something has happened; a whole series of events, in fact, she could not have made it from the apartment to the bus devoid of thought without anything at all happening but she cannot get hold of it. Maybe it was the loosening of certain emotional blocks, a small breakdown of the defense mechanisms when Willie gave her his revelation. Certainly she is not infallible; she has a great deal to learn about the art and science of social work, she may have over-reacted.

She has, in fact, a vague recollection of screaming: screaming and shouting and twisting as she left the apartment scuttling past Mrs. Buckingham and her broom, leaving Willie standing in isolation and penitence in the frame of the bedroom door. Some cursing as well. She must have cursed because she has some memory of their faces and the reactions were as if she had spoken curse words. But this is not important. Nothing that she did is important; there is no way to take it seriously. A fugue is a fugue … that is all there is to it … and the important thing is that she is seated on the bus, headed back toward the welfare center. Others in adjoining seats are looking at her strangely, some are peering into her fieldbook and shaking their heads, but this has nothing to do with her; only with the strange ethos of Bedford-Stuyvesant. Better to put all of this out of her mind. It is better to carry on as if none of this happened. The only thing to do is to see a doctor tonight — she can think of several in the neighborhood whose ground floor signs she has often seen — and that will be the end of that.

She is willing to concede, thinking the issue through quietly and rationally now, she is willing to concede the possibility that she has made certain mistakes. By all means she should have thought more of consequences before she performed certain acts; above and beyond that it is true that she might have been better off trying to get into graduate-school and obtaining a social work degree before she began to attempt to relate to clients in the way that she has over these past months.

But where was she going to go to graduate school? And how would she have financed it? And didn't the Department of Welfare give her the trust and opportunity to engage in casework? And above and beyond all of this, what could a school of social work have taught Elizabeth Moore that she did not instinctively know in her heart and was unable to verify every day from all of her experience?

Well, these are interesting questions: they will be worth a good deal of thought someday. When she has worked into the home economics job at Fordham Welfare Center she may have long afternoons free when all of the workers are in the field and she will be able to sit quietly and review her past life; these are definitely some of the questions which she will want to go over. Maybe she has erred, Elizabeth decides. She never had any pretensions to infallibility. She was better than the clients and knew that in the relative sense as compared to them she might be infallible but in the higher scheme she was definitely not. Where did she ever try to pretend that she was, anyway?

Time past. Not to be considered, not part of the situation. The bus lurches, it spills forth passengers, it takes in passengers, it proceeds on its route. Elizabeth looks past the dismal relief faces across from her and out the window, ponders her future. She will come back to the welfare center now. She is definitely out of the field; there are many disappointments she will leave behind her and much unfinished casework but unquestionably she cannot go to the field again. Not after today. She cannot be blamed for this.

Back to the welfare center. There, she will do her casework from her desk. In the long run, this will be the better way. She will write letters to all of her clients, those she has not seen that is:

Dear Mr. or Mrs. —
For reasons which are beyond my control I will no longer be your caseworker effective the earliest part of next week. To lose you is something which I do with the greatest of regret but I want you to know that you have filled a peculiar and vital place in my life and that I will miss you terribly and personally. I hope that in return I have been able to give you something which will make you miss me as well but you will, of course, have the courage to go on as will all of us. Relief is only a state of mind; you can overcome it. It is in your psyche but not your circumstances and you hold within yourself the power of your own liberation. If you will yourself from the relief class you can do so. You need not stay entrapped in this cycle of poverty and misery forever.

Not *Elizabeth Moore* with all of the stately, Victorian formality of that name which she has always hated (and wanted to break free from) but *Elizabeth* to show them what she really thinks of them. This first caress of intimacy, however distant, will touch them with warmth and they will respond. If only she had had the time to do the work herself! If only her time had not been so cruelly limited! If only she had been allowed to dedicate herself in the way she wanted! But there is no time for regrets. The regrets will come later. She has done the best she could.

The bus stops. It is at the corner of the welfare center. Elizabeth, wrapped within herself stands, holds her fieldbook and handbag, moves musing to the stairwell, steps down and out. Only when she is on the sidewalk does she become aware that there seems to be something of a disturbance in the vicinity of the welfare center, directly across the street.

Police are there. Prowl cars are there, flashing their deadly beams in and out of her eyes. Reporters seem to be there or at least a press car or two. The street is filled with noise, tumult. The entryway of the welfare center is blocked by a wooden stand and three policemen. Workers and clerks dangle their heads out of the second floor loft to see what is going on. Clients on the Intake level have hoisted themselves on benches and are looking through open spaces in the windows. Sirens flare. More police cars seem to be on the move.

Milling around the entrance to the welfare center are orthodox Jews. Elizabeth, in her stunned appraisal, believes that she is seeing what has long since been prophesied in the testaments: every Jew in the world must be there. Frock-coated and hatted, bearded and solemn, holding prayer books and wearing shawls, Jews are walking back and forth in front of the center, some of them pushing to move past the resistant police, others, in small, ambitious streams, trying to get in through the window.

Jews are up the street, they are down the street. Elizabeth, as she looks, realizes that they must be in the Intake section as well. Several hundred of them, as a matter of fact, seem to be in the Intake section; now a window bulges outward under pressure from police clubs or struggles and in the open, shattered glass she can look fully within. Jews are on the floor of Intake, milling around and shouting. They are not as relatively peaceful as the ones without. Those who have gotten within the Intake section are a hardier, more physical group of *chassids*. They are screaming. Some are chanting. Others appear to be seated on the floor in silent, terrible protest.

Elizabeth looks at all of this. She stands and considers it; might consider it forever. There is no reason to move. But just at the moment of timeless ascension, when she feels that she is moving upward and outward in relation to all of this, contemplating it in eternity, the Jews turn. First one, then two, then five and a hundred. Talking to themselves, gesticulating wildly. They focus upon her. Five hundred arms go in her direction. Police look at her as well. The workers from the second floor of intake looked at her. There are more sirens. A fire engine seems to be panting up the block.

"There she is!" she thinks she hears someone shout, "that's her, that's her!" and before Elizabeth can do anything else at all (not that there is really any reason to do anything else: what could she have done?) she is suddenly pursued by not one, not ten, not even a hundred but very possibly the entirety — it is hard to judge the right statistics — of the well-known Lubavitcher Congregation.

THE END

Barry N. Malzberg Bibliography

FICTION

Oracle of the Thousand Hands (1968)
Screen (1968)
Confessions of Westchester County
  (1970)
The Spread (1971)
In My Parents' Bedroom (1971)
The Falling Astronauts (1971)
Everything Happened to Susan (1972)
The Masochist (1972)
Horizontal Woman (1972; reprinted as
  The Social Worker, 1973)
Overlay (1972)
Revelations (1972)
Herovit's World (1973)
In the Enclosure (1973)
The Men Inside (1973)
Phase IV (1973; novelization based on
  a story & screenplay by Mayo Simon)
The Day of the Burning (1974)
The Tactics of Conquest (1974)
Underlay (1974)
Beyond Apollo (1974)
The Destruction of the Temple (1974)
Guernica Night (1974)
On a Planet Alien (1974)
Out from Ganymede (1974; stories)
The Sodom and Gomorrah Business
  (1974)
The Best of Barry N. Malzberg (1975;
  stories)
The Many Worlds of Barry Malzberg
  (1975; stories)
Galaxies (1975)
The Gamesman (1975)
Down Here in the Dream Quarter
  (1976; stories)
Scop (1976)

The Last Transaction (1977)
Chorale (1978)
Malzberg at Large (1979; stories)
The Man Who Loved the Midnight Lady
  (1980; stories)
The Cross of Fire (1982)
The Remaking of Sigmund Freud
  (1985)
In the Stone House (2000; stories)
Shiva and Other Stories (2001; stories)
The Passage of the Light: The Recursive
  Science Fiction of Barry N. Malzberg
  (2004; ed. by Tony Lewis & Mike
  Resnick; stories)
The Very Best of Barry N. Malzberg
  (2013; stories)

With Bill Pronzini

The Running of the Beasts (1976)
Acts of Mercy (1977)
Prose Bowl (1980)
Night Screams (1981)
Problems Solved (2003; stories)
On Account of Darkness and Other SF
  Stories (2004; stories)

As Mike Barry

Lone Wolf series:
Night Raider (1973)
Bay Prowler (1973)
Boston Avenger (1973)
Desert Stalker (1974)
Havana Hit (1974)
Chicago Slaughter (1974)
Peruvian Nightmare (1974)
Los Angeles Holocaust (1974)
Miami Marauder (1974)
Harlem Showdown (1975)

Detroit Massacre (1975)
Phoenix Inferno (1975)
The Killing Run (1975)
Philadelphia Blow-Up (1975)

As Francine di Natale

The Circle (1969)

As Claudine Dumas

The Confessions of a Parisian
  Chambermaid (1969)

As Mel Johnson/M. L. Johnson

Love Doll (1967; with The Sex Pros by
  Orrie Hitt)
I, Lesbian (1968)
Just Ask (1968; with Playgirl by Lou
  Craig)
Instant Sex (1968)
Chained (1968; with Master of Women
  by March Hastings & Love Captive by
  Dallas Mayo)
Kiss and Run (1968)
Nympho Nurse (1969; with Young and
  Eager by Jim Conroy & Quickie by
  Gene Evans)
The Sadist (1969)
The Box (1969)
Do It To Me (1969)
Born to Give (1969; with Swap Club by
  Greg Hamilton & Wild in Bed by Dirk
  Malloy)
Campus Doll (1969; with High School
  Stud by Robert Hadley)
A Way With All Maidens (1969)

As Howard Lee

Kung Fu #1: The Way of the Tiger, the
  Sign of the Dragon

As Lee W. Mason

Lady of a Thousand Sorrows (1977)

As K. M. O'Donnell

Empty People (1969)
The Final War and Other Fantasies
  (1969; stories)
Dwellers of the Deep (1970)
Gather at the Hall of the Planets
  (1971)
In the Pocket and Other S-F Stories
  (1971; stories)
Universe Day (1971; stories)

As Elliot B. Reston

The Womanizer (1972)

As Gerrold Watkins

Art of the Fugue (1970)
A Bed of Money (1970)
Giving It Away (1970)
A Satyr's Romance (1970)
Southern Comfort (1972)

NON-FICTION/ESSAYS

The Engines of the Night: Science
  Fiction in the Eighties (1982; essays)
Breakfast in the Ruins (2007; essays:
  expansion of Engines of the Night)
The Business of Science Fiction: Two
  Insiders Discuss Writing and
  Publishing (2010; with Mike Resnick)

EDITED ANTHOLOGIES

Final Stage (1974; with Edward L.
  Ferman)
Arena (1976; with Edward L. Ferman)
Graven Images (1977; with Edward L.
  Ferman)

Dark Sins, Dark Dreams (1978; with Bill Pronzini)

The End of Summer: SF in the Fifties (1979; with Bill Pronzini)

Shared Tomorrows: Science Fiction in Collaboration (1979; with Bill Pronzini)

Neglected Visions (1979; with Martin H. Greenberg & Joseph D. Olander)

Bug-Eyed Monsters (1980; with Bill Pronzini)

The Science Fiction of Mark Clifton (1980; with Martin H. Greenberg)

The Arbor House Treasury of Horror & the Supernatural (1981; with Bill Pronzini & Martin H. Greenberg)

The Science Fiction of Kris Neville (1984; with Martin H. Greenberg)

Uncollected Stars (1986; with Piers Anthony, Martin H. Greenberg & Charles G. Waugh)

The Best Time Travel Stories of All Time (2003)

www.ingramcontent.com/pod-product-compliance
Lightning Source LLC
Chambersburg PA
CBHW070956180726
48291CB00004B/1315